WITHDRAWN

The Ratbridge Chronicles

VOLUME 1

HERE·BE·MONSTERS!

AN ADVENTURE INVOLVING

MAGIC, TROLLS, AND OTHER CREATURES

OXFORD

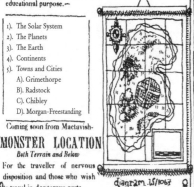

HERE·BE·MONSTERS!

AN ADVENTURE INVOLVING

MAGIC, TROLLS, AND OTHER CREATURES

WRITTEN AND ILLUSTRATED

by Alan Snow

OXFORD
UNIVERSITY PRESS

Great Clarendon Street, Oxford OX2 6DP

Oxford University Press is a department of the University of Oxford.
It furthers the University's objective of excellence in research, scholarship,
and education by publishing worldwide in

Oxford   New York

Auckland   Cape Town   Dar es Salaam   Hong Kong   Karachi
Kuala Lumpur   Madrid   Melbourne   Mexico City   Nairobi
New Delhi   Shanghai   Taipei   Toronto

With offices in

Argentina   Austria   Brazil   Chile   Czech Republic   France   Greece
Guatemala   Hungary   Italy   Japan   Poland   Portugal   Singapore
South Korea   Switzerland   Thailand   Turkey   Ukraine   Vietnam

Oxford is a registered trade mark of Oxford University Press
in the UK and in certain other countries

British Library Cataloguing in Publication Data

Data available

ISBN: 0-19-271992-0 (restricted edition)
ISBN: 0-19-271964-5 (hardback)

1 3 5 7 9 10 8 6 4 2

Printed in Great Britain by Mackays of Chatham plc, Chatham; Kent

The Ratbridge Chronicles

VOLUME 1

HERE·BE·MONSTERS!

IN WHICH WE LEARN A LITTLE ABOUT ARTHUR, BOXTROLLS, CABBAGEHEADS, AND STRANGE GOINGS-ON IN RATBRIDGE

To Edward, and with enormous thanks
to everyone who has helped along the way

HERE·BE·MONSTERS!

AN ADVENTURE INVOLVING
MAGIC, TROLLS, AND OTHER CREATURES

JOHNSON'S TAXONOMY OF TROLLS

Chapter 1	COMING UP!	13
Chapter 2	THE HUNT	25
Chapter 3	FROM ON HIGH	33
Chapter 4	INTO THE TOWN	37
Chapter 5	HERE BE MONSTERS!	51
Chapter 6	THE CEREMONY	71
Chapter 7	WHICH HOLE?	75
Chapter 8	SEARCH FOR A HOLE	83
Chapter 9	THE WET DRY DOCK	93
Chapter 10	THE RETURN	99
Chapter 11	A VISIT	105
Chapter 12	THE MARKET	121
Chapter 13	MADAME FROUFROU	131

Chapter 14	THE PATENT HALL	145
Chapter 15	GONE!	163
Chapter 16	PANTS AHOY!	177
Chapter 17	CABBAGEHEADS	197
Chapter 18	THE CHEESE HALL	201
Chapter 19	AN INCIDENT OUTSIDE THE NAG'S HEAD	209
Chapter 20	INSIDE THE CHEESE HALL	219
Chapter 21	THE DUNGEON	227
Chapter 22	BACK IN THE LAB	235
Chapter 23	OUT ON THE ROOF!	249
Chapter 24	BACK AT THE SHIP	257
Chapter 25	TEA AND CAKE	261
Chapter 26	AN ESCAPE?	273
Chapter 27	ATTACK ON THE SHIP	285
Chapter 28	THE POLICE	293
Chapter 29	EXODUS	305
Chapter 30	BACK BELOW THE CHEESE HALL	311
Chapter 31	THE STAND OFF	317
Chapter 32	THE MAN IN THE IRON SOCKS	327
Chapter 33	GOING DOWN!	335
Chapter 34	THE COUNCIL OF WAR	341

Chapter 35	UP AND UNDER!	355
Chapter 36	THE RABBIT WOMEN	363
Chapter 37	THE DOLL	373
Chapter 38	WET!	379
Chapter 39	THE TELLING	387
Chapter 40	A GLIMMER AT THE END OF THE TUNNEL	399
Chapter 41	THE KEYS	405
Chapter 42	THE TRAPS	415
Chapter 43	DEEP WATER	419
Chapter 44	THE SHAFT!	427
Chapter 45	THE GREAT ONE!	437
Chapter 46	THE NEXT VICTIM!	443
Chapter 47	HOW ARE WE GOING TO FIX IT?	451
Chapter 48	LET'S HIT THE TOWN!	457
Chapter 49	ATTACK ON THE CHEESE HALL	463
Chapter 50	MAGNETISM!	475
Chapter 51	THE BIG BANG	489
Chapter 52	SKINNED!	493
Chapter 53	REPAIRING THE DAMAGE	503
Chapter 54	HOME	511
Chapter 55	MEASURE FOR MEASURE	527

JOHNSON'S TAXONOMY
OF TROLLS AND CREATURES

Aardvark

Aardvarks are invariably the first animals listed in any alphabetical listing of creatures. Beyond this they have few attributes relevant here.

Boxtrolls

A sub-species of the common troll, they are very shy, so live inside a box. These they gather from the backs of large shops. They are somewhat troublesome creatures—as they have a passion for everything mechanical and no understanding of the concept of ownership (they steal anything which is not bolted down, and more often than not, anything which is). It is very dangerous to leave tools lying about where they might find them.

Cabbageheads

Belief has it that cabbageheads live deep underground and are the bees of the underworld. Little else is known at this time, apart from a fondness for brassicas.

Cheese

Wild English Cheeses live in bogs. This is unlike their French cousins who live in caves. They are nervous beasties, that eat grass by night, in the meadows and woodlands. They are also of very low intelligence, and are panicked by almost anything that catches them unawares. Cheeses make easy quarry for hunters, being rather easier to catch than a dead sheep.

Crow

The crow is a very intelligent bird, capable of living in many environments. Crows are known to be considerably more honest than their cousins, magpies, and enjoy a varied diet, and good company. Usually they are charming company, but should be kept from providing the entertainment. Failure to do so may result in tedium, for while intelligent, crows seem to lack taste in the choice of music, and conversational topics.

Fresh-water Sea-cow

Distant relative of the manitou. This creature inhabits the canals, and drains of certain West Country towns. A passive creature of large size, and vegetarian habits. They are very kind to their young, and make good mothers.

Rats
Rats are known to be some of the most intelligent of all rodents, and to be considerably more intelligent than many humans. They are known to have a passion for travel, and be extremely adaptable. They often live in a symbiotic relationship with humans.

Grandfather (William)
Arthur's guardian and carer. Grandfather has lived underground for many years in a cave home where he pursues his interests in engineering. All the years in a damp cave have taken their toll, and he now suffers from very bad rheumatism, and a somewhat short temper.

The Members
Members of the secretive Ratbridge Cheese Guild, that was thought to have died out after the 'Great Cheese Crash'. It was an evil organization that rigged the cheese market, and doctored and adulterated lactose-based food stuffs.

Rabbits
Furry, jumping mammals, with a passion for tender vegetables and raising the young. Good parents, but not very bright.

The Man in the Iron Socks
A mysterious shadowy figure said to be much feared by the members of the now defunct Cheese Guild. He is thought to hold a dark secret as well as a large 'Walloper'. His Walloper is the major cause of fear, but he also has a sharp tongue, and a caustic line in wit. History does not relate the reasoning behind his wearing of iron socks.

Rabbit Women
Very little is known about these mythical creatures, except that they are supposed to live with rabbits, and wear clothes spun from rabbit wool.

Trotting Badgers
Trotting badgers are some of the nastiest creatures to be found anywhere. With their foul temper, rapid speed, and razor-sharp teeth, it cannot be stressed just how unpleasant and dangerous these creatures are. It is only their disgusting stench that gives warning of their proximity, and when smelt it is often too late.

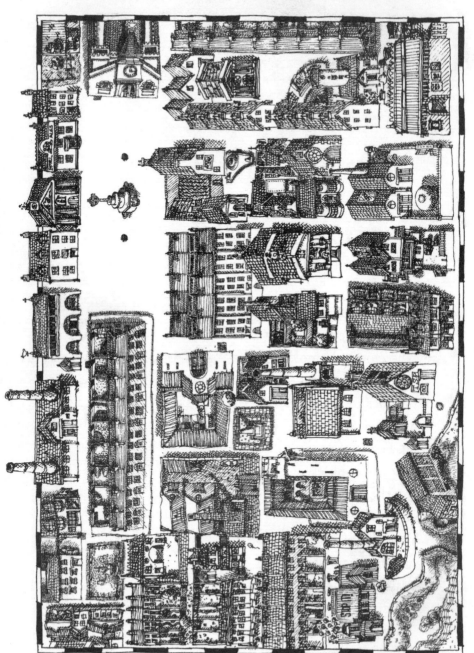

Ratbridge Town Centre

Ratbridge

Chapter 1

COMING UP!

It was a late Sunday evening and Ratbridge stood silver grey and silent in the moonlight. Early evening rain had washed away the cloud of smoke that normally hung over the town, and now long shadows from the factory chimneys fell across oily puddles in the empty streets. The town was at rest.

The shadows moved slowly across the lane that ran behind Fore Street revealing a heavy iron drain cover set amongst the cobbles.

Then the drain cover moved. Something was pushing it up from below.

One side of the cover lifted a few inches, and from beneath it, a pair of eyes scanned the lane. The drain cover lifted further, then slid sideways. A boy's head wearing a woven helmet with nine or ten antennae rose through the hole and glanced around. The boy shut his eyes, and he

A pair of eyes scanned the lane

listened. For a moment all was quiet, then a distant dog bark echoed off the walls. Silence returned. The boy opened his eyes, reached out of the hole, and pulled himself up and out into the lane. He was dressed very strangely. In addition to the helmet he wore a large vest knitted from soft rope, that reached the ground, and under that a short one-piece suit made from old sugar sacks. His feet were wrapped in layers of rough cloth, tied with string.

Fixed about his body by wide leather straps was a strange contraption. On his front was a wooden box with a winding handle on one side, and two brass buttons and a knob on the front. A flexible metal tube connected the box to a pair of folded wings, made from leather, wood, and brass, that were attached to his back.

The boy slid the drain cover back into place, reached inside his under-suit and pulled out a toy figure dressed just like him. He held the doll out and spoke.

'Grandfather, I am up top. I think I'll have to go gardening tonight. It's a Sunday, and everything is shut. The bins behind the inn will be empty.' He looked at the doll.

There was a crackle of static, and a thin voice came from the doll. 'Well, you be careful, Arthur! And remember, only take from the bigger gardens . . . and only then if they have plenty! There are a lot of people that can only survive by growing their own food.'

Arthur smiled. He had heard this many times before. 'Don't worry, Grandfather, I haven't forgotten! I'll only take what we need . . . and I will be careful. I'll see you as soon as I am done.'

'Grandfather, I am up top'

Arthur replaced the doll inside his suit, then started to wind the handle on the box on his front. As he wound it made a soft whirring noise. For nearly two minutes he wound, pausing occasionally when his hand started aching. Then a bell pinged from somewhere inside the box and he stopped. Arthur scanned the skyline, crouched, and then pressed one of the buttons. The wings on his back unfolded. He pressed the other button and at the same moment jumped as high as he could. Silently the wings rushed down and caught the air as he rose. At the bottom of their stroke they folded, rose, and then beat down again. His wings were holding him in the air, a few feet above the ground. Arthur's hand reached for the knob and he turned it just a little. As he did so he tilted himself a little forward. He started to move. Arthur smiled . . . he was flying.

He was flying

He moved slowly down the lane, keeping below the top of its walls. When he reached the end, he adjusted the knob again, and rose up to a gap between the twin roofs of the Glue Factory. Arthur knew routes that were safe from the eyes of the townsfolk, and would keep to one of these tonight on the way to the particular garden he planned on visiting. When it was dark or there was thick smog, things were easy. But tonight was clear and the moon full. He'd been spotted twice before on nights like these, by children, from their bedroom windows. He'd got away with it so far, as nobody had believed them when they said they had seen a fairy or flying boy, but tonight he was not going to take any chances.

He adjusted the knob

A horse started and whinnied as he flew over

Arthur reached the end of the gap between the roofs. He dipped a little and flew across a large stable yard. A horse started and whinnied as he flew over. He adjusted his wing speed and increased his height. The horse made him feel uneasy. At the far side of the yard he rose again over a huge gate, topped with spikes. He crossed a deserted alley, then moved down a narrow street flanked with the windowless backs of houses. At the far end of the street he slowed and then hovered in the air. In front of him was another high wall. Carefully he adjusted the knob, and rose very gently to the point where he could just see the ground beyond the wall. It was a large vegetable garden. Across the garden fell paths of pale light, cast from the windows of the house. Arthur looked towards it. One of the windows was open. From it he could hear raised voices and the clatter of dominoes.

That should keep them busy! he thought, scanning the garden again. Against the wall furthest from the house was a large glass lean-to.

He checked the windows of the house again, then rose over the wall and headed for the greenhouse, keeping above the beams of light from the house. He came to rest in front of the greenhouse door.

Silently Arthur turned off and folded his wings. He opened the door, and a soft rush of warm perfumed air brushed his face. It was a mixture of smells—some familiar, some not.

Dark leafy forms filled the greenhouse. Some were suspended from the roof, while others climbed almost invisible strings. Some larger ones just hogged the ground. As Arthur entered he recognized tomato plants climbing the strings, and cucumbers and grapes hanging from above.

He moved past all these, and made his way to a tree against the far wall.

It was a tall tree with branches only at its top. Dangling from a stem below the branches was what looked like a stack of huge fat upside-down spiders. It was a large bunch of bananas. As Arthur got closer he caught their scent. It was beautiful.

Arthur could hardly contain his delight. Bananas! He tore one from the bunch, then peeled and ate it ravenously. When he had finished it, he turned and checked the house. Nothing had changed. Turning back to the tree, he reached inside his under-suit and pulled out a string bag, then reached up to the banana bunch and pulled eagerly. It was

What looked like a huge stack of fat upside-down spiders

not as easy to pick the full bunch as it had been to pull off a single banana, and Arthur found he had to put his full weight on the bunch. A soft fibrous tearing sound started, but still the bunch did not come down. In desperation, Arthur lifted his feet from the ground and swung his legs. All of a sudden there was a crack and the whole bunch, along with Arthur, fell to the ground. The tree trunk sprang back up and struck the glass roof with a loud crack. The noise sounded out across the garden.

'Oi! There is something in the greenhouse,' came a shout from the house.

Hearing the shout, Arthur scrambled to his feet, grabbed the string bag and looked out through the glass. No one was in the garden yet. He rushed to collect up as many of the

bananas as possible, shoving them into the bag. Then he heard a door bang and the sound of footsteps. He ran out of the greenhouse into the garden.

A very large lady with a very long stick

Clambering towards him over the rows of vegetables was a very large lady with a very long stick. Arthur dashed over to one of the garden walls, stabbed at the buttons on the front of his box, and jumped. His wings snapped open and started to beat, but not strongly enough to lift him. He landed back on the ground, his wings fluttering behind him. Arthur groaned—the bananas! He had to adjust the wings for the extra weight. But he was not ready to put the bananas down and fly away empty-handed—they were too precious. Still clutching the string bag with the bananas in one hand, he grabbed for the knob on the front of the box with the other hand, and twisted it hard. The wings immediately doubled their beating and became a blur. Just as the woman reached the spot where Arthur stood, he shot almost vertically upwards, just avoiding her outstretched hand. Furious, she swung her stick above her head and, before he could get out of range, landed a hard blow on his wings, sending him spinning.

'You little varmint! Come down here and give me back my bananas!' the woman cried. Arthur grasped at the top of the wall to steady himself. The stick now swished inches below his feet. He adjusted the wings quickly, and made off over the wall. Shouts of anger followed him.

Arthur felt sick to the pit of his stomach. Coming up at night to collect food was always risky, and this was the closest he'd ever been to being caught. He needed somewhere quiet to rest and recover.

I wish we could live above ground like everybody else! he thought.

Now he flew across the town by the safest route he knew—flying between roofs, up the darkest alleys, and across deserted yards, till finally he reached the abandoned Cheese Hall. He knew he would be alone here.

The Cheese Hall had been the grandest of all the buildings in the town and was only overshadowed by a few of the factory chimneys. In former times, it had been the home of the Ratbridge Cheese Guild. But now the industry was dead, and the Guild and all its members ruined. The Hall was now boarded up and deserted. Its gilded statues that once shone out across the town were blackened by the very soot that had poisoned the cheese.

The Cheese Hall

Arthur landed on the bridge of the roof, and settled himself amongst the statues. As he sat catching his breath it occurred to him that maybe he should inspect his wings for damage. The woman had landed a fairly heavy blow, but Arthur decided it would be too dangerous and awkward to take his wings off high up here on the roof, and besides they seemed to be fine. Something distracted him from his thoughts—a noise. It sounded like a mournful bleat, from somewhere below. He listened carefully, intrigued, but heard no more. When he finally felt calm again, he stowed the bananas behind one of the statues, climbed out from his hiding place, and flew up to the best observation spot in the whole town. This was the plinth on the top of the dome that supported the weathervane and lightning conductor.

A complete panorama of the town and the surrounding countryside, broken only by the chimneystacks of the factories, was laid out before him. In the far distance he could just make out some sort of procession in the moonlight making for the woods. It looked as though something was being chased by a group of horses.

The plinth that supported the weathervane and lightning conductor

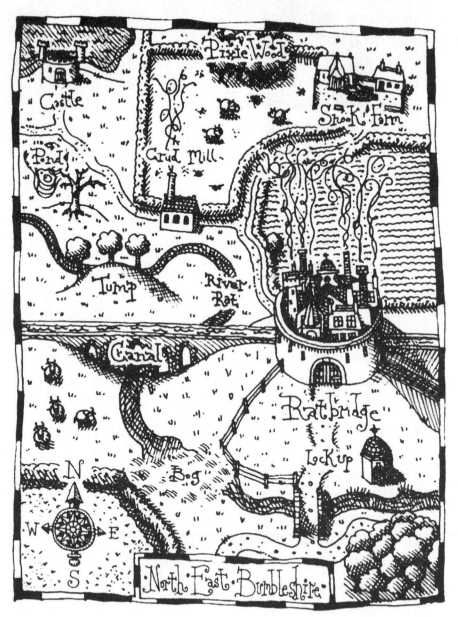

North East Bumbleshire

Three large barrel cheeses broke from the undergrowth

Chapter 2

THE HUNT

Strange sounds were filtering through the woods—scrabblings, bleatings and growlings—and, strangest of all, a sound closely resembling bagpipes, or the sound bagpipes would make if they were being strangled, viciously, under a blanket. In a small moonlit clearing in the centre of the woods the sounds grew louder. Suddenly there was a frantic rustling in the bushes on one side of the clearing, and three large barrel cheeses broke from the undergrowth, running as fast as their legs would carry them. Hurtling across the clearing, bleating in panic, they disappeared into the bushes on the far side of the clearing, and for a moment all was still again.

Suddenly a new burst of rustling came from the bushes where the cheeses had emerged, along with a horrid growling noise. Then a pack of hounds burst out into the open. They were a motley bunch, all different shapes and sizes, but they all had muzzles covering their snouts, and they all shared the awful reek of sweat. The hounds ran around in circles, growling through their muzzles. One small fat animal that looked like a cross between a sausage dog and a ball of wire wool kept his nose to the ground, sniffing intently. He gave a great snort, crossed the clearing, and dived onwards after the cheeses. The other hounds followed.

They were a motley bunch, all different shapes and sizes

The weird bagpipe sound grew closer, accompanied by vaguely human cries. Then there was a louder crashing in the undergrowth and finally the strangest creature yet arrived in the clearing. It had four skinny legs that hung from what looked like an upturned boat made from a patchwork of old sacking. At its front was a head made from an old box, and on this the features of a horse's face were crudely drawn. A large angry man rode high on its back.

'Which way did they go?' the man screamed.

An arm emerged from the sacking and pointed across the clearing. The rider took his horn (made from some part of a camel), and blew, filling the clearing with the horrible

A large angry man rode high on its back

bagpipe-like sound. Then he raised the horn high in the air and brought it down hard on his steed.

'Hummgggiff Gummmminn Hoofff!' came muffled cries of pain from below.

The creature started to move in a wobbly line across the clearing, picking up speed as the rider beat it harder. More men on these strange creatures arrived in the clearing, following the sound of the horn. They were just in time to catch the lead rider disappearing. They too beat their mounts. As they did, shouts of 'Tally-ho!' and 'Gee-up!' could be heard over the cries from the beasts below.

The front legs of the last of these creatures came to a sudden halt. However, the back legs kept moving and, inevitably, caught up with the front legs. There was an Ooof! and a sweaty red face emerged from the front of the creature. The head looked up at the rider and spoke.

'That's it, Trout! I have had enough! I want a go on top.'

'But I only got a "turn" since the start of the woods, and

A sweaty red face emerged from the front of the creature

you had a long go across the fields,' moaned the rider. Another face now emerged from the back end of the creature, and joined in.

'Yes! . . . and Gristle, you tried to make us jump that gate!'

'Well, I'm not going on, and I'll blame you two if we get in trouble for getting left behind,' said the face at the front.

'All right then!' the rider said with a pout.

He jumped down, and as he took off his jacket and top hat, the creature's body lifted to reveal two men underneath. The

The creature's body lifted to reveal two men underneath

man at the front unstrapped himself, and the rider took his place. The body lowered itself and the new rider put on the jacket and hat, and climbed with some difficulty into the saddle.

'Don't you dare try going through the stream,' the back end of the creature demanded.

'All right, but make sure we catch up,' said the new rider. 'You know the rules about being last!'

He then grabbed a large twig from an overhanging branch, snapped it off, and belted the back end of his mount. With a short scream and some cursing, the creature set off. Quiet returned to the clearing.

The woods now disgorged a weird procession. First the cheeses, then after a few moments the hounds, followed by the huntsmen. Baying filled the night air as the hounds got a clear sight of their quarry. Fear drove the cheeses faster. The hounds gained on them and as they did the cheeses' bleating became ever more mournful . . .

With a short scream and some cursing, the creature set off

A weird procession

Then the first of the cheese-hounds struck. One of the smaller cheeses was trailing a few yards behind the rest. It was an easy target. In one leap, the hound landed its front paws on the cheese. Whimpering and bleating, the cheese struggled to get free, but it was no good. Its legs buckled, and it collapsed on the grass. The dog rolled the cheese onto its side with its snout, and held it down firmly with his paws. Most of the other hounds raced after the other fleeing cheeses, but a few dogs paused long enough to worry the trapped cheese, growling threateningly. As they did so the leader of the hunt laboured up on his mount and clonked them mercilessly with his horn.

Then the first of the cheese-hounds struck

'Back to the chase, you lazy dairy-pugs!' he yelled. 'Gherkin! Deal with this 'ere cheese!'

'Yes, Master!' replied a stubby rider close behind. He slowed his mount, stopped close to the cheese, and climbed down. Throwing a piece of dried bread to the ground to distract the hound, Gherkin put a boot on the cheese to keep it pinned down, then took some string from his pocket and

Gherkin dealing with the cheese

tied it firmly to the cheese's ankle. Keeping a tight hold on the string, Gherkin climbed back on to his mount.

'Right, my boys, it's a gentle ride home for us,' said Gherkin, stirring his mount back towards the town.

'It might be a gentle ride home for you, Gherkin, but it's a damnable long walk for us!' a muffled voice grunted from under the saddle. Still, off they set with the cheese in tow. The hunt was now in the distance, picking off the rest of the cheeses. Their mournful cries were being replaced by a resigned silence.

Off they set with the cheese in tow

The Cheese Hall

He grabbed his doll from under his suit

Chapter 3

FROM ON HIGH

Arthur watched it all from his perch on top of the Cheese Hall. The procession drew closer to Ratbridge and now he could make out most of the creatures involved. It slowly dawned on him what was happening. It was a cheese hunt!

He grabbed his doll from under his suit, and raised it to his mouth.

'Grandfather! Grandfather! It's Arthur. Can you hear me?' There was a crackling and his grandfather replied.

'Yes, Arthur, I can hear you. What's happening?'

'I think I can see a cheese hunt!'

There was a pause, then Grandfather spoke again. 'Are you sure? Cheese hunting is illegal. Where are you?'

'I am sitting on top of the Cheese Hall. I am . . . ' Arthur decided to gloss over earlier events. ' . . . having a break. I can see the whole thing. Riders and hounds chasing and catching cheeses.'

'But they can't! It's cruel, and illegal!' Grandfather sputtered. 'Are you sure there are riders on horses?'

'Yes, Grandfather. Why?'

'Because all the cheese hunting horses were sold off to the Glue Factory after the great Cheese Crash.'

'Well, they do seem to be riding horses . . . but there's something rather odd about them,' Arthur told him.

'They do seem to be riding horses'

'What is it?'

'They're very ungainly, and somewhat oddly shaped . . . I can see that even from here. Who do you think is doing the hunting?'

'I am not sure,' said Grandfather. 'Where are they now?'

'They are approaching the West Gate.'

'Well, they must be from the town then. If we could find out who was responsible, perhaps we could do something to put a stop to it. Do you think you could have a closer look without being seen?'

'Yes, I think so,' Arthur said, starting to feel excited.

'Well, keep up on the roofs, and see if you can follow them.' Grandfather paused. 'BUT . . . be very careful!'

'Don't worry, I will be.'

'And call me if you find out anything.'

'All right. I'll speak to you later. And, Grandfather . . . I've got some bananas.'

'Err . . . Well . . . err . . . I rather like bananas . . .' Grandfather's voice trailed off.

Arthur put the doll away and wound his wings again. Here at last was a chance for some real adventure.

Here at last was a chance for some real adventure

Cheese hunting is illegal!

He pulled out a large black iron key

Chapter 4

INTO THE TOWN

By the time the hunt reached the West Gate, they had nine cheeses in tow. The hounds were exhausted. As the chase was over, their muzzles had been removed. Snatcher, the leader of the hunt, manoeuvred his mount till he was within arm's length of the thick wooden gate. He pulled a large black iron key out of his topcoat, leaned over and unlocked it. Gristle, on the horse behind him, dismounted and swung the gate open.

Arthur flew from the Cheese Hall to a rooftop near the gate, and settled out of sight behind a parapet. He looked down.

In the street below the hunt wove its way into town. It was a terrifying sight. Strange four-legged creatures were carrying very ugly men in very tall hats. A pack of manky hounds sniffed around behind them, and just visible in the

He looked down

shadows were short tubby yellow cheeses tied with pieces of string to some of the riders. One of these cheeses stumbled on the cobbles and let out a bleat.

'Quick!' hissed Snatcher. 'Muffle 'im! We don't want to get caught.'

One of the riders threw a large sack over the cheese and it fell silent. The rider scooped up the sack and the procession continued on its way.

Arthur moved along the parapet till he reached the end of the building. An alley divided him from the next house. He

The procession continued on its way

pressed the buttons on the front of his box, rose silently and flew towards the next house. He was proud of himself—he had not made a single sound that had attracted their attention. But what he had not accounted for was the position of the moon. As he crossed the alley his shadow fell across the street.

Cheeses have many predators, but the one that they fear most is the Cheese Hawk. The merest hint of anything large and flapping will send cheeses into a blind panic. Arthur's flapping shadow was too much for them. All hell broke loose.

Arthur's flapping shadow was too much for them

One cheese let out a sharp cry. This set off the other cheeses. The riders were caught off guard, and had the strings ripped from their hands as the cheeses bolted . . . straight under the legs of the 'mounts'. Two of the mounts tripped over the cheeses and collapsed, throwing their riders to the ground. The riders following them were unable to halt their mounts and they too all piled into the heap. The hounds now went crazy. In their excited state, with no muzzles to hold them back, they set upon all the available human limbs sticking out of the heap. This caused much screaming and wailing. In the middle of the confusion, only Snatcher and his mount were left standing. He looked up and caught Arthur in his stare.

They all piled into a heap

'What do we have 'ere?' he said to himself with a mixture of malice and curiosity.

Arthur watched the commotion in shock. He twisted round to get a better look and in the moment of doing so, it became clear that the blow from the banana woman's stick had damaged his wings.

There was a snapping sound and he felt himself jerk to one side . . . then start to drop. He was falling! Arthur grabbed for the knob and twisted it hard. Still he dropped. His broken right wing was just dragging limply above him like a streamer. Snatcher was driving his mount towards the ground below him. In a last desperate attempt, Arthur reached for the handle on the side of the box and started to wind for all he was worth. The remaining wing sped up. Harder and harder he wound. His descent slowed to a stop . . . just above Snatcher.

Just above Snatcher

Still Arthur wound, harder and harder. Then he felt something grab his ankle. Arthur tried to pull away. There was a cackling from below.

''Ow ingenious! I always rather fancied flying,' came a voice.

'Let me go!' cried Arthur.

'I shall not!' came the reply, and Arthur felt a sharp tug, swinging him around, and the tip of his broken wing poked Snatcher straight in the left eye.

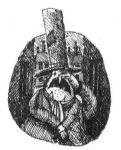

'Wwwaaaahhhh!'

'Wwwwwwwwwwwwaaaaaaaaaaaaaaaaaahhhh!!' Snatcher cried,

releasing his grip on Arthur's ankle and putting a hand to his eye. As soon as he was released Arthur rose a little. Still winding he kicked off from one of the walls and started down the alley. Behind him he could hear a very pained Snatcher.

'Faster, faster, get the little tyke!' screamed Snatcher.

Though he kept winding, there was no way Arthur could get high enough to escape over the roofs—his damaged wing could barely keep him above the ground. To get back to the drain, he would have to make his way through the streets and alleys, he thought wildly. But the cheese-hounds were now snapping below him, and he wound faster still, trying to keep above their reach . . .

Snapping below

Ahead of him the alley faded into darkness, and he turned through an archway into a yard beyond. With a start of relief, Arthur realized he knew where he was. The yard backed onto the lane where the drain—and the way home—was. He had a chance of getting there, if his wings would just hold out long enough. The wall dividing him from the lane was only a few feet higher than he was flying. He might just make it. The barking grew louder again. Arthur wound and adjusted the knob at the same time, twisting it with all his might and willing himself over the wall.

But the remaining wing could not take any more. With a sharp tearing noise, the leather tore away from the wing spars. Arthur frantically reached out for the wall, but it was no good. He was falling—and the cheese-hounds were waiting for him below. Dropping to the ground, he spun round to face the drooling hounds, bracing himself for the worst. There was no way he could fight them off. But they held back, seeming to be a little scared by the flailing wing spar.

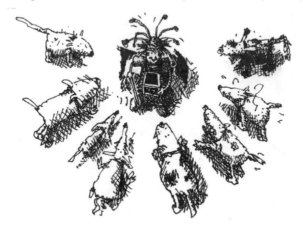

He faced the drooling hounds

For a wild moment Arthur wondered if he could somehow beat them back, but then there was a crunching noise from the box and the skeleton of the last wing stopped. The hounds started to spread out in a circle around him. They were growling and snapping, looking for a chance to pounce. Desperately, Arthur tore one of the wing spars from his back, and spun around to confront any dog that seemed to be getting closer. Every time he did, the hounds on the other side would start to creep forward. He noticed a water butt in the corner of the yard, next to the back wall. Perhaps if he could manage to get onto that, he might have a chance. Fending off the dogs, he moved towards the butt. The hounds moved with him. Then Arthur's heart sank again. Snatcher entered the yard. He quickly dismounted and walked towards Arthur, holding a hand over his injured eye.

'No you don't, you little vermin. I have plans for you! . . . And your wings,' he wheezed.

'No you don't, you little vermin'

The man's eye now was so swollen that it had closed.

'It's just as well that you poked me in me glass eye,' Snatcher hissed, 'or I'd have had to come up with something even more unpleasant than I've got planned for you!'

Snatcher snarled and made a lunge for Arthur. Arthur jumped back, and bumped into the butt. He was completely cornered.

'Now, boy, give me those wings of yours. I am very interested in contraptions! Take 'em off now! Now!' Snatcher ordered.

Arthur slowly reached for the buckle on one of his shoulders.

'Faster, boy!' Snatcher snapped. 'Get 'em off quick, or I'll be setting the hounds on yer!'

Arthur released one buckle, then another and finally the last one at his side. The wings were now loose.

Snatcher grabbed the wings

'Give 'em 'ere!' Snatcher hissed.

Arthur slipped the wings over his head, and as he did so Snatcher grabbed them.

'Clever, very clever . . . might well be useful!' Snatcher mused as he turned the remains of the wings over in his huge hands.

Arthur stood with his back against the water butt, glancing from the snapping dogs to Snatcher. Grandfather had warned him so many times about being careful. Now, having made just one mistake, he was in real trouble for the first time in his life. The dogs took their chance and moved closer as Snatcher's attention was not on them.

Then one of the larger hounds made a lunge for him. Arthur kicked out just in time and caught the dog's nose with his toe. The dog pulled back with a whimper, and Snatcher looked up.

Arthur kicked out just in time

'You just keep him there, me pugs.' He smirked, and turned back to his inspection.

Arthur slowly moved his hands back onto the butt then, stealthily, always keeping an eye on Snatcher, he pulled himself up till he was sitting on the edge of it. The hounds started to growl and strain forward, but Snatcher was so absorbed in the wings that he absent-mindedly shushed them. So, careful not to make a

sound, Arthur raised his knees till his heels were resting on the edge of the butt.

The hounds started to growl and strain forward

He glanced up at the top of the wall, and one of the hounds let out a bark. Snatcher looked up and realized what was happening. He let out a cry of rage just as Arthur jumped up, turned, grabbed the top of the wall and pulled himself over it.

He fell flat to the ground on the other side, and winded himself. He lay for a few seconds trying to catch his breath, and listened to the shouts of anger and barking from over the wall.

'Get round the back and 'ave im! You mutts!' Snatcher bellowed. There was the sound of leather on dog and then a loud howling.

He fell flat to the ground

Arthur scrambled to his feet and started for the drain cover at the far end of the lane. Then he heard the hounds coming round the corner. He wasn't going to make it. He ducked into a doorway in the wall, then peeped back out. Snatcher, surrounded by hounds, stood right by the drain cover. There were more footsteps and the rest of the riders appeared.

Snatcher, surrounded by hounds, stood by the drain cover

'I think he went down here! Must live down below! Go and get the glue and an iron plate!' Snatcher ordered. A group of the hunters disappeared.

Snatcher turned and scanned the alley. 'OK, the rest of you search the alley, just in case.'

The men stood for a moment while hounds sniffed the air. Then the little dog that looked like a cross between a sausage dog and a ball of wire wool started to make his way down the alley directly towards Arthur. Arthur pressed his back against the door. This time there really was no way out. A shiver of fear went through him at the thought of what Snatcher would do to him when he got hold of him. Suddenly he felt the door give way behind him. Something grabbed him around the knees, pulled him through the doorway, and the door slammed shut.

Arthur pressed his back against the door

The shop

It framed a boxtroll

Chapter 5

HERE BE MONSTERS!

Arthur found himself standing in total darkness. The overwhelming relief at having got away from Snatcher and his hounds was mixed with the awful fear that he might have been dragged into something even worse. Who or what had pulled him through that door and why? A soft gurgling noise came from somewhere behind him. He turned round towards it, and trod on something. There was a squeak, a scuffling of feet, and the sound of a doorknob being turned. Light broke in as a door opened. It framed a boxtroll, its smiling head protruding from its large cardboard box.

Arthur had seen boxtrolls before, underground. He would occasionally come across them as he explored the dark passages, caverns, and tunnels. Boxtrolls were timid creatures and always scuttled away as soon as they noticed his presence. This was the first time Arthur had seen one close at hand, and it now stood smiling, and beckoning to him.

Arthur walked towards it hesitantly. The boxtroll turned and scampered up a huge heap of nuts and bolts that covered the floor of the room ahead. As it reached the top, it stopped and picked up a handful of the nuts and bolts. Arthur stared as it lifted them to its mouth and kissed them. It then sprinkled them back over the heap, and grinned at him. Arthur had heard that boxtrolls loved everything mechanical, and he'd seen their work everywhere underground, draining the passages, and shoring up the tunnels and caves.

Beckoning to Arthur again, the boxtroll turned and scuttled out of the doorway on the other side of the room. Arthur clambered over the heap and followed it into a small hallway. Ahead of them was a panelled door. The top panels were made of glass, and through them a warm yellow light shone. The boxtroll knocked on the door.

'Come on in, Fish!' a muffled voice replied.

The boxtroll turned again to Arthur and smiled. Then it opened the door, walked a few steps into the room, and cleared its throat.

'Well, what is it, Fish? What treasures have you brought to show us this evening?' A man's voice came from somewhere inside the room. 'Come on then, let's have a look!'

The boxtroll reached back. It took Arthur's hand and led him into the room.

Arthur's jaw fell open. From amongst the cages, tanks,

The boxtroll turned again to Arthur and smiled

boxes, old sofas, clocks, brass bedstead, piles of straw, heaps of books, and who knew what else, stared four pairs of eyes. There were two more boxtrolls sitting on a shelf, a small man with a cabbage tied to the top of his head, and an old man. The old man sat in a huge high-backed leather armchair. He was wearing half glasses and a grey wig, and was smiling at Arthur.

'Hello. Who do we have here?' the old man enquired in a gentle voice.

Arthur blinked. The old man waited patiently.

'I'm Arthur!' he finally said.

'Well, Arthur, are you a friend of Fish?' the old man asked.

The old man sat in a huge high-backed leather armchair

Two other boxtrolls made spluttering noises. The boxtroll holding Arthur's hand turned to him, squeezed his hand, and made a happy gurgling sound.

'Yes,' said the old man, 'I think you are!' He looked sternly at the two boxtrolls on the shelf. 'And Shoe and Egg should know better than to snigger at Fish!' The two boxtrolls fell silent, their faces turning bright red.

Arthur looked around the room. It was packed to overflowing. If you took a junk shop, added the contents of a small zoo, then threw all your household possessions on

The two boxtrolls fell silent, their faces turning bright red

top, it would start to give you an idea of what it was like. It smelt a little of compost. But it was warm and quiet, everyone looked friendly—and, best of all, there were no hounds snapping at him.

He had no idea where he was, but he did know that he felt safe. Safe enough to ask a question himself.

'Please, sir, may I ask you who you are?' asked Arthur.

'Certainly, young man!' the old man grinned. 'I am Willbury Nibble QC . . . Retired! I was a lawyer, but now I live here with my companions.'

Arthur looked about. 'What is this place?'

'Oh, this place was a pet shop, but now I rent it to live in. And these are my friends,' Willbury said, looking around at the creatures. 'You have met Fish already it would seem, and these two reprobates,' he nodded at the other boxtrolls, 'are Shoe and Egg.'

The boxtrolls on the shelf smiled at Arthur. Then the old man turned to the last creature—the little man with the cabbage on his head. 'And this is Titus. He is a cabbagehead.'

The cabbagehead scurried behind the old man's chair.

'I am afraid he is rather nervous. He'll get used to you, though, and then you will find him charming.'

'I am afraid he is rather nervous'

A cabbagehead! Grandfather had told Arthur stories about cabbageheads. Legend had it that they lived in the caverns deep underground. It was said that they grew strange vegetables there, and worshipped cabbages. This had something to do with why they tied cabbages to their heads. Even Grandfather had not seen a cabbagehead, they were so shy.

Arthur thought to himself for a moment then asked, 'Your friends are all underlings, so why do they live with you?'

Willbury smiled with bemusement. 'What do you know about underlings, Arthur?'

'I know that the boxtrolls look after the tunnels and plumbing underground. But I don't know much about cabbageheads,' said Arthur.

They lived in the caverns deep underground

'Well, I am not sure I entirely approve, but our boxtroll friends here act as scouts.' Willbury gave the boxtrolls a funny look.

'Scouts?' asked Arthur.

'Yes. It would seem that the boxtrolls have a need for certain supplies to help with their maintenance of the Underworld. So Fish, Shoe, and Egg wander the town looking for . . . "supplies"! When they find them they "prepare" the item for removal—loosen it, unbolt it, unscrew it, whatever. That's why there is such a large heap of nuts and bolts in the back room. God help me if I was ever visited by the police.'

'They "prepare" the item for removal'

He looked rather severely at the boxtrolls, then resumed speaking. 'They leave signs for the other boxtrolls. You may have seen strange chalk marks on the walls about town. These are there to guide the other boxtrolls to the "supplies" so they can make a quick getaway!'

A quick getaway

Arthur looked across at Fish, who grinned and nodded.

'Yes,' said Willbury, rather sternly. 'I don't think I approve at all. Our friends the boxtrolls have a rather strange attitude towards ownership. Have you not noticed that most of your arrows point at someone else's property?'

The boxtrolls looked rather guilty. Arthur felt a little guilty himself remembering the bananas he had left on top of the Cheese Hall.

With all this talk of 'supplies' Arthur thought it was time to change the subject. 'And your friend Titus?'

Willbury beamed. 'He is researching gardening. The cabbageheads are always trying to improve their methods of cultivation. So occasionally one of them spends some time up here studying human gardening methods. Titus has been here a few weeks. Egg and Shoe discovered him one night sleeping in a coalbunker and brought him back. He's been here for a few weeks writing up a report on gardening. When he's finished he will go back to the Underworld.'

Willbury looked behind his chair and said coaxingly, 'Titus, I think our new friend might like to see your report if you would like to show it to him.'

The cabbagehead shot from behind Willbury's chair to a barrel that stood in one corner of the shop. There was a hole cut in its side just big enough for Titus to clamber through. He disappeared and re-emerged carrying something. He ran back and hid behind the chair. A hand offering a small green notebook appeared.

The pages were covered with tiny writing and drawings

Willbury took the notebook and opened it. Arthur leaned over to look. The pages were covered with tiny writing and the most beautiful drawings of plants.

A squeak came from behind the chair. Willbury closed the notebook, winked at Arthur, and passed it over his shoulder to an outstretched hand. The notebook disappeared.

'Now, Arthur, please sit down, if you wish.' Willbury lifted his feet from a footstool, and pushed it towards Arthur. Arthur sat.

'So what brings you here?' asked Willbury.

Arthur suddenly felt overwhelmed. He didn't know where to begin. Fish came forward, and started talking.

Arthur suddenly felt overwhelmed

'Hummif gommmong shoegger tooff!!!'

'I think it would be better if Arthur explained what's happened himself, Fish,' said Willbury. He smiled encouragingly at Arthur. 'Are you in trouble?' asked Willbury.

'Yes,' whispered Arthur. There was a pause.

'Well, let's hear what kind of trouble it is. We'll try to help you if we can. I have spent my whole life trying to sort out trouble for other people,' said Willbury.

Arthur hesitated, then decided he could trust Willbury. 'Yes, I am in trouble. I live underground with Grandfather . . . and now they've blocked my hole back. It's the only way I know to get home . . . And they have taken my wings!' Speaking the words aloud made Arthur realize fully what a terrible situation he was in. Would he ever be able to get back to Grandfather?

'All right,' said Willbury, looking concerned. 'I think you had better tell me the full story.'

Arthur started. 'I'm from the Underworld . . . well, I have lived there since I was a baby.'

Willbury looked curious. 'You live underground?'

'Yes . . . Me and my grandfather live in a cave . . . well, three caves actually. One we use as a living room and kitchen, another is Grandfather's bedroom and workshop, and the smallest is mine. It's my bedroom.' Arthur looked around the shop. 'It's warm and cosy, a bit like this place.'

'Well, three caves actually'

'But why do you live underground?' Willbury asked in a puzzled voice.

Arthur paused for a few moments. 'I'm . . . I'm not really sure. Grandfather always tells me he'll explain when I'm older.'

'And what about your parents?'

Arthur looked sad. 'I don't know . . . I am a "foundling" I think.'

'But your grandfather?'

'Oh . . . He's not my real grandfather, he just found me abandoned on the steps of the workhouse, when I was a baby, and took me back to live with him. He's raised me like he was my father, but because he's so much older than my father would be I call him "Grandfather".'

'So has he always lived underground?'

Arthur thought for a moment. 'No, he said he lived in the town when he was younger . . . But he doesn't talk about it . . . ' Arthur's voice trailed off.

Willbury decided to change the subject a little. 'You say "they" have blocked your hole back to the underground and taken your wings? Who is "they"?'

Arthur spoke mournfully. 'I saw these men hunting cheese and I went to have a look, but my wings broke and the hunters took them and then I escaped, and was trying to get back down underground when they blocked up my hole.'

'But what were you doing above ground? And what wings? I don't understand,' said Willbury.

Arthur decided to tell Willbury all. His face grew red. 'I was gathering food. It's the only way we can survive. My grandfather is so frail now that I have to do it. And he made me some wings so I could get about the town easily.'

'Your grandfather made you wings?'

'Yes, he can make anything. He made my doll as well so I could talk to him while I am above ground.' Arthur reached inside his under-suit and pulled out the doll to show Willbury.

Willbury's eyes grew wide. 'Do you mean to say that you can talk with your grandfather, using this doll?'

'Yes,' said Arthur.

'Does it still work?' asked Willbury.

Arthur looked at the doll closely

'Yes . . . I think so.' Arthur looked at the doll closely—it didn't look damaged in any way.

'When did you last speak to your grandfather?'

'An hour or so ago when I was sitting on top of the Cheese Hall.'

'On top of—oh, never mind. Does he know what's happened to you or where you are?'

'No . . .' said Arthur.

'Well, I suggest you speak to your grandfather right now to let him know you are all right, and that you are here!' Willbury insisted. All the eyes in the room fixed on Arthur and the doll. 'And when you have spoken to your grandfather, I should like to talk to him, if I may?' asked Willbury.

Arthur nodded. He wound the tiny handle on the box on the front of the doll. There was a gentle crackling noise, and then Grandfather's voice broke through.

'Arthur, Arthur, are you out there?'

'Yes! Yes! It's me! Grandfather, it's me! Arthur!' Arthur yelped. It was such a relief to hear Grandfather's voice.

'Arthur! Where are you? I've been so worried. Are you all right?' Grandfather's voice sounded shaky.

'I followed the cheese hunt like you told me to. I did try to be careful, Grandfather, but the huntsmen tried to catch me . . . They took my wings! And sealed up the drain! But I've escaped and found a safe place . . . and someone who can help me!' Arthur reassured him. 'I'm in an old shop, with a man called Willbury. He wants to speak to you.'

'Certainly—please pass the doll to him,' Grandfather told Arthur. Arthur gave the doll to Willbury, who had been looking at it a little uneasily. Willbury cleared his throat.

'Good evening, sir'

'Good evening, sir. This is Willbury Nibble speaking. I have Arthur with me in my home. I haven't heard the full story, but it sounds as if he has had a terrible time. I would just like to say that you have my word as a gentleman, that while your grandson is in my charge I shall do all within my power to keep him safe. I shall also endeavour to help him return to you, as soon as maybe!'

'Thank you, Mr Nibble!' replied Grandfather. 'If you could help Arthur get back to me safely, I would be very grateful!'

Arthur moved closer to the doll. 'Grandfather, how am I going to get back now that the huntsmen have blocked up the drain?'

For a moment there was just a gentle hissing and crackling from the doll, then they heard Grandfather's voice again. 'I know there are other routes between the town and the Underworld. But I don't know where they are. They belong to other creatures.' His voice sounded sad.

'Sir,' replied Willbury, 'I have a number of boxtrolls and a cabbagehead living with me. They may know of a way!'

Willbury looked up and was met by nodding heads. Even Titus had come out of hiding and was nodding.

'Yes! It seems they do,' said Willbury. 'I will have them help us guide Arthur back to you!'

'Thank you!' came the voice from the doll.

Arthur looked at the creatures gratefully. Of course—it was such a simple answer. He needn't have been so worried. Then Willbury spoke again.

'I think it might be a bit risky with these blackguards who chased Arthur roaming about. I suggest we wait till early tomorrow morning, then Fish and the others can find Arthur a hole.'

'I agree, Mr Nibble. I think Arthur has had enough excitement for one evening.' Then the voice from the doll paused for a moment. 'Getting Arthur back is my first concern. But I am worried about his wings. Without them he won't be able to collect food for us safely . . . '

'I understand your concern, sir. I am not sure where they are or how we might get them back, but I will think on it. It's getting late now, so I suggest that we all get some sleep. Do you have enough food for the moment?' asked Willbury.

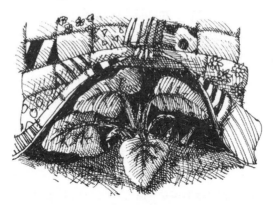

'I have several large clumps of rhubarb'

'Yes, I have several large clumps of rhubarb, growing under the bed,' said Grandfather.

'Good. We'll give Arthur a good supper, and there is plenty of space for him to sleep here.'

'Thank you so much, Mr Nibble. And Arthur, look after yourself . . . I need you back!' said Grandfather.

'I will, Grandfather. Goodnight,' replied Arthur.

'Goodnight, Arthur, and I shall see you in the morning.'

The doll fell silent, and Arthur took it back from Willbury. He kissed it and tucked it in his under-suit.

'Why don't we have a little something to eat, and Arthur can finish telling us his story,' Willbury suggested, looking at Arthur. Then, turning to Titus, he said, 'Titus. Get the big forks!'

A huge smile shot across Titus's face, and he disappeared back inside the barrel for a moment. He returned carrying massive three-foot forks and brought them over to Willbury. Willbury leant down and Titus whispered in his ear.

'Yes, Titus! Go and get the buns . . . and the cocoa bucket.' Willbury nodded.

Titus bounded out of the door at the back of the shop and returned carrying a huge plate of buns and a large zinc-plated bucket full of cocoa. He set them by the fire and the other creatures, Willbury, and Arthur gathered around him. Willbury hung the bucket on a hook over the fire and after a few minutes it was slowly bubbling. Everybody took a fork and started to toast the buns. When the buns were crisp, they dipped them in the cocoa before eating them.

Arthur finished his story as they ate. He told of how he would come up every night to gather food, but of how as it was a Sunday he had to go 'gardening'. Then rather shamefacedly he told of his raid on the greenhouse and how he had been struck by the woman, of his flight to the Cheese Hall, and how he had seen the hunt, and how he had tried to spy on them, then all that had followed—his wings breaking, the evil leader of the hunt, the hounds, and how he had escaped over the wall into the lane.

The boxtrolls listened in awe as they sucked on their buns, and Titus got so caught up in the story that he hid behind Willbury when Arthur mentioned the hounds. Arthur finished his tale and looked towards Willbury, who was staring into the fire.

'It has been quite an adventure, Arthur. I think we should get to bed,' said Willbury. 'Let's just finish off the cocoa.'

Willbury took the cocoa off the fire. When it had cooled a little they took it in turns to drink straight from the bucket. Arthur felt much better.

Drinking cocoa straight from the bucket

'Now, let's get our heads down. We need to be bright and fresh for the morning!' said Willbury.

The creatures found places for themselves around the room and nestled down. Willbury made up a bed for Arthur under the shop counter, out of old velvet curtains. Arthur took off his hat and climbed in. Willbury tucked another curtain around him.

'You sleep well, Arthur. I have an idea where we might make enquiries about your wings.'

Willbury left Arthur to settle and the light in the shop went out. Arthur pulled the soft velvet covers over his head. The curtain felt heavy and gave off rather a comforting dusty smell. Arthur lay quietly in the darkness and started to think. It will be good to get back to Grandfather tomorrow . . . But my wings . . . I can't lose those . . . I wonder what Willbury meant when he said he had an idea?

His thoughts became slower as sleep overtook him. Soon all that could be heard was gentle snoring.

Soon all that could be heard was gentle snoring

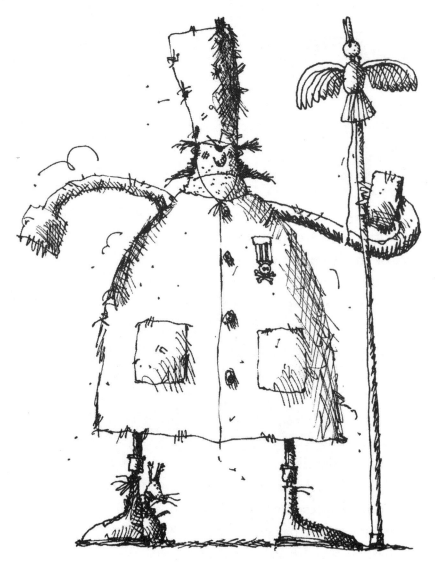

Snatcher

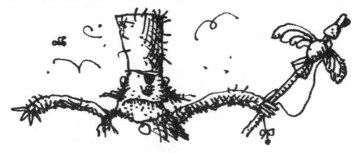

Snatcher raised the pole

Chapter 6

THE CEREMONY

Across the town from where Arthur slept, deep within the heart of the Cheese Hall, the huntsmen and their mounts were getting changed. All stripped down to their long johns, and hung their outer garments on pegs. From cases that were stored under the benches that bordered the room they took out outlandish furry capes, hats, and some battered musical instruments. They donned the clothes, picked up the instruments, and then made their way through a small wooden door into a large hexagonal chamber. This was some twenty feet across, about thirty feet high, with a vaulted ceiling. In the centre of the floor was a deep circular hole. If one had looked into the hole, one might have seen a bubbling mass of sticky yellow cheese far below. This was the Fondue Pit.

Watching from a balcony, about halfway up one wall, was Snatcher. He was dressed in the same furry robes and hat as the other huntsmen, but in his hand he held a wooden pole.

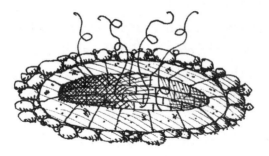

The Fondue Pit

At its tip was a gilded duck. A piece of string went from the duck's head to Snatcher's hand. When the huntsmen had settled down, Snatcher raised the pole and waved it slowly over his head. The huntsmen started to play on their instruments. Some had drums and others strange horns. The noise was awful and grew louder and louder, till Snatcher pointed his duck stick at the hole, and pulled the string. The huntsmen immediately stopped playing. The duck's mouth opened and emitted an eerie quack. The quack faded away, leaving only the sound of bubbling molten cheese. Snatcher spoke.

'Members of the Guild, we are on our way to wreaking revenge on this appalling town. Soon we will be unstoppable!'

The men assembled in the chamber cheered. Snatcher raised his duck stick and the crowd grew silent.

'It is time to feed the Great One! . . . Gristle, lower the cage,' Snatcher's voice boomed.

The duck stick

From somewhere above there was a clanking of chains, and the bleating of a cheese. Slowly a cage came into view. In it was one of the cheeses gathered from the hunt. The crowd watched in silence as the cage went lower and lower until it disappeared into the pit. After a few more seconds the bleating became more frenzied. Then suddenly it stopped, and the chain went slack.

There was another clank from high above, the chain tightened, and slowly an empty cage emerged from the pit. A few strands of cheese stretched, then broke from the bottom of the cage.

Snatcher raised the duck stick. Again it opened its mouth and quacked.

'More cheese, Mr Gristle!' Snatcher intoned.

Slowly a cage came into view

A model of Ratbridge

He sat up and banged his head

Chapter 7

WHICH HOLE?

Arthur woke up with a start. He sat up and banged his head on the wooden shelf above him. Then he remembered where he was. Pale daylight filled the space between the counter and the wall behind it. A face popped into view, and smiled at him.

'Good morning, Fish!' Arthur said, rubbing his head.

Fish gurgled in a friendly way and disappeared. He returned a moment later carrying the cocoa bucket. Arthur swung himself from under the counter and took the bucket.

He returned a moment later carrying the cocoa bucket

It had only a couple of inches of the rich dark liquid in the bottom. Obviously, he realized, he must be the last one up. He lifted the bucket and drank the lot. Fish giggled, then took the bucket back. Arthur wiped his mouth on the hem of his string vest and burped.

'Thank you. I needed that.'

Willbury appeared behind the counter wearing a worn dressing gown of green silk.

'Good morning, Arthur. I think we had better get ready. It's still early, but it's market day, so the streets will get busy quite soon, and I know the underlings prefer it when there are not many people about.'

'We have made a model of the town'

Arthur stood up, followed Willbury and Fish out from behind the counter, and almost walked into a pile of books. Arthur looked down to see a complex pattern of books covering most of the floor. The other creatures stood around its edges.

'What's this?' asked Arthur.

'It's Ratbridge,' replied Willbury. 'My friends here don't really understand maps, so we have made a model of the town with all its buildings and streets. This way we can plan our expedition.'

Arthur looked again at the books on the floor. There before him lay every street and building, defined by books and other objects from the shop. It was astonishing! He looked about and got his bearings. Then he pointed to a small dictionary. 'That's where we are!'

'Yes!' laughed Willbury. 'It works quite well, doesn't it?'

'Well, where have we got to go?'

The underlings started chattering, and each of them pointed at a different part of the 'town'. There seemed to be some difference of opinion.

'The underlings all have favourite holes,' said Willbury. 'I think that we will have to work this out.' He then addressed the underlings. 'I will give each of you a six groat coin, and I want you to place it where your hole is.'

Willbury took a small leather bag from out of his pocket and handed each of the underlings a shiny silver coin. The creatures then carefully leaned over the model of Ratbridge and placed their coins. Willbury surveyed the positions of the holes.

Willbury handed each of the underlings a shiny silver coin

'I rather like the idea of Titus's hole. It's nice and close,' he finally declared. The boxtrolls all laughed. Willbury looked at them, puzzled.

'What is it? What's wrong with Titus's hole?' he asked.

The boxtrolls squeaked and made signs at Arthur and Titus.

'Oh, of course,' said Willbury. 'Titus's hole would be too small for Arthur.' He turned to Titus. Titus reluctantly nodded.

Willbury turned to the boxtrolls. 'Well then, what do you suggest?' Fish seemed the most insistent. He kept pointing at his coin, which was placed amongst books that made the shape of houses and gardens near the edge of town.

Willbury's eyes traced a route from the shop to Fish's coin. 'It seems to me that Fish may have a point. Arthur should have no trouble getting down a boxtroll hole . . . And we could get there very quietly down these back streets.' Willbury indicated the route with a walking stick. 'If we find there are too many people about we can always divert and make our way to one of the other holes. We'll set off right after breakfast.' He turned to Arthur. 'I am sure your grandfather is anxious to see you again.'

Arthur paused. 'But what about my wings?'

'Yes . . . well . . . ' replied Willbury. 'I told you I had an idea. Based on what you said about the man who took them, it occurred to me that he must be someone who knows about mechanical things and the like. I know a person who knows most people in that line. Finding her may take some time as I have not seen her about recently, so I think it better that we get you back to your grandfather first.'

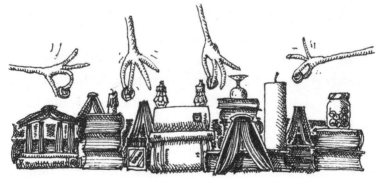

The creatures placed their coins

Arthur's heart sank. 'I am not sure how I am going to be able to collect food for Grandfather if I haven't got wings.'

'Well, you don't need to worry about that. I'll go to the market this morning and get you some food. I have to go anyway as we are out of buns!' Willbury looked around indulgently at the creatures. He turned back to Arthur. 'Come back tonight and I will have plenty for you to take back to the Underworld.'

Then Willbury gave Arthur a rather disapproving look. 'Mind you, I don't hold with taking other people's things. None of this would have happened if you hadn't helped yourself to that lady's bananas. Now, everybody collect up these books and put everything away, and I'll make breakfast.'

'I don't hold with taking other people's things'

Arthur, the boxtrolls, and Titus set about tidying the floor. When they had finished they hovered round the fireplace where Willbury was using the cocoa bucket to make porridge.

'I am afraid it may taste a little chocolatey,' apologized Willbury.

'I think I should rather like that,' replied Arthur, and the other creatures nodded in agreement.

Willbury grinned. 'Well, then I shall add more cocoa and sugar. It will cut out the need to make cocoa afterwards. Titus, would you be so good as to fetch the bowls and spoons?'

After finishing the cocoa porridge, which everyone declared a success, Willbury disappeared into the back room for a few moments, and reappeared dressed. Then he unbolted the front door, and the little band set off through the deserted streets.

Willbury was using the cocoa bucket to make porridge

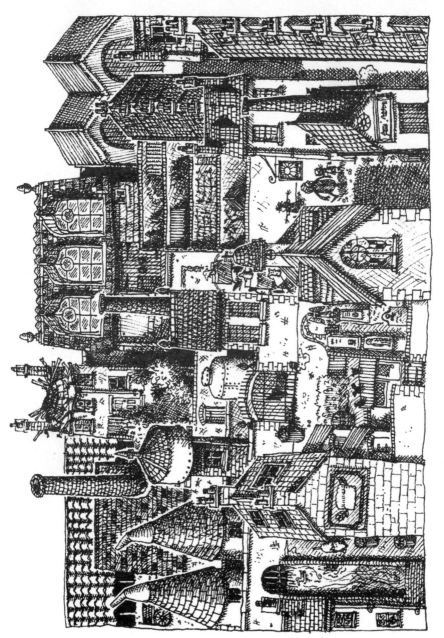

The group made its way through the back streets of Ratbridge

At each corner the boxtrolls checked for humans

Chapter 8

SEARCH FOR A HOLE

The boxtrolls trotted ahead as the group made its way through the back streets of Ratbridge. At each corner the boxtrolls checked for humans, then waved the group on. As yet they had the town to themselves. When they passed a carpentry workshop, Willbury pointed to some blue chalk marks on the cobbles.

The boxtrolls trotted ahead

'I think Fish has been here recently,' he said to Arthur. Arthur's eyes followed the direction of the arrow drawn on the floor. It pointed to a pale strip of brickwork where a drainpipe had once been fixed. 'Yes, I really must have words with them,' Willbury added.

The group moved on. Within ten minutes they were approaching the site of Fish's hole.

Fish, taking the lead, stopped by a door in a garden wall.

He signed to the others to keep quiet and follow him. He pushed at the door and they all made their way into an overgrown garden. It was clear that the house that it belonged to was deserted. Everyone followed Fish up the garden path, carefully avoiding brambles. He led the way to a brick outhouse, and opened its door. Then he let out an anguished squeak.

Fish stopped by a door in a garden wall

The others crowded round to see what had upset him. A large rusty iron plate covered the floor inside. Some kind of dried black glue bulged from around its edges.

Fish turned to them and started to make gobbling noises.

'Confound it!' said Willbury. Then he looked at the boxtrolls. Shoe and Egg were comforting Fish.

Some kind of dried black glue bulged from around its edges

'Let's see if we can lift it,' said Willbury. 'If we get a large stick we could try to force it under the edge.'

Arthur spotted an old spade in the brambles, and hurried to fetch it. Willbury smiled.

An old spade

'Good thinking, Arthur. I think Fish is the strongest one here. Give him the spade, and let him try.'

Arthur handed the spade to Fish, who tried to push it

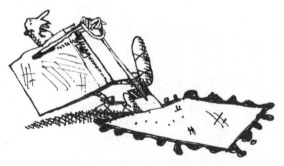

He made no impression

under the edge of the iron plate. But the glue was so hard that even after a great deal of effort he made no impression.

'I don't think we should worry too much, Fish. The hole must have been found when someone was doing repairs on the house, and they just covered it up,' said Willbury consolingly. 'Let's try another hole.'

Fish frowned. He threw the spade down in a rather bad-tempered way.

'Fish! That is not the sort of behaviour I expect from a boxtroll. Pick that up and leave it neatly against the wall, please,' Willbury said sternly.

Fish looked huffy, but did what he was told.

'Shoe, I think your hole is the closest one to here. Let's go there,' Willbury continued. Then he put his hand on Arthur's shoulder. 'Don't worry. We'll have you back home before you can say Jack Robinson.'

The group set off again, this time following Shoe. Fish trailed behind, muttering to himself and kicking every pebble he found in his path.

The butcher's shop

They passed through a few more streets, then arrived outside a butcher's shop. Shoe led them up the side alley next to the shop, and into a walled yard. On one side was a derelict pigsty. Shoe looked about to check that nobody was watching them, then opened the pigsty's gate and went inside. He came back out looking worried. He took Willbury's hand, and led him into the sty. Arthur and the others followed. Old straw had been pushed up around the edges of the sty revealing another large iron plate.

'Oh dear!' muttered Willbury. 'This looks bad. Two holes both sealed up!'

'Three if you count mine,' said Arthur.

'You're right, Arthur. This seems more than a coincidence,' said Willbury, sounding worried.

Arthur was also starting to feel worried. He moved forward and took a long look at the iron plate. 'This is how the huntsmen sealed up my hole last night.' Suddenly getting home did not seem so straightforward after all.

On one side was a derelict pigsty

'I'm beginning to suspect these things could be connected. We had better go and check the other holes forthwith,' said a perturbed Willbury.

Egg now came forward and gurgled to Willbury.

'Yes, Egg! Let's check your hole. Hopefully we'll have more luck there.'

They left the pigsty and emerged up the alley onto the street. A few people were now out and about, pushing handcarts towards the market. They didn't seem to pay any attention to Arthur, Willbury, and the creatures, but the boxtrolls looked uneasy. And Titus nervously tried to keep Arthur between himself and the humans.

Egg led them to a rubbish heap behind the Glue Works, where he immediately started pulling pieces of junk away from one end of the heap. After a few moments he stopped. Sunlight glinted off an iron plate . . .

In silence Egg turned and looked back at them. The boxtrolls started to make an agitated mewing sound. Willbury walked over to the iron plate and stared. Arthur joined him, feeling increasingly alarmed.

'Why would anyone do this?' he asked.

'I am not sure . . . but I have got a very bad feeling about it. We should check Titus's hole to see if the same thing has happened there.' Willbury turned and spoke to Titus, who was trembling all over. 'Can you show us your hole, please?'

Titus nodded his head and the group set off again, this time at a real pace. The streets were now filling but although the boxtrolls still seemed very nervous of the passers-by, and tried to keep to the shadows, Arthur noticed that in fact nobody seemed to take much notice of them at all. Titus was so concerned about getting to his hole that he hardly noticed the onlookers, and even dared to lead them.

They went up and down so many streets that Arthur wasn't sure where they were any more. Titus moved more and more quickly. Then he disappeared around a corner into an alley. The others turned the corner to see Titus in the distance, running towards a drain. Before he reached it, he stopped.

The sun was glinting off a large iron sheet covering the drain. The others caught up, to find Titus whimpering to himself. This time, for several seconds no one said a word.

Titus hardly noticed the onlookers

Finally, Willbury spoke. 'I'm so sorry, Arthur, but I am not sure what I can do. This is terrible . . . and I don't think we know of any more holes.'

Arthur did not know what to say. The thought of never going home again was too much to bear.

Willbury took Arthur's hand and gave it a squeeze. The underlings stood in silence and stared at the iron plate. Then Fish made a noise.

'GeeeGoooW!'

The other boxtrolls turned to look at him and repeated the noise. 'GeeeGoooW! GeeeGoooW! GeeeGoooW!'

Fish turned to Willbury and started to jump up and

down, suddenly filled with energy again. The other boxtrolls joined in. Even Titus was nodding eagerly.

'GeeeeGooow!'

'What is it?' asked Willbury.

The underlings all pointed down the street.

Willbury perked up. 'I think they know of another hole, Arthur.'

The uunderlings nodded.

'Well, let's go!' said Willbury. And they set off at a trot.

The wet dry dock

A fresh-water sea-cow

Chapter 9

THE WET DRY DOCK

Not far from the back of the Cheese Hall was a disused dry dock. This was connected to the canal by a short channel. It was no longer dry as its huge wooden gates were open and hanging from their hinges. The hulks of several narrow boats were partially submerged in the murky water that filled it, and the occasional bubble rose up and broke the weedy surface. If you listened very carefully you might have heard a low rumbling mooing sound coming from its depths.

Willbury and Arthur looked expectantly at the boxtrolls. The boxtrolls stared into the water. Then more bubbles broke the surface. The boxtrolls grinned and started to clap their hands excitedly. Fish looked up and down the footpath and spotted a clump of grass. He ran to it, pulled it up, and tossed it into the water, near where the bubbles had emerged. It sank slowly. And just as slowly, something large moved under the water.

Fish spotted a clump of grass

Arthur was startled. 'Quick, Willbury! Did you see that?'

'Yes I did . . . I'm not sure what it is.'

Fish, Shoe, and Egg were now running up and down the bank, gathering vegetation. When they had built a small heap they nodded to each other, gathered it up, and threw it in the water. Some of it sank, but most of it floated. They all waited.

A large hairy pink muzzle broke the surface of the water, right in the middle of the floating vegetation.

'Oh my word!' said Willbury. 'I have never seen one of those before.'

Something large moved under the water

A large hairy pink muzzle broke the surface of the water

'What is it? What is it?' Arthur asked impatiently.

'I believe it is a fresh-water sea-cow!'

The boxtrolls nodded. The fresh-water sea-cow lifted its head above the water, revealing two large gentle eyes and a pair of short horns. The creature was huge. Arthur stared in awe at its large black and white body floating beneath the water. It started to vacuum up the greenery with its huge floppy nose. With a couple of breathy sucks the food was gone. The sea-cow sank back down till only its eyes and horns were visible above the water. It looked very sad.

Fish held out some dandelion leaves

Fish crept closer to the water's edge, crouched down and held out some dandelion leaves. Slowly the sea-cow moved towards him, raised its head, and sucked in the leaves. Fish's hand got covered in slobber, but he kept very still. Then very carefully he reached out with his other hand and patted the sea-cow's nose. The group watched in silence.

Fish now made gentle gurgling noises as he patted the pink muzzle, and the sea-cow held still. Then it let out a deep sigh. Fish made a mewing sound and the sea-cow replied with another sigh.

Fish's hand got covered in slobber

Arthur tugged on Willbury's arm. 'I think he's talking to it!'

They watched for a few minutes as the boxtroll and the sea-cow made conversation. Then the sea-cow sank back into the water and disappeared. Bubbles rose from the pool and then all was still.

Fish stood back up. He looked very upset.

'What is it, Fish?' asked Willbury.

Fish started to jabber. As he did so, Willbury leaned

down, and Titus began whispering in his ear. Arthur realized that Titus was translating what Fish was saying to Willbury.

Willbury looked more and more uneasy. When Fish had finished Willbury turned to Arthur.

'Something tragic has happened. That poor sea-cow!' Willbury's voice trailed off.

'What is it?' asked Arthur quietly.

'Well, the fresh-water sea-cows live in waterways under the town. They use a tunnel that extends from the dry dock to come out into the canal to feed. That sea-cow has three calves. A few days ago she left them here to play while she went off to forage in the canal. When she returned the calves were gone . . . and the tunnel blocked . . . '

Fish slowly nodded his head. The group stood very still.

'What can we do?' asked Arthur.

'I'm not sure, Arthur. I'm not sure,' said Willbury very quietly. Then he turned to the underlings. 'Do you know of any more holes?'

The underlings slowly shook their heads.

Willbury gazed into the water of the dock for a while then spoke. 'I really have no idea what is going on. I think it best if we all go back to the shop.'

He started to walk back up the path. The others followed in silence. As they trailed through the now crowded streets, Titus gripped Arthur's hand. Things did not look good.

Willbury

'Grandfather! Are you there?'

Chapter 10

THE RETURN

As soon as they were inside the shop Willbury turned to Arthur. 'I think we had better call your grandfather. He needs to know what's going on.' Arthur nodded in agreement.

He reached under his shirt and took out the doll, wound the handle, and soon the familiar crackling could be heard.

'Grandfather! Are you there?'

Grandfather's voice came back straight away.

'Arthur, where are you? Are you underground yet?'

'No . . . I am not,' Arthur replied. 'We have tried, but all the underlings' holes have been blocked up.'

There was a pause. Then they heard Grandfather again.

'Where are you now?'

'I am back at the shop with Mr Nibble.'

'Can you let me speak to him, please?'

Arthur passed the doll to Willbury.

'Every entrance has been sealed up'

'Hello, sir,' said Willbury.

'Hello, Mr Nibble . . . this doesn't sound good at all. Have you any idea what is going on?'

'Frankly . . . no. We have tried five entrances to the Underworld, and every one has been sealed up. With Arthur's that makes six.'

'Do you think that lot who chased Arthur last night are sealing the holes to stop Arthur getting back underground?'

'I don't think so. Some of the holes have been sealed up for some time. It's not just about Arthur and his wings.'

There was another pause.

'Do you have any clue who this bunch of ruffians who chased Arthur were?' asked Grandfather.

Willbury thought for a moment. 'I don't, but there is someone I know who is well up in the world of inventions. She knows everyone with an interest in mechanics in Ratbridge. She might know the man who took Arthur's wings.'

'If you could follow that lead up I would be very grateful.'

'I have to go to the market for food, and will go to find my friend after that,' replied Willbury.

There was another silence. Then Grandfather spoke again.

'This business with the cheese hunting? It's been illegal for years now. In the old days it was the Cheese Guild that did the hunting, but the Guild was said to have died out when the trade was banned.'

'Do you think it might be something to do with that?' asked Willbury.

'Years ago, when I lived above ground, there were rumours about the Cheese Guild. Nothing specific . . . just the odd story of "Goings On" . . . secret meetings and the like.'

There was a long pause

Willbury looked quizzical. 'If you don't mind me asking—why do you live underground?'

There was a long pause. When Grandfather finally replied, there was a steely tone to his voice that Arthur had never heard before. 'I was accused of a crime that I did not commit. I have had to take refuge here ever since.'

Arthur felt his skin prickle as he stared at the doll. This was the closest he had ever come to finding out the reason for their life underground. Would Grandfather say more? What sort of crime could have driven him underground for so long? He looked up and found Willbury's gaze upon him. Then Grandfather continued.

'I have kept it from Arthur as I felt he was too young to understand. But please believe me when I say you have my word as a gentleman that I am an innocent man.'

'I believe you, sir,' said Willbury. Then looking at Arthur he spoke again. 'We shall leave it at that. I think Arthur may be old enough to understand. But I also think it better he hears this sort of thing from you face to face.'

'Thank you,' came the voice from the doll.

Willbury looked at Arthur one more time, then asked another question. 'On a more immediate matter. Do you have enough food, Grandfather?'

'Yes. The rhubarb seems to be thriving. I think I have a few days' supply.'

'Well, hopefully we can get this matter sorted out very quickly. I am sure Arthur will be back with you soon.'

'I do hope so,' said Arthur quietly.

'Yes . . . We will go and see my friend this morning. I am sure she will be able to help,' said Willbury.

'Can you call me as soon as you know anything?'

'I will make sure that Arthur calls you as soon as we have any information.'

'Thank you . . . And, Arthur, YOU TAKE CARE . . . I need you back.'

'All right, Grandfather!' said Arthur. He took the doll from Willbury. 'I will be very careful . . . and I will be back . . . Soon!'

Arthur was trying to sound positive, but actually he felt very unsure now of when he was going to get home—if ever.

'Speak to you later then,' said Grandfather.

'Goodbye . . . till later!' Arthur put the doll away.

'Right!' said Willbury firmly. 'I think we need a good feed. I can always think better on a full stomach. Let's draw up a shopping list.'

Arthur could tell that Willbury was as worried as he was, but that he was trying to keep everyone's spirits up. If he could put a brave face on the situation, then Arthur would too. The boxtrolls and Titus needed him to be strong, so he tried to raise a smile as they all sat down around the shop. Willbury took out a quill and a scrap of paper from under his chair.

Then there was a knock.

Willbury took out a quill and a scrap of paper

A rather grubby man

Everyone turned to the door

Chapter 11

A VISIT

Everyone turned to the door. Through the window they could see the tall shadow of a figure standing outside.

Willbury put his finger to his mouth. 'Quiet!' he whispered. 'It may be the hunters looking for Arthur. Arthur, quick, hide behind the counter.'

Arthur obeyed without hesitation. He never wanted to see the huntsmen again if he could help it. The memory of their leader's sneering face still made him shudder. He got back down into the space where he had slept the night before. There was a crack in the woodwork, and by placing his eye close to it he could still see the shop door. He watched as Willbury unlocked the door and stepped back.

A rather grubby man wearing a frock coat and a top hat stood on the doorstep. He was holding a large box in his arms, and on the ground by his side was a bucket.

A bucket

'Excuse me, sir,' he said in an oily voice. 'My name is Gristle, and I represent the Northgate Miniature Livestock Company. I was wondering if you might be interested in buying some rather small creatures?'

Willbury looked quizzically at the box, and then stared at the bucket. 'Er. Umm. You know this is not a pet shop any more?' he said slowly. 'What are they?'

'They are the very latest thing! Miniatures! Little versions of some of the pet industry's best sellers.'

Mr Gristle put down the box and, with a flourish, took off the lid. Willbury took a look at the contents of the box, and couldn't help smiling.

'They're beautiful!' he said, squatting down. Then he frowned. 'But they don't seem very happy.'

'No,' replied Gristle. 'I think it's a by-product of the breeding.'

The underlings had become curious. They moved shyly closer to have a look.

'You wouldn't like to do a swap, would you?'

'You wouldn't like to do a swap, would you? I'm looking for BIG creatures,' Gristle said, eyeing up Willbury's companions. All the big creatures pulled away again, and hid behind Willbury.

All the big creatures hid behind Willbury

'Certainly not!' Willbury blurted, outraged. Then his curiosity got the better of him. 'What's in the bucket?'

Arthur was also immensely curious, but couldn't see what was happening now as Willbury and the underlings were obscuring his view. He would have to wait, he told himself.

Willbury took out his leather coin bag

'A little spotty swimming thing. I believe it's from Peru,' said Gristle.

'How much do you want for them?' asked Willbury.

'How would five groats sound?' said Gristle, rather hopefully.

'It would sound very expensive!' replied Willbury.

'Well, three groats, five farthings. It's my last offer. I can always take them to the pie shop,' Gristle smirked.

Willbury looked shocked. The underlings gasped collectively. Willbury took out his leather coin bag and gave Gristle the money.

'Thank you, squire! Are you sure you don't want to part with any of your BIG friends?' Gristle asked again.

'Absolutely not! Now, be off with you!' Willbury had taken a distinct dislike to Mr Gristle. He lifted the box and the bucket into the shop, and closed the door on the salesman.

The letterbox flipped open.

'I really am very interested in your BIG friends, sir. I'm sure we could come to some arrangement?' said the disembodied voice of Mr Gristle.

'Go AWAY!' said Willbury, starting to get angry.

The letterbox closed for a moment, and then a ten groat banknote appeared, held by two long thin grubby fingers.

'Pretty please,' whispered Gristle.

The fingers started to wave the note. Willbury took a lone cucumber from the vegetable box that was kept on the floor.

'I'm warning you. GO AWAY! I do not sell friends!' Willbury was turning red.

Another banknote held by another pair of fingers slipped through the letterbox, and started waving.

'Oh, go on!'

'Oh, go on! Twenty groats. They are only dumb old underlings,' the voice said.

This was too much for Willbury. He raised the cucumber and brought it down on the letterbox flap. There was a 'Splut!' as the cucumber hit the flap, a 'Snap!' as the flap

closed on the fingers, and a scream from outside. The fingers
and the banknotes disappeared.

'You'll be sorry for this!' came a muffled shout from outside. Then they heard the sound of footsteps hurrying away.

A silence fell over the shop. Willbury turned and spoke.
'You can come out now, Arthur.'

Arthur joined the group huddled around the box and bucket

Arthur joined the group huddled around the box and
bucket. He peered into the box. The bottom was covered
with straw, with half a turnip, covered in tiny bite marks,
lying in one corner. Standing amongst the straw were a
number of tiny creatures. There was a cabbagehead and a
boxtroll, both about five inches high, and three trotting
badgers. Most trotting badgers were the size of large dogs,
but these were the size of mice. All the creatures in the box
were shaking with fear.

Three trotting badgers

Fish leaned over the box, and made a low, cooing noise. The tiny boxtroll looked up and started squeaking. Fish looked puzzled. He looked up at Shoe and Egg, who also seemed puzzled. It was obviously a boxtroll, but they couldn't understand what it was saying. Shoe grunted softly. Fish nodded, raced out of the room, then raced back in again. In his hand was a brass nut and bolt. He laid them in the straw next to the tiny boxtroll. The tiny boxtroll made some more squeaking sounds, then picked up the nut and bolt, kissed them and gave them a hug. The big boxtrolls smiled.

The tiny boxtroll

A small splash came from the bucket. Everyone turned to see ripples spreading over the surface of the murky green water.

'I wonder?' Willbury muttered to himself.

He reached for a small piece of the shattered cucumber, and dropped it into the bucket. For a moment it hung just below the surface. Then a tiny head emerged from the murk and started to nibble the cucumber. As the creature fed, more of it came into view. Its body was short and stout, a bit like a very small seal. It had horns and a large floppy nose, and its skin was white with black patches.

'Oh my!' said Willbury. 'It's a tiny fresh-water sea-cow.'

'It's so small!' said Arthur. 'You don't think it's one of the calves the mother lost?'

'No, no. They would be much bigger than this,' Willbury said. Then he muttered to himself. 'Peru, did he say? I didn't think that they had them in South America.'

He looked up at Fish. 'Will you and Titus go and get the old fish tank, from the back of the shop? Fill it with fresh water. We need to get this little one out of the dirty bucket.'

The sea-cow started to explore its new home

Fish and Titus fetched the tank and placed it on the counter, then started to fill it with jugs of water. Willbury laid an old stoneware jar on its side in the tank. There was some pondweed in the bucket, so he took that out and placed it in the tank too. When the tank was three quarters full, Willbury told Fish and Titus to stop. Then he lifted the bucket onto the counter, rolled up his sleeves, and gently lifted the sea-cow out into the tank. With a plop the little creature entered the water. It swam straight to the bottom of the tank and disappeared into the jar. They all stood around the tank and watched. After a minute or so, a nose emerged.

'Keep very still,' said Arthur quietly. He was practically holding his breath, not wanting to disturb the tiny creature.

Slowly the sea-cow swam out and started to explore its new home.

'Now we must find homes for our other friends,' Willbury said. 'I want Fish, Shoe, and Egg to look after the little boxtroll, and Titus, you can look after the tiny cabbagehead.'

The big boxtrolls looked very happy. Willbury picked up the little boxtroll (who was still hugging the nut and bolt) and passed him to Fish. The other boxtrolls crowded around. After a great deal of billing and cooing they set off around the shop to give their new friend a tour.

Titus looked nervous. Willbury lifted the tiny cabbagehead up to his nose. He took a sniff and smiled, then offered it to Titus to smell. Titus leant forward and took a tiny sniff.

Willbury picked up the little boxtroll

After a moment a smile spread over his face too. He then lowered his face to the tiny cabbagehead and allowed it to smell him. The tiny cabbagehead gave a little squeak, and jumped onto Titus's shoulder.

'Why don't you show him where you live?' suggested Willbury.

Titus's eyes grew bright. He clutched the tiny cabbagehead to his chest, shot across the room, and disappeared through the hole in his barrel.

Willbury smiled. 'Titus really needed a companion!'

Suddenly there was a scuffling from the box and the trotting badgers scurried across the floor and disappeared into a mouse hole in the skirting board.

'Oh dear!' said Willbury.

Arthur picked up the box and turned it over. One corner had been chewed away, leaving a small hole.

'That's the problem with trotting badgers! They are really wild . . . and have REALLY sharp teeth,' said Arthur. 'Grandfather always warned me to stay away from the outer caves and tunnels where they live. He says "You can get in real trouble with a trotting badger!"'

'Oh! Well, do you think these little ones will be all right?' asked Willbury.

Titus with the tiny cabbagehead

'If they are anything like the big ones they should have no problems. It's the mice in that hole that I feel sorry for . . . trotting badgers will eat anything.'

'Well, we'll leave out some milk and biscuits for them later. Maybe if we keep them fed they'll leave the mice alone. I don't think there is anything else we can do,' said Willbury looking at the hole in the skirting board.

He turned and picked up the quill and paper from his chair. 'Now I think we should finish this shopping list, get to the market, and then find my friend.'

Arthur and Willbury sat down again. As soon as the boxtrolls realized what was going on they joined them.

'How are you getting on with your new friend?' he asked them.

Fish gurgled and pointed at a matchbox on the mantelpiece, then at the little boxtroll who Shoe was now holding.

'Oh! You have called him "Match". How very appropriate,' said Willbury.

The boxtrolls and Arthur giggled.

'Now what would everybody like to eat?' asked Willbury.

Shoe nudged Egg, who then reached inside his box somewhere and produced a folded piece of paper. He handed it to Willbury. Arthur watched as Willbury unfolded it. Drawn very neatly on the paper were pictures of all the foods that the boxtrolls wanted, grouped together by type.

'Thank you, Egg!' said Willbury, studying the pictures. 'I notice that you are rather light on vegetables. You know they are good for you.'

The boxtrolls moaned. Willbury turned towards the barrel in the corner. 'Titus! Could you come out? I think we need some help with the shopping list.'

Titus appeared, carrying the little cabbagehead, and took up position standing next to Willbury.

'So, Titus, do you have any suggestions for vegetables?'

The boxtrolls looked glum while Titus's eyes lit up. He leaned over and started to whisper in Willbury's ear.

Willbury was soon struggling to keep up. The list grew very long. The boxtrolls looked increasingly unhappy. Then Willbury raised a hand and Titus stopped.

'I think that is enough vegetables. Thank you, Titus.'

Titus looked at the little cabbagehead and whispered again to Willbury.

'Yes. I am sure I can get your friend a Brussels sprout.' Willbury caught the boxtrolls making faces at each other. 'You could take a few tips from cabbageheads on diet.' Willbury looked back down at the paper they had given him. 'Boxtrolls cannot live by . . . cake, biscuits, treacle, boiled sweets, toffee, shortbread, pasties, anchovies, pickled onions, raspberry jam, and lemonade . . . alone!'

The boxtrolls looked rather guilty. Willbury turned to Arthur. 'What would you like to eat?'

'We had better get off'

'Do you think we could have some more cocoa and buns?'
he asked rather sheepishly.

Willbury raised one eyebrow. 'Well, only as part of a
properly balanced diet . . . ' he began. Then he giggled. 'I was
going to get them anyway.'

Arthur smiled.

'And I think I shall get myself a few pies . . . ' said Willbury,
finishing the list and putting down his quill.

'Right, we had better get off. I think it best if we leave the
underlings and their new friends here.'

Three men in top hats and mufflers, sitting on a large cart

Willbury put on his coat while Arthur stood waiting by
the shop door. Arthur had never been to market, and he was
rather excited by the idea. But when Willbury opened the
door, there was an immediate shock. The street was
thronging with people. Arthur was astonished. He had never
been above ground in the middle of the day before. He never
dreamed that there could be so many people in the world.
Suddenly he felt rather frightened.

'Keep close, I don't want to lose you,' said Willbury.
And off they set.

What they failed to notice was that across the street were three men in top hats and mufflers, sitting on a large cart. As Willbury and Arthur headed towards the market, the men climbed down. One lifted a large metal bar from the back of the cart. The other two took out some old sacks. The men then walked shiftily towards the shop, all the time checking to see that nobody was watching them.

The men walked shiftily towards the shop

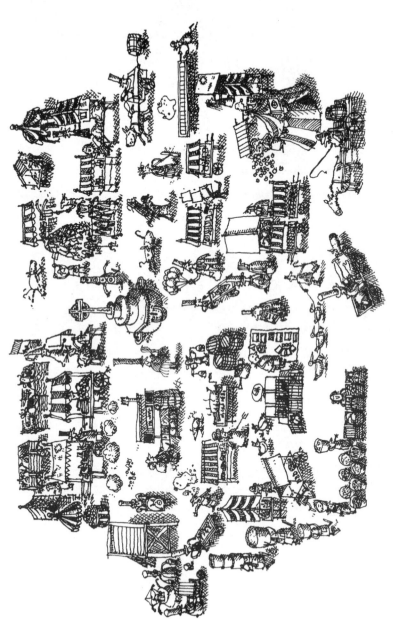

Early morning in Ratbridge market

Willbury led Arthur through the streets of Ratbridge

Chapter 12

THE MARKET

Willbury led Arthur through the streets of Ratbridge towards the market. Arthur had never been anywhere so crowded. There were tradesmen and women, farmers, shopkeepers, dogs, chickens, pigs, street sellers, buskers, and more children than he had ever seen in his life. On his night-time expeditions he had rarely seen children and when he had, he'd had to hide. But now they took no notice of him as they played. Some of them were kicking a leather ball the size of a cabbage about, while others were chasing each other, or fiddling with sticks in puddles. Arthur felt a little jealous at the easy way they laughed and spoke with each other.

'Willbury?' asked Arthur.

'Yes, Arthur?'

'What do children do?'

'You know. Play with friends, and go to school, and the like . . . '

Arthur was not sure he did know. He looked at the children. 'I don't think I have any friends.'

Willbury stopped and turned to him. 'I think you do! What about Fish . . . and Egg and Shoe . . . and Titus . . . and me?'

Arthur smiled, and they walked on. It was so noisy! There was shouting, barking, horses' hooves on cobblestones, the rumble of cartwheels, and over everything was the cackling of the ladies . . .

There were an awful lot of ladies doing an awful lot of cackling. And as they cackled, they tottered slowly down the streets, their bottoms wobbling behind them. Arthur had not seen bottoms like these before. From the way the ladies paraded their 'derrières' it seemed that to have an interesting behind was very much the thing! Round ones, cone-shaped ones, pyramidal ones, cuboid ones, and some that defied description. All large, and wobbling like jellies.

The ladies seemed perturbed by the bottoms of their rivals and kept taking furtive looks at the competing behinds. And they had plenty of time for these observations as they moved so slowly. This was because they wore ridiculously high shoes, which seemed to have been specially designed to make walking close to impossible.

Arthur could not help overhearing the conversation of two of the ladies.

There were an awful lot of ladies doing an awful lot of cackling

'Hark at her,' said one to another.

'Which one do you mean? That Ms Fox?' replied the other.

'Yes! Coming on hoity-toity with her new hexagonal buttocks,' said the first, with more than a hint of jealousy.

'No? And on shoes like that! She thinks she's the bee's knees, and she doesn't even realize that hessian went out weeks ago!'

Arthur had no idea what they were talking about. He looked up at Willbury, slightly bewildered. Willbury smiled, leaned towards him, and whispered, 'Fashion victims!'

Approaching the market the streets became more and more crowded. Arthur found it very exciting. As they entered the market square they were met by a wall of rather shabby people.

*As they entered the market square they were met by
a wall of rather shabby people*

'Hang on very tightly to my hand, Arthur!' said Willbury
as he pushed into the throng.

Arthur grabbed Willbury's hand and hung on. Slowly
they squeezed their way through the jostling mass of bodies.
Arthur could see very little except when there was a break in
the crowd and for a moment he would catch sight of the
stalls . . . He was amazed! He had never seen such a profusion
of things. Stacks of sausages, bundles of new and second-
hand clothes, strange tools and gadgets, bottles of grim
looking medicines, stacks of broken furniture, toys, clocks,
pots and pans . . . The list went on and on. Even when he
couldn't see much about him the smells kept flooding into
his nostrils. Some were familiar, some new, some sweet and

some very, very unpleasant. Arthur felt boggled by it all.
How strange the town seemed by day. Occasionally
Willbury would guide them towards a stall where he would
buy food, and then off they would set again on their journey.
As the shopping amassed Arthur helped Willbury with the
bags, which were making it increasingly harder to move
through the market.

Finally they broke free of the crowds and Arthur found
himself standing by the cross in the very centre of the
market.

Willbury led him towards a pie stall which stood against
the market cross. Around it was a group of people wearing
oily overalls, chewing on pies, chatting, and drawing on
blackboards attached to the stall. Built into one side of the
stall was a strange copper drum with a chimney. A man
behind the stall was shovelling coal into the drum through a
door in its base.

Around it was a group of people wearing oily overalls, chewing on pies

'Are you hungry?' Willbury asked Arthur. 'The pies here are simply the best in Ratbridge. Would you like to try one?'

Arthur looked at the group around the stall tucking into their pies and decided that he was very hungry indeed.

'Yes, please!' he answered.

The man behind the stall looked up and smiled at Willbury.

'Good day to you, Mr Nibble, sir. Is it the usual? A nice turkey and ham special for yourself?' the man asked Willbury. 'And what would the young man like?'

'Yes, a turkey and ham would be very nice, thank you, Mr Whitworth,' replied Willbury. 'I recommend that you try one as well, Arthur.'

'Yes, please!' said Arthur again.

Mr Whitworth opened a door in the top of the copper drum and scooped out two large steaming pies with his spade. He flipped them onto a stack of newspapers on the counter, put down the spade and then wrapped a few sheets of the newspaper around the pies.

'Will there be anything else, Mr Nibble?' asked Mr Whitworth.

'Just a bit of information. I am trying to get in touch with Marjorie. Do you happen to know where she is?' replied Mr Willbury.

'Haven't you heard? She's been camping down at the Patent Hall for weeks, ever since they lost her application,' answered Mr Whitworth.

Mr Whitworth opened a door in the top of the copper drum and scooped out two large steaming pies with his spade

'Lost her application?' Willbury sounded alarmed.

'Yes. Marjorie took her application and prototype for some new invention of hers for approval, but the man who was checking them disappeared for lunch with them. And never came back . . . Now Marjorie's stuck there—if she leaves the queue she could lose her invention for ever!'

'How awful! We must go and see her straight away.' Willbury hesitated for a moment. 'I'll take her six of your finest pork and sage, please! She'll need to keep her strength up. How much is that?' asked Willbury, offering a silver coin.

'They are two groats each, Mr Nibble. But I'll not be taking your money. We are all doing what we can to help poor

Marjorie. It may be a small thing but pies are vital to keeping one together. If you take them down to the Hall for her I'll not be charging you for the pies for you and the boy either.'

Mr Whitworth pulled six more pies and a small cake from the oven, wrapped them, and then placed them in a sack with the two turkey and ham pies.

'The cake is for you, young man.' Mr Whitworth smiled and winked at Arthur.

'Thank you!' said Arthur.

'Yes! It is very kind of you, Mr Whitworth. Thank you indeed!' said Willbury.

Mr Whitworth pulled six more pies and a small cake from the oven, wrapped them, and then placed them in a sack with the two turkey and ham pies

Mr Whitworth passed the sack to Arthur. 'You look like a strong lad. If you run out of energy you can always eat one.'

Happily Arthur took the sack and swung it gently over his shoulder. Then with a parting wave to Mr Whitworth they picked up the shopping bags and set off into the crowd again.

IS THAT THEOREM CAUSING CONFUSION?
IS THAT HYPOTHESIS BEFUDDLING YOUR BRAIN?

You need brain food! Try a pie!!! From

WHITWORTH'S SCIENTIFIC PIES

Choose from today's finely-balanced range:

Turkey and ham

Turkey and ham in precisely equal quantities, with a catalyst
of four-sevenths of a teaspoon of the strongest English mustard

Pork and sage

The finest Ratbridge Old Spot pork combined with a compound
formed of four-fifths fresh sage, one-tenth ground cloves,
one tenth ground black pepper

Venison and redcurrant jelly

A combination of venison with a precisely-set jelly
formulated from 19 redcurrants per pie

Rhubarb and ginger

An amalgam of rhubarb and ginger, with one third of an ounce of cardamom,
and heated for 47 minutes to a temperate 108 degrees centigrade

All pie vessels are formed from pastry which has been made from flour
specially milled to a density of thirty-six pounds per cubic foot.

Madame Froufrou

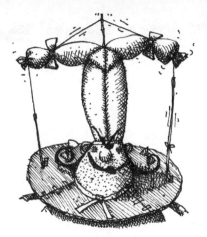

A very strange woman

Chapter 13

MADAME FROUFROU

Arthur and Willbury set off across the market in the direction of the Patent Hall, Arthur trying to keep up with Willbury as they pushed their way through the crowds again. As they reached the edge of the market the crowds became even denser until finally they could no longer find their way through, and were forced to come to a stop.

They were in the middle of a large crowd of ladies, all of whom seemed in a state of high excitement. It was clear there was something unusual going on.

'What do you think is happening?' Arthur had to raise his voice to make himself heard above the sound of chattering and twittering.

'I am not sure. There seems to be a platform with someone on,' Willbury called back.

Willbury then guided Arthur in front of him. The crowd parted a little and Arthur could see a high wooden platform. On it stood a very strange woman. She wore a dress that looked as if it was made from skinned sofa and cardboard, an enormous pink wig, and a pair of rubber gauntlets. She also had a patch over one eye.

'Who is it?' asked Arthur. Despite never having seen a woman dressed in such a way before, Arthur felt the woman was oddly familiar, but for the life of him, he didn't know where from.

The woman standing next to them overheard Arthur's question. 'Don't you know? It's Madame Froufrou . . . the fashion princess!'

Willbury and Arthur looked at each other, shrugged their shoulders, and turned back to watch.

The strange woman raised her arms to quiet the crowd and the din died down. The ladies of the town were now all aquiver, and some let out squeals of delight.

'What has she got this week?' one whispered.

'I heard it's something really special . . . and totally new,' replied another.

'I can hardly bear it,' said the first. 'I missed out last week and they haven't let me in the tearooms since.'

The woman on the platform glowered at the crowd. A silence fell, but was broken by the sound of a large wooden box being slid up onto the stage. The woman started to speak.

'Today, my little fashion friends, Madame Froufrou 'as a real treat for you.'

Little cries of 'Magnifique!' 'Wunderbar!' 'I must have one' 'I must have two', came from the crowd.

The lady on the platform gave a smirk. She leaned over to the box, opened a door in its lid, and reached in with her large rubber-gloved hand. She paused, then looked about the crowd, and gave them what was supposed to be a look of delight. Then slowly she pulled out a tiny creature. It was a miniature boxtroll.

Then slowly she pulled out a tiny creature

The crowd let out a gasp of admiration. Arthur turned to Willbury. They both looked shocked.

'It's just like the ones Gristle brought to the shop! What do you think is going on?' asked Arthur.

'I am not sure, but I don't like it!' replied Willbury. 'Let's watch.'

Madame Froufrou started to speak again. ''Ere I 'ave a lickle lap creature, just the very sort the finest ladies of Pari are clamouring for as we speak. I 'ave a very limited supply and I'm afraid that some 'ere will be left in a sad and lonely fashion backwater.'

She paused and stared at the crowd. A soft pitiful moaning started from all around Arthur and Willbury.

'I cannot 'elp this, but it is for you to decide whether you are a woman of tomorrow or merely a ugly frump . . . with no sense of taste . . . or chance of social position!'

At this the ladies of the town started a desperate squeaking.

Then someone cried: 'Me, me, sell one to me!'

Others immediately joined in the cry. 'ME, ME, Me, No! Me, ME!'

The noise grew so loud that Arthur had to put down his shopping and put his hands over his ears.

Madame Froufrou raised a hand. The cries halted and all that could be heard was the snapping of opening purses, and coins being counted.

'I cannot be kind to you all . . . My supplies are very limited.'

Someone in the audience let out a miserable whimper.

'Should Madame Froufrou choose the ladies at the front to give the opportunity to buy these sweet treasures?'

Cries of 'No! No! No!' came from the back of the crowd.

A fashionable lady of Pari

'Should I choose only those who are wearing this week's pink?' asked Madame Froufrou, grinning.

'No! No! No!' came the cries from all but those who wore pink.

'I think I shall do as they do in Pari,' said Madame Froufrou.

'Yes! Yes! Yes!' cried the ladies. 'Do what they do in Pari!'

'Yes, I shall do what they do in Pari. I shall do what is the latest thing . . . and select only from those who are . . . fashionably . . . RICH!' Madame Froufrou came to a halt and several ladies in the crowd fainted.

She scanned the crowd. 'Now, there is a question you must ask yourselves. Am I fashionably RICH? If you are not . . . you must cast yourself from this world of glamour and

retire to your true miserable and rightfully low position.'
She glowered at the crowd.

There was silence for a moment then cries of 'I am rich! I
am rich! I am rich!' came from the ladies around Arthur and
Willbury.

Again Madame Froufrou raised her hand and silence
returned.

'What a joy it is to be in such fashionable company.
But . . . I have a feeling that hiding amongst us are some . . .
DOWDY FRUMPS!'

A dowdy frump

Arthur noticed that the women around him all started to
tremble with fear.

Madame Froufrou paused a long time for dramatic effect,
then spoke again. 'I shall have to weed them out . . .

BUT HOW?' There was another very long pause as she peered around the crowd. 'I have an idea . . . an idea that will show up the dowdy frumps hiding amongst us!'

Several more ladies in the crowd fainted.

Madame Froufrou started again. 'Could the fashionable ladies here please raise their hands and display the most fashionable quantities of money they can . . . And please do check that those around you are fashionable!'

Hundreds of hands shot up and started to wave money

For a few moments all that could be heard was the rustling of banknotes and clinking of coins. Then hundreds of hands shot up and started to wave money. The ladies looked nervously around. Madame Froufrou now took out an enormous pair of binoculars and started to scan the crowd.

'As I look at you all, I am shocked that one whole area is obviously harbouring the dowdy trying to pass themselves off as fashionable . . . '

Nervous twitching broke out.

'I shall turn my back for a moment and let them crawl away . . . for if they are still here when I turn back . . . I shall

POINT THEM OUT!' With that she turned her back.

The ladies now struggled to find every last penny to hold up in an attempt to avoid being labelled a frump.

Madame Froufrou turned slowly back and smiled. 'Ah! I see they have fled! It is only the stylish that remain.'

'Yes! Yes!' cried the crowd in relief.

'Well, it is time for us to impart the new and ultimate accessory upon those who deserve it! Come hither, Roberto and Raymond.'

Two men dressed in dirty pink suits climbed onto the stage.

'These are my French fashion specialists and they are here to help me select those who are the most fashionable. Roberto and Raymond, please take out your fashion scopes and wands . . . Divine those that are expectable!'

Two men dressed in dirty pink suits climbed onto the stage

Roberto and Raymond pulled out what looked like binoculars made from toilet rolls, and fishing rods with small buckets hung on the end. Looking through their binoculars they started to scan the crowd.

Looking through their binoculars they started to scan the crowd

Roberto's gaze fixed upon a particularly full hand and he turned to Madame Froufrou. 'Madame, I think I see a fashion angel,' he said, indicating the 'angel' in the crowd.

'Yes, it is true! A woman of grace and virtue! Now my angel, if you would place your offering in the bucket affixed to our fashion wand, and take a numbered ticket, I shall invite you to collect your very precious new lifestyle accessory from the stage, and lo . . . You shall be a queen amongst women!'

Roberto took out a grubby ticket from his pocket and put it in the bucket at the end of his wand. Then he swung the wand out over the crowd to the angel's outstretched arm. The woman pushed all of her money into the bucket, took the ticket, and squeaked as she made her way towards the stage. Looks of hatred and envy followed her. The bucket swung back over the crowd and disappeared. When the angel had made her way to the stage Madame Froufrou passed the tiny boxtroll down to her in exchange for the ticket.

Madame Froufrou passed the tiny boxtroll down to her in exchange for the ticket

Roberto and Raymond began selecting more members of the crowd and exchanging tickets for cash, while Madame Froufrou stood by the wooden box and collected the tickets, and handed out more miniature boxtrolls. The crowd of ladies rapidly thinned, as they handed over their cash, collected their new pets, and set off in small groups to parade them.

Then Arthur and Willbury watched as Madame Froufrou turned to what remained of the crowd.

There were now only three ladies, Willbury, and Arthur left. The remaining women still held their handfuls of cash aloft, as they quietly wept.

Madame Froufrou saw Arthur and for a moment fixed him with a rather steely gaze, before turning her eye on the ladies.

'Do you know her?' whispered Willbury.

'I am not sure, but there is something about her. I get the feeling that I have met her before,' Arthur muttered nervously.

'And from the look of it, I think she thinks she knows you!' Willbury replied.

Madame Froufrou was now asking Roberto and Raymond some questions. They answered and she turned back to her remaining customers.

'We have I am afraid sold out of our little friends in the box, but it is not my way to let you POOR ladies go home with no chance of social position. It seems I have a late special offer.'

The remaining ladies let out their breath. Roberto and Raymond disappeared down behind the stage and after a few moments three large zinc buckets were passed up.

Arthur stared at the buckets, then turned to Willbury. 'You're not thinking what I am thinking about those buckets, are you?'

Willbury was looking shocked. 'If I am, this is definitely more than a coincidence!'

'Come closer, ladies. In these vessels are some very special creatures that have only come into fashion in the last few minutes . . . ' Madame Froufrou whispered.

The remaining ladies suddenly started to look happy again as they made their way to the front of the stage.

'Yes! The very, very latest. Fresh-water sea-cows! Dredged from the banks of the Seine. These creatures are the very height of chic in the bathrooms of Pari and Milan.'

The ladies started to giggle, and Willbury picked up his shopping. 'Quick, Arthur. Grab your things. I am going to have words with this Madame Froufrou.'

Arthur picked up the sack and shopping bag, and followed Willbury towards the platform.

'Excuse me, madam!' called Willbury. Madame Froufrou looked up at Willbury, then down at the ladies, then back at the approaching Willbury.

'I am sorry, ladies, but I have to go.' She snatched the money from the outstretched hands. 'Help yourselves to the buckets.' Then she turned and jumped off the back of the stage.

'Excuse me, madam! Where do you think you are going?' shouted Willbury. 'I want words with you!'

Arthur followed Willbury as he ran round to the back of the platform.

Madame Froufrou and her assistants were gone.

After a few moments Willbury spoke. 'You said she looked familiar. Do you know where you might have seen her?'

'I'm not sure where I could have seen her before. I know it's strange, but I got the same feeling when I was looking at her, that I got when the leader of the cheese hunt cornered me. She could have been his twin sister.'

'Very strange . . . ' Willbury paused to think. 'Something is very wrong . . . And weird. I think we had better go and find Marjorie. Maybe she can throw some light on things.'

Madame Froufrou and her assistants were gone

Outside the Patent Hall

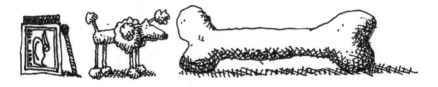

A miniature French poodle

Chapter 14
THE PATENT HALL

Willbury and Arthur made their way up the side streets towards the Patent Hall, and as they went they talked.

'Before today I'd never seen, nor even heard of, miniature boxtrolls, cabbageheads, sea-cows, or trotting badgers. And now miniatures seem to be everywhere. It's very odd,' said Willbury.

'I suppose there are different types of creature in different countries,' said Arthur.

'True. I've heard of miniature French poodles, so I guess France might be the home of a lot of small things,' added Willbury. 'But I don't like something about what's going on. Think how unhappy those poor creatures were when they arrived at the shop . . . And as for Madame Froufrou . . . Well! The less said about her the better!'

'I just don't understand what is going on,' said Arthur. He felt bewildered and rather sad.

'Yes, it is all rather odd,' replied Willbury. Then he paused for a moment as he thought. 'This business of the hunt leader and Madame Froufrou looking like brother and sister is strange. I wonder if all this bother is tied up in some way?'

'Do you think your friend Marjorie might be able to help?' asked Arthur.

'I do hope so,' replied Willbury. 'She might not be able to shed any light on this matter of the miniature creatures, but I suppose we should concentrate on our own problems at the moment. Getting you back to your grandfather, and getting your wings back. As I said, Marjorie knows pretty well everybody who has anything to do with mechanics in the town. I am hoping that she will help us track down your wings.'

'Who is Marjorie?' asked Arthur.

'Marjorie was my clerk. Very bright woman. She used to deal with patent claims mostly. Invariably she could understand most inventions better than their creators, so when I retired she decided to go into inventing, rather than sticking with law. She has a natural aptitude for it. A lot of the legal stuff can be very boring so I was not surprised. Anyway, with all the legal work she did with patents and now with her own inventing, she knows everybody who has anything to do with machines and the like. Though it is quite a secretive world, if you are trusted like she is, you do get to hear what is going on.'

'Marjorie was my clerk'

'So do you suppose she might hear where my wings are?'

'That is what I was hoping, but even supposing we do get your wings back, we still have to get you back underground.' Willbury looked sad.

'Yes . . . I have been thinking about Grandfather . . . ' Arthur's voice trailed off.

Willbury put a hand on Arthur's shoulder to comfort him. 'There have to be other ways to get you back into the Underworld.'

'There are,' said Arthur. 'But I just don't know where!'

Willbury stopped in his tracks. 'What do you mean? Have you heard of other routes to the underground?'

'Yes,' said Arthur.

'Arthur, this could be very important. Tell me everything!'

'Well, lots of creatures live underground, and not just under Ratbridge . . . A lot of their tunnels are linked up. It might be possible to get down one of the tunnels outside Ratbridge, and get back to Grandfather. But I just don't know where the other tunnels come out above ground . . .

And it might be dangerous,' Arthur replied.

'Dangerous?' Willbury sounded surprised.

'Yes. I was always warned to stay away from the outer tunnels. Trotting badgers live in some of them . . . and they can be very, very nasty. Grandfather lost a finger to one when he was younger.'

A trotting badger

'Are trotting badgers the only creatures that have tunnels outside the town?' asked Willbury.

'No. There are rabbits . . . and rabbit women.'

'Rabbit women? I thought they were just a myth.'

'No! They exist. I saw them once when I was exploring . . . well, not actually them . . . I found a home cave,' replied Arthur.

'Home cave?'

'It's a place where they live. You can tell it's a home cave by the things they leave about—scraps of food, ash, rabbit droppings, and suits the rabbit women have knitted from rabbit wool.'

'So do you know where the rabbit women's holes are? Could we find one?' asked Willbury.

A rabbit woman knitting rabbit wool

'No.' Arthur looked very sad. 'I don't think so. They are very, very secretive, and keep themselves very much to themselves. They have to . . . to avoid the trotting badgers.' He paused. 'Besides, the rabbit women are so good at tunnelling that their holes could be miles away.'

It had started to drizzle. They both felt glum and fell silent as they walked. Soon they came to a small cross roads and Willbury pointed down one of the streets.

'This way. The Patent Hall is not far now.'

'By the way, what is a patent?' asked Arthur.

'Oh! That was my speciality as a lawyer.' Willbury perked up a little. 'A patent is a legal certificate given by the government to the inventor of some new device or idea or process. The patent says that because it is their idea they are the owner of that invention. This gives them the right to use their invention without others copying it without their permission. The patent will last for some years and that way the inventor can profit from their invention.'

'Does that mean that if I had invented string, I could charge everybody who made or sold string?'

'Yes, Arthur, if you had invented string you would be a very, very rich man.' Willbury chuckled.

'So what happens at the Patent Hall?'

'It's a government office where inventors go to get patents. They have to prove that their ideas work and are totally new.'

They turned up another side street and there in front of them stood the Patent Hall. It was a fine building with a frontage that looked like a Greek temple. Arthur had noticed it before when he had been flying, but approaching it on foot it seemed far bigger than he remembered. There was a queue of inventors that started in the street, led up the steps, past the pillared entrance, and disappeared through a huge pair of oak doors. The members of the queue all carried carefully

wrapped bundles and looked round nervously at Arthur and Willbury as they passed by.

'Why are they looking at us like that?' asked Arthur.

'They are all worried that someone might steal their ideas before they are registered and patented,' said Willbury. 'There are people that come here specially to try and get their hands on new ideas, and rob the poor inventors of their patents.'

Willbury led Arthur up the steps of the Patent Hall, and in through the doors. Just inside was a desk where a man was handing out tickets to people in the queue. Beyond was a large crowded hall. Down either side of the hall was a series of tents, each with a number on. The tents were made of thick canvas that had seen better days and was now covered in burns and a multitude of stains. Strange noises, and the odd flash of light, came from several of the tents. Outside each of these tents stood a queue of even more nervous-looking inventors.

'That is where the inventors give the initial demonstrations. If they get through that they are sent upstairs to have their inventions checked for originality,' said Willbury.

At the far end of the hall was a large staircase and by it stood a group of very shifty-looking men. Arthur caught Willbury giving them a very suspicious glance.

'Failed Patent Acquisition Officers! Scum!' Arthur was shocked by Willbury's mutterings.

'Who is?' asked Arthur.

'That lot at the foot of the stairs!' Willbury pointed an accusing finger. 'They are the very scum of the mechanical world. Technical vultures! They hit a man when he's down, and by the time he recovers they have either made off with his invention or have him so tied up in contracts that he either has to buy them off or hand the whole thing over to them. Vermin! They should be locked up!'

'How do they do that?' asked Arthur.

'Well, if an inventor isn't granted a patent because his idea is not fully developed or the patent officers just don't understand it, the inventor can get very upset and disheartened . . . and that lot . . . ' Willbury pointed his finger again at the group at the bottom of the stairs. ' . . . that lot . . . move in on him.'

The Failed Patent Acquisition Officers had spotted Willbury pointing at them, and were now trying either to hide behind the tents or slide along the walls and out of the entrance.

Willbury's voice grew louder. 'Every day they assemble there at the bottom of the stairs, waiting for their chance to spring . . . They watch for unhappy faces leaving the tents,

The very scum of the mechanical world

then . . . with all the slime they can muster they approach the man and offer him "sympathy"! They might take him round the corner for a cup of tea, offer him a biscuit or piece of cake, tell him they might have a few bob to help him out and take his project further, ask him to just sign a little document to show they are pals and will be willing to have fun together . . . and before he knows what's hit him he doesn't own the clothes he stands up in! The scum then turn the screw. They make the man finish his project under the threat of legal action, then sell it on once it's patented . . . without a single penny going back to the inventor.'

Willbury's voice could now be heard throughout the hall. He took a turnip from his shopping bag and threw it at the last of the Failed Patent Acquisition Officers, who was disappearing out of the main doors.

There was a yelp from outside, and some of the older inventors cheered.

He took a turnip from his shopping bag and threw it

'Very satisfactory!' said Willbury, rubbing his hands. 'When I was a lawyer it was a favourite pastime of mine to break the grasp of those filth. I have very happily kicked their posteriors on a number of occasions! And if there was one thing that would persuade me to come out of retirement it would be the opportunity to kick a few more.'

Arthur looked a little startled.

'Now,' said Willbury, 'let us find Marjorie!'

Willbury looked around the hall, walked over to one of the queues, and asked, 'Does anybody know where Marjorie is?'

Several arms pointed up to the balcony on the first floor. Arthur and Willbury set off up the stairs. When they reached the top Willbury led Arthur to a small desk at the far end of the balcony. A small tent was erected by the side of the desk, and outside it in a deckchair sat a very unhappy looking woman, reading a book of mathematical tables. Willbury coughed and the woman looked up.

*A small tent was erected by the side of the desk, and outside
it in a deck chair sat a very unhappy looking woman*

'Good morning, Marjorie,' said Willbury. 'I would like
you to meet a good friend of mine: Arthur. How are you?'

The woman dropped the book of tables to her lap, then
spoke. 'Not well, Mr Nibble. Not well. I have been stuck
here for months . . . and things are not looking good!' She
paused for a moment, then stood up and reached out a hand
to Arthur. 'I am sorry. It is very impolite of me. I am pleased
to meet you, Arthur. It's just everything has gone wrong for
me.'

Arthur took her hand, shook it, and gave her a
sympathetic smile.

'I did come here to ask you for some help, but before we

get onto that can you tell me what has happened to you?' asked Willbury.

'I came here three months ago with my new invention, did my initial demonstration downstairs, and then was sent up here to see a Mr Edward Trout. He had to check the machine for originality. I was a bit dubious when he said he was taking it away for inspection. Then he didn't come back!'

'What! He disappeared?' asked Willbury.

'Yes! That's right. I can prove that I gave him a machine because I've got a receipt, but because my receipt has no description of my machine on it, I can't prove what it is that they have got of mine. They keep trying to get rid of me by sending out junior clerks with any old rubbish they can find in the warehouse! But I won't leave until they give me back my invention!'

'Oh dear, dear me!' said Willbury. 'This is terrible. How have you managed to survive?'

'Yes, it is terrible, but the other inventors have been very good about it. They have brought me food when they can . . . and this tent and chair. I have just about got enough to live on, but I can't spend the rest of my life here.'

The receipt

A junior clerk with a piece of rubbish from the warehouse

Willbury looked very concerned. 'No . . . no, you can't.'

Marjorie spoke again. 'The clerk who disappeared has apparently now left the employment of the patent office, and I am very scared that he just ran off with my invention.'

'Ran off with your invention? What was it?' asked Willbury.

Marjorie looked around furtively, then she whispered to Willbury, 'I know I can trust you Mr Nibble . . . but at this point I think it better that no one knows!'

'Oh!' said Willbury. 'If you are sure. Is it the sort of invention that others might want to steal?'

'Yes! Mr Nibble, it is fantastic,' Marjorie whispered. 'It is the culmination of the last two years' work . . . But in the wrong hands it could be very dangerous . . . and now it has either been stolen, or lost!' Marjorie was looking very upset, and Willbury took her hand in his.

Arthur caught Willbury's eye, and pointed to the sack.

'You will never get in to see him Mr Nibble!'

'I know it may be of little comfort, but we have brought you some pies from Mr Whitworth,' said Willbury. 'Arthur, could you get them out while I go and have a word with the Head Patent Officer, Mr Louis Trout.'

'Louis Trout?' said Marjorie. 'It was an Edward Trout that went off with my machine.'

'I had heard that Louis Trout's son had joined the office. It must have been him,' said Willbury. 'I am sure that he will know exactly what has happened.'

'You will never get in to see him, Mr Nibble!' said Marjorie. 'I have been trying for weeks.'

'I think I shall! He knows me from a certain legal case . . . and if I let one or two things drop in conversation with his receptionist I think he will see me very quickly.'

With that Willbury left Arthur and Marjorie, and disappeared into the grandest of the doors along the balcony.

Marjorie's eye fixed on the sack. 'Err . . . um. What flavour pies are they?'

'We've got six pork and sage, a couple of turkey and ham, and Mr Whitworth gave me a cake as well. You can share that with me if you want?' offered Arthur.

Suddenly Marjorie looked a lot more perky. 'It's not one of Mr Whitworth's mulberry cakes, is it?'

'I am not sure,' replied Arthur. 'Why?'

'You wouldn't be offering to share it if it was,' Marjorie jested.

Arthur reached inside the sack and pulled out the smallest of the bundles, then unwrapped it. The cake was pink and dotted with small pieces of fruit.

'It is!' declared Marjorie. 'Joy upon joy. Do you really not mind sharing it?'

Arthur grinned. 'I don't mind.' And he broke the cake in two and passed half to Marjorie. She stared at the cake and after a few moments closed her eyes and took a bit of it. Arthur watched her, then did the same. As soon as the cake entered his mouth the flavour burst over his tongue. Marjorie was right—it was a joy. He opened his eyes to see Marjorie stuff the rest of her half of the cake into her mouth at one go.

'You must be very hungry?' asked Arthur. Marjorie nodded, then after a deep swallow spoke again.

'Now I remember food! My stomach thought that my throat had been cut. Do you mind if I get stuck into a pork and sage pie . . . or two?'

Arthur reached inside the sack again and pulled out the

rest of the parcels. He unwrapped one and noticed it had a pig made of pastry stuck on the top.

'I guess this must be pork and sage then?'

'Yes. Mr Whitworth always puts a sign on his pies so you can recognize what's inside.' Arthur passed her the pie. 'I have to thank you for bringing these to me. It is very kind.'

Something occurred to Arthur. This was the first woman he had ever spoken to and he felt a little bashful. He watched as Marjorie tucked into the pie, then there was a noise from along the balcony. Willbury had reappeared and was looking very flushed and angry.

'What's the matter, Willbury?' asked Arthur.

'Pack up your things, Marjorie! The Head Patent Officer, Mr Louis Trout, has taken early retirement and gone off to set up a new business with his son . . . the man who disappeared with your invention!'

Marjorie lowered the pie from her mouth, swallowed, then spoke. 'They've stolen my machine!'

'I am sorry but it looks as if it might well be that way,' said Willbury.

'What do I do?' asked Marjorie. 'Do I stay here and wait for ever, or do I go in search of the Trouts . . . and for ever lose my chance of recovering my invention here?'

Willbury spoke in a soft voice. 'I think the chances of getting your machine back here at the moment are almost nil. Your last chance is to file an official complaint . . . Come with us now and I will help you draft one. And besides,

'What do I do?' asked Marjorie

I think we need your help. If you come with us I'll explain why.'

They collected up their things and then they set off back across the town to the shop. Marjorie was muttering about what she might do if she ever caught up with the Trouts, Arthur was worrying about Grandfather and his wings, and Willbury had a face like thunder. And then things got worse . . .

Willbury, Arthur, and Marjorie stood in the doorway of the shop and just stared

Even Willbury's armchair had been broken and upended

Chapter 15

GONE!

Willbury, Arthur, and Marjorie stood in the doorway of the shop and just stared. The door had been broken from its hinges, and inside the comfortable untidiness had been reduced to a broken shambles.

'Oh no!' Willbury whispered under his breath. 'What's happened?'

Arthur felt shocked, and a little afraid. He reached up and took Willbury's hand. The room was a pitiful sight. The bookcases were overturned, the curtains torn, and newspapers and books were scattered over the floor. Even Willbury's armchair had been broken and upended.

Arthur felt Willbury's grasp suddenly grow tight. Willbury cleared his throat then called out. 'Fish! Titus! Egg! Shoe! Where are you?' He was met with silence. He spoke again but this time there was real worry in his voice. 'Where are the creatures?'

Arthur broke free of Willbury's grip and ran across the room to look behind the counter, then he ran out through the door to the back room and hall. He returned looking very glum. 'They're not here.'

Willbury walked forward into the centre of the shop, and stopped. He reached down and picked up a torn piece of cardboard, raised it to his nose, and sniffed.

He raised the torn piece of cardboard to his nose and sniffed

'Fish!' he muttered, and clutched the piece of cardboard to his chest.

Arthur walked forward to Willbury. Willbury looked down at Arthur. 'Something awful has happened!'

Suddenly Arthur noticed that his feet felt cold. He looked down and realized that he was standing on a piece of sodden carpet. There by his feet was the fish tank on its side. He leaned down. In the shadow of the earthenware jar lay the miniature sea-cow. It didn't move, and Arthur was not sure if it was still alive. Willbury followed Arthur's gaze and dropped to his knees.

'Quick, Arthur, fetch a jug full of water!'

Arthur ran out to the back of the shop, found a jug, filled it, and rushed back. Willbury slowly righted the tank as he filled it from the jug. The sea-cow floated on the surface of the water. They all stared at her body, hoping they were not too late. After a few moments it twitched and started to move.

'Thank God!' said Willbury. 'I hope it's going to be all right. Arthur, go and get more water.' He gently lifted the tank and placed it back on the counter. Arthur refilled the jug, and soon the tank was full.

Willbury slowly righted the tank as he filled it from the jug

'Where do you think everyone is?' asked Arthur.

'I am not sure . . . ' said Willbury as he looked about. He lifted a bookshelf upright and started to place a few books back on it. Marjorie joined him.

'What shall I do?' asked Arthur.

'Would you see to that water?' Willbury pointed at the damp patch on the carpet. 'Collect up some newspapers, and use them to soak it up.'

Arthur walked towards some newspapers that lay strewn across the floor. Lifting a handful of them, he suddenly let out a gasp. There, huddled on the floor, shaking uncontrollably, was the miniature boxtroll.

'It's Match!' cried Arthur to Willbury.

The tiny boxtroll ran straight at Arthur and threw its arms around his ankle. Arthur looked down at Match, and something shiny on the carpet caught his eye. It was Match's nut and bolt. Arthur reached down and gently picked up Match, then with his other hand picked up the nut and bolt and passed it to Match's outstretched arms. Match took the nut and bolt and snuggled into Arthur.

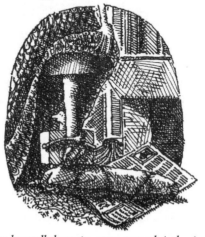

The tiny boxtroll threw its arms around Arthur's ankle

'That's right. You take care of Match,' said Willbury.

Marjorie looked at the miniature boxtroll, then walked over and looked in the tank. She did not say a word but looked very uneasy.

'What is it, Marjorie?' asked Willbury.

'Nothing.' Marjorie paused. 'Where did these tiny creatures come from?'

'I bought them this morning from an awful man called Gristle . . . ' Willbury stopped. 'He wanted to buy Fish . . . and the other big creatures. He was desperate to get his hands on them. I wonder if he was behind this? If so, he is going to pay for it!'

'We saw miniature creatures today at the market, too,' Arthur said. 'Willbury, do you think that Gristle has something to do with Madame Froufrou?'

'I am not sure, but whatever is going on, we have got to get Fish and the others back!' declared Willbury. 'I don't know why Gristle wanted them, but I can't help feeling they're in terrible danger.' He looked around the room again and his eyes fixed on the barrel in the corner. 'Titus!' he exclaimed and rushed to the barrel. Willbury got down on his knees and peered through the hole in the side.

'Oh dear, you poor thing!' said Willbury. He reached inside the barrel and pulled the tiny cabbagehead out. 'Titus may be gone . . . but his little friend is still with us.'

Willbury held the miniature cabbagehead in his hand and gently stroked it. It too was shaking.

Willbury held the miniature cabbagehead in his hand and gently stroked it

'Poor thing,' Willbury said mournfully.

As Willbury, Arthur, and Marjorie were fussing over the tiny cabbagehead, thinking about how to comfort him, there was a sudden coughing from the shop doorway. They spun round, fearful of who they would see there. But the sight that greeted them was quite unexpected—it appeared to be a large basket full of dirty washing supported by a pair of legs.

A large basket full of dirty washing supported by a pair of legs

'Good morning! Need any washing done?' The washing lowered itself to the floor, and from behind it stepped a smiling man with a platform made of sticks fixed to his head. On the platform sat a large and friendly-looking rat, wearing a spotted handkerchief tied around his head.

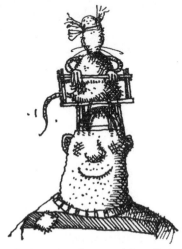

On the platform sat a large and friendly-looking rat

'This is Kipper,' the rat said, indicating the man below, 'and my name is Tom. Business card, please, Kipper!'

The man with the platform fixed on his head pulled out a tiny business card from his pocket, passed it to the rat, who then held it out. Willbury walked forward, took the card and read it.

First Mate Tom R.N.L.

The Ratbridge Nautical Laundry

We wash whiter and boil things brighter

No load too big or filthy

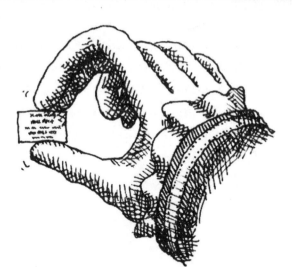

The tiny business card

Willbury was not sure whether to address the rat or the man beneath.

'It's all right,' said the man called Kipper. 'I'm just the muscle round here. You deal with the boss.'

'Boss?' cried the rat. 'Not boss! This is a working co-operative. We are all equal in the Ratbridge Nautical Laundry. It is true that I deal with the customer interface, and you deal with the load management. But you know that last week when we tried it the other way round . . . it all went horribly wrong!'

'True enough, Tom. You're rubbish at shifting things and I am rubbish at organizing stuff. Anyway, sir,' Kipper said turning to Willbury, 'if you would like to deal with Tom here, as he is the brains of this outfit, I shall just stand beneath until required.'

'Yes,' said Tom the rat. 'Now, may we be of any service to you? You are very lucky as this week is our "Big Smalls Promotion". As we are new in this area, the Ratbridge Nautical Laundry is offering a special introductory offer to new customers. As much underwear as you like boil washed, free . . . if you get two shirts and a pair of trousers . . . '

Tom stopped. Kipper had just poked him in the ribs.

'I think our friends here have got more on their minds than cheap deals on getting their underwear washed,' said Kipper.

Tom looked at Willbury, Arthur, and Marjorie, then about the shop.

'Oh, my Gawd! What's happened here? Closing down sale?' he asked.

'No, I think we have been raided and our friends snatched,' replied Willbury.

'Oh!' said Tom. 'Please excuse my patter.' He looked genuinely concerned. 'When did this happen?'

'In the last hour or so. We've just got back from town, and this is what we found on our return,' said Willbury.

'Did you say your friends are missing?' asked Kipper.

Willbury looked slowly about the room. 'Yes, our dear, dear friends are missing.'

'How many were there?' asked Tom.

'Four—Fish, Shoe, Egg, and Titus,' said Arthur.

'They're three boxtrolls . . . and a cabbagehead,' added Willbury.

'Boxtrolls and cabbageheads?' asked Tom. 'What, like those creatures?'

Tom pointed to Match, who Arthur was still holding, and to the tiny cabbagehead that Willbury was trying to comfort.

'Yes,' said Willbury. 'Only much, much bigger.'

'Oh dear!' said Tom. 'How terrible!'

Then Kipper spoke. 'We've had three of our crew disappear in the last couple of weeks . . .'

'What?' cried Willbury. 'This has happened to you as well?'

'Yes. When the first one disappeared we thought he might have just run away, but last week two more disappeared, and we're sure that something bad has happened to them . . . The last two were good mates . . . not the type to run off,' said Kipper.

The first to go was a very unpopular rat called Framley

'What happened?' asked Arthur. 'Did you have a break-in like this?'

'The first to go was a very unpopular rat called Framley. He was a nasty piece of work so nobody was sorry to see the back of him. He just disappeared one day from the laundry,' said Kipper.

'That Framley . . . If he hadn't gone I think he would have been booted out, anyway,' added Tom. 'We were all a little wary of him, to be honest—felt he could turn violent at any time. But then last week we lost two more rats. This time it was Pickles and Levi. They were really good blokes. Disappeared on a shopping trip.'

'This is very peculiar!' said Willbury. 'Have you got any idea where they might have gone?'

'I think you should talk to the captain,' said Tom. 'He's started an investigation. Why don't you come back with us to the ship?'

Kipper looked up at Tom, and Tom corrected himself. 'Erm . . . laundry?'

'Well . . . ' Willbury looked around the shop. 'I hate to leave the shop like this. But if you think your captain might be able to help us get our friends back, then of course that's more important than this mess.'

'Don't worry about clearing this place up. We can send a party from the laundry to tidy up for you,' said Kipper.

'That is very kind of you, but . . . ' said Willbury.

'Not at all. We insist!' replied Kipper. 'The crew really

enjoy tidying things up and cleaning. It's all those years at sea.'

'Well, thank you,' said Willbury. 'Do you mind if we go and talk to your captain right now? We need to get to the bottom of this as quickly as possible.'

'Certainly! Follow us,' replied Tom. 'Up Kipper and home! And don't spare the horses!'

Kipper took up the huge laundry basket and pulled its straps over his shoulders.

Arthur turned to Willbury. 'What about Match, the sea-cow, and Titus's little friend?'

'Take them with us. We can't leave them here.' Willbury slipped the tiny cabbagehead into the top pocket of his jacket.

'Marjorie. Do you think you could put the sea-cow back in the bucket with some water? We can't leave her alone.'

'Certainly,' said Marjorie. She took the bucket the sea-cow had arrived in, and after a bit of gentle fussing, she managed to get her out of the tank and into the bucket with some water.

Off they set to the laundry. As they walked, Arthur held Match tight to him and talked to him in a gentle voice.

'Don't worry, Match, we'll get the others back. It's all going to be all right.'

Match seemed comforted by Arthur's words, but Arthur wondered to himself if they were true.

The Ratbridge Nautical Laundry

The pink and white ensign flown when washing is on the boil

Chapter 16

PANTS AHOY!

The canal ran along the backs of factories. Once it had been Ratbridge's main commercial link with the outer world. Barges had brought coal and other raw materials to the town, and had taken goods manufactured there out to the world. The canal had bustled with life. But since the coming of the steam railway, it had not been much used, except by unambitious fishermen, and small boys with model boats. Then a few weeks ago a large ship had somehow lodged itself under the canal bridge, and as its crew needed an income, and because of their limited skills, they had 'launched' the Ratbridge Nautical Laundry. The crew was unusual in that it consisted of a mixture of sailors and rats, working as equal partners together. Rumour had it that they had a long and interesting history, and that before they turned their hands to laundry they had been an altogether less respectable crew, but nobody in Ratbridge knew that much about them yet.

Rain was just starting to fall as the little group led by Kipper and Tom turned onto the towpath. Ahead of them was a very peculiar sight. The aft of the wooden sailing ship filled the canal. Steam rose from a tall chimney positioned on the main deck, and wafted through what looked like ragged sails that were fluttering from the rigging. As they drew closer they could hear a rhythmical hissing and throbbing of machinery. Arthur felt Match twitching. He looked down and saw that Match was becoming very excited.

'What is it, Match?' The miniature boxtroll pointed towards the steam and squeaked.

There was something large and green moving slowly up and down amongst the steam.

'You've got a beam engine!' exclaimed Marjorie, almost dropping the bucket with the fresh-water sea-cow in.

Kipper turned back and smiled. 'Yes. It's a really big one!'

'Where did you get it from?' Marjorie sounded excited.

Kipper looked a little nervous, and Tom spoke. 'Er . . . We acquired it . . . on a recent trip to Cornwall . . . '

'How do you acquire a beam engine?' asked Marjorie.

'With a great deal of pushing and shoving . . . ' replied Kipper.

'Can't say much, but it was superfluous to the needs of its owners,' said Tom.

'And we won't be going back there on holiday any time soon,' Kipper added. Tom looked a bit shifty. Willbury gave them a rather suspicious look.

'What's a beam engine?' Arthur asked.

'It's a sort of steam engine, but it usually stays fixed in one place. Instead of moving things like a railway engine, it uses its power to work machines,' Marjorie explained. Her eyes were shining. 'It's a most incredible invention.'

They were approaching the gangplank that ran from the towpath onto the deck of the ship. Arthur looked up and realized the 'sails' were in fact hundreds of pieces of washing, pegged onto the rigging and flapping in the breeze.

'All aboard!' cried Kipper, and the little group made their way up onto the deck of the Ratbridge Nautical Laundry. Sitting on the rails that ran down both sides of the deck sat some twenty miserable-looking crows.

'What's up, Mildred?' asked Tom.

'Rain!' answered one of the crows. 'We just got this load hung out when it started.'

'Aren't you going to take it in?' asked Tom.

'Doesn't seem much point as it is already wet,' said Mildred. 'Besides, where are we going to put it? The hold is full of dirty washing, the bilges have got another load in, and the crew quarters are packed with boxes of washing powder.'

Miserable-looking crows

Tom turned to Willbury, Arthur, and Marjorie. 'I'll take you down below to try and find the captain, but first we need to check in this washing. Kipper . . . the hatch!'

Kipper walked to a large hatch set in the deck, and put the basket down. Then he stamped three times on the deck, and the hatch opened. A friendly-looking rat jumped out, and spoke.

'Morning, Kipper! Morning, Tom! Got the list to go with this lot?' he asked as he pointed to the washing in the basket. Kipper produced a long strip of paper, and handed it to the rat.

'Can you be very careful with the big woolly underpants, Jim?' said Tom. 'I know that wool has a tendency to shrink, and the lady who the pants belong to can only just get them on as it is.'

Jim saluted. 'Aye, aye. Me and the boys will take it from here!' Then he called down the hatch. 'Oi! Lads! Another load . . . and keep an eye on the big pants!'

Suddenly ten more rats jumped out of the hatch, and manoeuvred the basket full of washing down through the hole. The hatch door closed.

'Have you seen the captain?' Tom asked Jim.

'Yes. He is in his cabin sorting out the lists and invoices. Follow me!' Jim turned and walked aft towards another hatch. The others followed.

There were some steps inside the hatch, and as they made their way down them Arthur asked Tom a question.

'Who were those birds?'

*Suddenly ten more rats jumped out of the hatch,
and manoeuvred the basket full of washing down through the hole*

'Oh, the crows deal with drying and folding. They are part of the crew. They're very fussy and even fold socks up properly. What happens is that some of us go out into the town and collect the clothes in baskets. As we collect the washing we write it all down on a list so we know who everything belongs to. Then we take it all back to the ship. Jim here then collects the lists, and the rats he works with divide the washing into different colour and fabric loads. That's so we don't get colours running or clothes shrinking. Then the bilge crew put the loads into the bilges and we pump water in from the canal. We add soap powder, and about half a barrel of peppermint toothpaste and then stoke up the beam engine. When the wash is finished, the bilge crew pass the washing up on deck and the crows hang it up to dry. When it's dry, the crows fold it and the rats pack it back in baskets to be delivered back to its owners.'

The party had reached the bottom of the stairs and were making their way along a narrow passageway. Jim pointed to a series of pictures that hung on the walls of the passage.

'These are the portraits of our captains.'

'There are rather a lot of them,' replied Arthur.

'Yes. We elect a new one every Friday,' said Tom. 'We are very democratic. There is a long tradition of pirates . . . er . . . ' Tom stopped mid sentence, looked embarrassed and corrected himself again, ' . . . laundries electing their own captain.'

They reached the end of the passage and Jim knocked on the door.

'Come in!' came a cry. Jim opened the door and there behind a huge desk covered in charts and laundry slips, sat a rat with a huge hat on.

'I've got the latest list for you, captain,' Jim said and handed the list over. 'And these are some visitors that Tom

and Kipper have brought back.'

'Aye! Aye!' said the captain, as he surveyed the group that had entered the cabin. 'Who do we have here? Not a complaint about washing, I hope?'

'No, captain, these good people,' said Tom, pointing at Arthur, Willbury, and Marjorie, 'have had a spot of bother. Some friends of theirs have disappeared.'

'Oh dear! We have got something in common then,' said the captain, sounding concerned.

'We may have indeed,' said Willbury. 'May I introduce myself and my friends here. I am Willbury Nibble, and these are my friends Arthur and Marjorie.'

Match gave a squeak. Willbury had forgotten to introduce the tiny creatures.

'Oh, I am very sorry. And this is Match . . . and er . . . a cabbagehead friend in my top pocket here . . . and there is a tiny fresh-water sea-cow in Marjorie's bucket.'

The captain

'Good to meet you all,' said the captain, doffing his hat. He looked curiously at the miniature creatures for a moment, then asked, 'How many friends have you lost?'

'Four. Some boxtrolls and a cabbagehead,' answered Willbury. 'They disappeared . . . or were rather snatched some time after Arthur and I went to the market, and to find my friend Marjorie this morning.'

'How many friends have you lost?'

'How sure are you that they have been snatched?' asked the captain.

'I am very sure. When we got back to the shop where they lived with me, the place was wrecked. It looked as if there had been a struggle,' answered Willbury.

'When our "colleague" Framley disappeared there were no real signs of a struggle. But it was hard to tell, as his corner of the crew's quarters is always such a mess. He was a right lazy critter . . . and unpleasant with it,' replied the captain.

'His corner of the crew's quarters is always such a mess'

'He's about the biggest, ugliest, laziest rat you have ever seen!' added Kipper.

The captain went on, 'It's only his expertise in the sorting of laundry that we really miss!'

Tom, Kipper, and Jim nodded their heads.

'When did you notice that he'd gone?' asked Willbury.

'On Friday nights we always have a meeting. We elect a new captain, and do the profits share.'

'If there is any money,' said Kipper glumly.

'We have been making a few groats, but so far most of our money has gone back into washing powder and toothpaste.

Framley is very, very fond of money and had been making noises about going off, because he wasn't making enough here. That week after the share-out we realized that a few coppers were left over, so we took a roll-call and found Framley was missing. We looked everywhere, but couldn't find him. So we guessed he must have had a better offer.'

'It's only his expertise in the sorting of laundry that we really miss!'

'Tom mentioned that a couple of other rats have gone missing?' said Willbury.

'Yes, it was Levi and Pickles. About a week later they went shopping in the town and never came back. We miss them . . . Pickles is my brother,' the captain said fondly. 'We sent out search parties, but there was no sign of them.'

'Do you have any clues as to who might have got them?' asked Willbury

'This is what I have been investigating. At first I didn't think we had any enemies as we lead such a quiet life, but . . .

There was an incident a few weeks back. We had a visit from a rather odious man by the name of Mr Archibald Snatcher, and a couple of his sidekicks. He said he wanted to welcome us to Ratbridge on behalf of the "New Cheese Guild". The captain that week was a man called Charley. He greeted the visitors and gave them tea and biscuits. Over tea this Snatcher asked if the crew would like to join his guild. Only he was not interested in us rats joining the guild, only the humans! He was really rather unpleasant about rats. Said we couldn't be trusted in the presence of cheese and that we were vermin. Awful he was! So we showed him and his friends a long walk off a short plank . . . and they took a dip in the canal.'

'So we showed him and his friends a long walk off a short plank'

Kipper and the rats all giggled, but stopped when the captain raised a hand.

'There was something else that happened when they first came on board. It was all rather odd considering he had such a low opinion of rats. Framley had been picking on smaller rats and crows all morning, and finally just as Snatcher arrived, a fight broke out between Jim here, and Framley.'

'I was trying to stop Framley bullying some of the clothes sorters. He turned on me,' said a rather distressed Jim. 'He got really nasty and went for my throat. If Kipper here had not pulled him off, I don't know what he would've done.'

'Anyway it all blew over, what with the visit from strangers and things. But Snatcher had been watching Framley fighting, and afterwards said something to him.'

'Do you know what he said?' asked Willbury.

'I asked Framley, and he said that Snatcher offered him a job,' replied the captain.

'It does seem strange,' said Willbury.

'Yes, it does,' said the captain. 'But if he was interested in Framley, how come Levi and Pickles disappeared as well? They were perfectly happy here.'

'What did Snatcher say about this guild of his?' asked Arthur.

'Not very much. Just that it was some sort of mutual organization for the benefit of its members . . . and he kept making jokes about it having "big" plans for Ratbridge,' said the captain. Then he addressed Willbury. 'Now can you tell me a little more about what happened to you this morning?'

Willbury paused to think for a moment. ' . . . We had a visit this morning before we went shopping. But from the sounds of it, it was not from your friend. This was from a slimy man who was trying to sell miniature creatures. He seemed very interested in buying my friends, but I sent him packing. Said his name was Gristle.'

'It was me what was serving them tea.'

'Gristle!' said Jim. 'I think that that was the name of one of Snatcher's sidekicks!'

'Are you sure?' asked Arthur.

'It was me what was serving them tea. I am sure he called one of them Gristle when he was asking him to pass the sugar,' replied Jim.

'Then I think all the disappearances are linked,' said Willbury. 'What did this Snatcher look like?'

'Big bloke with sideburns . . . and a glass eye,' replied Jim.

Arthur looked at Willbury. 'It's him! The leader of the hunt . . . '

'Yes,' replied Willbury. 'I think we know who has got your wings . . . and our friends!'

An air of unease filled the cabin.

'Where does this Snatcher hang out?' Willbury asked the captain.

'That's what I have been investigating! There is a building called the Cheese Hall that Snatcher mentioned. He said he wanted to restore it to its former glory.'

'Yes, I know it,' said Willbury. 'But it has been deserted for years!'

'I was there last night on the roof,' said Arthur. 'I thought I heard something inside!'

Everybody turned to look at Arthur. Then the captain spoke again.

'Interesting. I had someone go down and have a look at that place. I'll get him to come and tell you everything he told me.' The captain turned to Jim. 'Do you think you could go and find Bert?'

Jim disappeared out of the door to the cabin.

'Have you contacted the police?' Willbury said.

There was a silence in the cabin, while the crew of the nautical laundry looked awkward.

Willbury addressed the captain. 'I see. Does this have something to do with your beam engine?'

'Er . . . Yes . . . and a few other things. We have a strange relationship with the police,' the captain replied, while trying to avoid Willbury's gaze.

There was a noise from the corridor, and the captain looked relieved. Jim had returned with Bert.

'Ah! Bert,' the captain said. 'Would you like to fill my new friends in on what you told me about the Cheese Hall?'

'Certainly, Guv!' Bert lifted a beret he was wearing and pulled a small notebook out from under it. 'Three weeks ago tonight—the second of September at nine thirty-three p.m.

'—I approached the Cheese Hall from the southern side, after instruction to do same. I was wearing a green vest and had eaten three . . .'

*Bert lifted a beret he was wearing and
pulled a small notebook out from under it*

The captain stopped him. 'Bert! Get to the point!'

'All right then!' Bert looked rather disappointed. 'Something is going on in there! The place is boarded up and is supposed to be up for sale . . . but I saw lights, and heard Things!'

'What things?' asked Willbury.

'Strange, bleating, moaning things!' Bert replied dramatically.

'I heard something like that when I was there,' said Arthur. 'I thought it could have been cheeses.'

'Did you manage to have a look inside?' asked Willbury.

'No.' Bert sounded rather sorry that he couldn't help. 'There was no way I could get in as the place is built like the Bank of England. It's mouse and rat proof . . . I asked the local mice. Guess a Cheese Guild would want to keep their cheese safe!'

'Did you try knocking on the front door?' asked Willbury.

'All right then!' Bert looked rather disappointed.

Bert looked rather embarrassed. 'I didn't think of that.'

'I find the direct approach often works. It might be well worth a go, and we have little to lose,' said Willbury.

'We should storm the place!' said Kipper.

Willbury looked a little shocked. 'We might find ourselves in even worse trouble if we do go down that route . . .'

'So when do you think we should go?' asked Tom.

'Can't we go now?' said Arthur. 'We have got no idea what they might be doing to our friends.'

'I agree,' said Willbury. 'But if they are up to no good in the Cheese Hall it might be as well not to raise their suspicions. I think I should go alone and see what I can find out.'

'I don't like that idea,' said the captain. 'Anything could happen to you. If you go to the door, the rest of us can hide out of sight, but we should be at hand, just in case there is any trouble.'

'How about we hide in the Nag's Head Inn, opposite the Cheese Hall? We can watch through the windows,' said Tom.

'I think we should get the whole crew together for this,' said Kipper.

'Well, what are we going to do then?' asked Arthur.

'OK, well, I suggest that Mr Nibble waits here for ten minutes to allow the rest of us to get to the Nag's Head, then he comes down and tries knocking on the front door of the Cheese Hall. We'll watch from the pub.'

Willbury turned to his friends. 'Marjorie, I'm so sorry you've got caught up in this. I promise we'll try to solve your problem as soon as we find our friends. Why don't you and Arthur stay here and look after the tiny creatures while the rest of us go to the Cheese Hall?'

Marjorie shook her head. 'I'd like to come. I might be able to be useful and I—well, I'd like to help if I can.'

'I'm coming too,' said Arthur in a determined voice. 'Fish and Egg and Shoe and Titus are my friends.'

'Very well,' said Willbury reluctantly. 'But I do think it best if we leave Match, the cabbagehead, and the poor sea-cow here on the ship. They could easily get hurt if there was any trouble.' He turned to the captain. 'Do you have somewhere they could safely stay?'

The captain thought for a moment. 'We have a rather plush box that used to house the sextant before Kipper dropped it over the side. The boxtroll and the cabbagehead could use that.'

Kipper was going red, and looked as if he was about to cry.

'Don't worry, Kipper. Nobody knew how to use it

anyway.' The captain got down off his chair and pulled a pile of papers off a mahogany box on the floor. Then he opened it. It was lined with deep red padded velvet.

Kipper dropped it over the side

'It's a bit too small for a rat to sleep in but I am sure it would suit your friends here. Will the sea-cow be all right stopping in her bucket for the moment?'

'I think so. Maybe we could find something larger for her later,' said Willbury. He lifted the tiny cabbagehead out of his pocket from where it had been watching the proceedings and placed it gently in the padded box. It immediately lay down and closed its eyes. Then Arthur leant down and allowed the boxtroll to join the cabbagehead. Match looked round the box and noticed a number of small spare parts fixed to the inside of the lid. He smiled, put his nut and bolt in one corner of the box, then set about quickly removing all the spare parts and piling them up with his nut and bolt. Then he cuddled up to the pile and closed his eyes.

'Do you think we should leave them anything to eat?' asked Arthur.

'Would ship's biscuits do?' asked the captain. 'They are a bit hard but we could break them up.'

'I think they would do very well, if you have any spare,' replied Willbury.

The captain climbed back on his chair and opened one of the desk drawers. He took out two biscuits and placed them on the desk, then picked up a rock that was acting as a paperweight and gave the biscuits a sharp blow. The biscuits shattered into small pieces and the captain collected them up.

'What should I do now?' he asked.

'I think if you sprinkle some in the bucket and put the rest in a heap in the sextant case, that would do for the moment,' said Willbury.

The captain followed Willbury's instructions, then brushed off his hands.

'Thank you. I am sure they will be very happy now,' said Willbury. 'If you put the bucket down next to the box, Marjorie, I think we can be on our way.'

After a few minutes' organization, the entire crew of the Ratbridge Nautical Laundry, accompanied by Arthur and Marjorie, set off for the pub. As Willbury stood on the deck waiting, rain dripped from the washing above.

*The party of cabbageheads making their
way upwards, to have words with the boxtrolls*

Things were becoming positively soggy!

Chapter 17

CABBAGEHEADS

Meanwhile, far below the streets of Ratbridge, there was much activity too. Over the last week or so the cabbageheads under Ratbridge had been very happy. The water supply had been much better than usual. But now things were becoming positively soggy.

They lived, and gardened, in a vast cavern several hundred feet under the streets of the town, and as it was at the deepest point of the network of tunnels, water collected there. Just in the last few days, too much water had started to gather. The special lowlight cabbages were swimming in water, and it was getting worse.

So a meeting was held, and it was decided that a party would go up and politely ask the boxtrolls to turn off the water for a few days.

Four of the largest workers set off up the tunnels in search of a boxtroll to talk to. As they made their way up through the tunnels it became clear that the boxtrolls had not been doing their job very well. Water was leaking everywhere. The cabbageheads muttered to each other that this was not a bit like the boxtrolls, letting things fall into this state. What could be causing them to neglect their job like this? Perhaps they had acquired some new piece of machinery which they were busy playing with, allowing themselves to be distracted from their duties, the cabbageheads whispered.

When they'd travelled some distance, they climbed up on a dry rock for a rest, and had a cabbage sandwich each. This was their favourite food, and was made of a cabbage leaf sandwiched between two more cabbage leaves.

A cabbage sandwich

As they ate their sandwiches one of them noticed that the rock they were sitting on was covered in netting. Nudging his companion, he pointed to the netting in puzzlement. All the cabbageheads seemed baffled, and twittered nervously to one another.

Then, without any warning, there was a twang, and before they could blink, the net whipped up in the air with them all in it.

They hung in the net for hours, trembling as water dripped down on them. They had no idea what or who could have caused this terrible thing to happen. Then they heard the sound of approaching feet, and it slowly grew lighter as flickering candles appeared. The lights got closer and they could see a group of men, wearing tall hats and carrying sacks over their shoulders.

The cabbageheads in the net

The men lowered the net and dumped the cabbageheads in the sacks.

'These ain't going to be enough.'

'We got a few boxtrolls in the other traps last time!'

'Let's just hope we ain't caught any more trotting badgers!'

'Too right!' And off the party set. Within moments all that was left in the tunnel were a few uneaten cabbage sandwiches lying on the floor.

Willbury paused, then pulled the knob

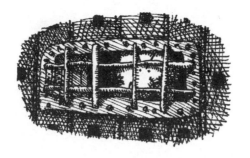

A pair of eyes peered out

Chapter 18

THE CHEESE HALL

The door of the Cheese Hall stood at street level, and was made from very solid-looking oak. Large iron studs were fixed at regular intervals across its surface, and at head height was a metal grille that covered a small hatch. Willbury approached it rather nervously. To one side of the door frame was a metal knob shaped like a cheese. Beneath it a dirty brass plaque read 'pull'. Willbury paused, then pulled the knob.

The sound of a cheese bleat could be heard distantly through the door. Willbury raised an eyebrow. Of all the knockers and bells he had knocked, pulled, or pushed, this was certainly the strangest. Then he heard steps, the hatch flew open, and a pair of eyes peered out.

'Yes!' snapped a voice. 'What d'yer want?'

'I . . . er . . . would like to talk to someone,' replied Willbury.

'You buying or selling?' The voice sounded very annoyed.

Willbury thought for a moment. 'I am not really buying . . . or selling.'

'Well, you ain't no interest to us then. Now naff off!' And the hatch snapped shut.

Willbury stood for a moment, rather perplexed, then he looked back towards the pub where the others were hiding. The window of the pub had most of the crew's faces pressed hard against it. He waved at them to get them to hide properly, and they reluctantly disappeared.

The window of the pub had most of the crew's faces pressed hard against it

He turned back to the door and pulled the knob again. The bleating started but was cut short by the sound of a thump, then the hatch swung open again.

'What d'you want now?' snapped the voice.

'Would it be possible to talk to someone about cheese?' Willbury asked.

'No! Cheese is our business, and information about cheese is confidential. I told you to naff off, so go on . . . Take a walk!' The hatch slammed shut.

Willbury was left standing in the rain, staring at the door. He was not quite sure what to do. He had not expected a warm welcome, but nor had he expected this total failure. He looked up at the building. Wooden boards were nailed over most of the windows, but from between gaps in the planks several pairs of eyes were staring down at him.

'I am being watched,' he muttered. He turned and nonchalantly walked across the street and into the Nag's Head.

As soon as he walked inside he was surrounded.

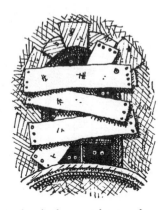

From between gaps in the planks several pairs of eyes were staring at him

'What they say then?' asked the captain.

'Not a lot!' said Willbury.

'Did you ask if they had our friends?' asked Kipper.

'I didn't really get round to that. They were not very chatty,' Willbury admitted. 'I wonder what our next step is?'

'Storm them with grappling hooks!' said a very enthusiastic Bert.

'We ain't got no grappling hooks, and anyway it looks a pretty tough building to storm,' Tom replied.

'Well, we could go back to the ship and get the cannon?' said Kipper.

'I don't think that the police are going to put up with members of the local laundry letting off cannons in the street,' said Willbury.

'I don't think that the police are going to put up with members of the local laundry letting off cannons in the street.'

'And we ain't got no gunpowder,' said Jim regretfully.

'Maybe there is another way in,' suggested Arthur.

'There is one other way in. The mice told me about it,' said Bert. 'If you look right up at the roof, you can see a pair of doors, with a crane that sticks out just above them. It's like one of them Dutch ones they use for lifting pianos into attics and the like. I don't think there is any way we can use that, as it's controlled from inside the building.'

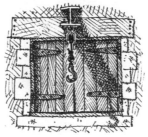

'If you look right up at the roof, you can see a pair of doors'

One of the other rats raised his hand. 'S'cuse me, but ain't they got a sewer?'

'The mice say the Cheese Hall has got its own cesspit and well. They're not connected up to the main systems, so it's impossible to use those to get in. The place is like a fortress!' said Bert.

'Well, how are we going to find out whether they got our mates then?' asked Tom.

'How about we kidnap one of them and torture 'im!' said Jim.

'Yeah!' agreed Bert.

'I don't think that's quite the right thing to do,' said Willbury. 'I think we have no choice but to watch the place and see what happens. An opportunity may present itself.'

'Does that mean we all get to stay in the pub?' said Kipper hopefully. Tom shot him another disapproving look.

'We just need someone here where they can see the entrance. How about we rent a room and set up watch?' said Arthur.

'Sounds like a very good idea to me,' said Willbury.

'And cheaper than keeping the whole crew in the pub,' added the captain.

There was a fluttering and Mildred made her way to the front

'We could keep in touch if crows act as messengers and fly back and forth to the laundry,' said Tom.

There was a fluttering and Mildred made her way to the front.

'I would like to volunteer to act as messenger,' said Mildred.

'Thank you,' said Willbury. 'And who would like to take first watch?'

'I will,' said Arthur.

'I don't think so,' replied Willbury.

'It's not going to be dangerous just looking out of a window,' pleaded Arthur. 'And besides, it was my idea. I know I can do this, Willbury, please let me.'

'All right then, but you are only to watch. I think it best though that someone else stays with you,' said Willbury.

Kipper broke in. 'Let me and Tom look after Arthur! We won't let him get into trouble.'

'All right. But if anything happens you are just to send a message back to the laundry,' insisted Willbury. 'I want to go back with the rest of the crew to check that the little creatures are all right.'

'Me too,' said Marjorie. 'The poor little things seemed so frightened . . . '

Willbury walked over to the bar.

'Excuse me, do you have a room I can rent?' he asked the landlady.

'I am afraid we only have a small one in the attic left, as it is market day,' she answered.

'Does it have a window on the street?' asked Willbury.

'Yes. Who's it for?' she asked.

Willbury pointed out Arthur, Tom, Kipper, and Mildred. The landlady looked rather unsure. 'The crow will have to perch on the curtain rail and it will be extra if boots are worn in bed.'

'Certainly,' said Willbury, and he handed over the money.

The landlady showed Arthur, Tom, Kipper, and Mildred to the room, while Willbury, Marjorie, and the rest of the crew returned to the Nautical Laundry.

The landlady

The Nag's Head

The sign of the Nag's Head

Chapter 19

An Incident Outside the Nag's Head

Arthur, Tom, Kipper, and Mildred returned downstairs to the bar and ordered some food. Then they settled at a table in the window of the bar. The rain fell, and slowly it grew dark outside.

By ten o'clock they retired to the attic, having finished fourteen games of Old Maid, twenty-seven games of dominoes, and building a large castle from the crusts of toasted sandwiches.

A large castle from the crusts of toasted sandwiches

Mildred perched on the curtain pole and went to sleep

'Shall I light a candle?' asked Arthur.

'No,' said Tom. 'Best not to. But why don't you open the window, then we will be able to hear if anything is happening, and we'll be able to put our feet up.'

Arthur opened the window and looked down. Nothing was happening. Tom and Kipper took one of the two single beds and lay down. Mildred perched on the curtain pole and went to sleep. Arthur stood by the window watching. Soon all he could hear was the rain, and Kipper snoring.

Arthur took out his doll, and quietly wound it up.

When it was ready, Arthur whispered, 'Grandfather. It's Arthur! Are you still awake?'

A sleepy voice broke through the crackling. 'Yes, Arthur.'

'How are you?' Arthur asked.

'I could be better,' came the reply. 'It is getting very damp down here. It's playing havoc with my rheumatism. The boxtrolls don't seem to be keeping up with the maintenance. But maybe I am just getting old and grumpy.'

'You stay in bed and keep warm.'

'What about you, Arthur? What's happening up there?' Grandfather asked.

Arthur told him everything that had happened. When he had finished his grandfather remained silent.

'Grandfather . . . Grandfather . . . Are you still there?' Arthur called.

Then his grandfather spoke. There was no longer any trace of sleepiness in his voice. 'Listen to me, Arthur. You are not to do anything rash. That is an order! I don't want you to do anything but watch. Mr Archibald Snatcher is a very dangerous man!'

'You know him?' asked Arthur.

'Oh yes . . . I know him . . . ' Grandfather's voice sounded angry. 'And he is the reason we live down here!'

'What!' Arthur was shocked.

'Trust me, Arthur. Stay well away from that man.'

'But what did he . . . ' Arthur broke off as there was a noise from the street below. 'Sorry, Grandfather . . . but something is happening.' Arthur peered out of the window. Below in the street a shaft of light fell from the open door of the Cheese Hall. Slowly a procession of horses and riders were making their way out into the street. It was the hunt.

'I've got to go, Grandfather.'

'Arthur! Arthur! Be careful!' Grandfather called.

'I will be. Don't worry. I'll talk to you later.'

The doll fell silent, and Arthur tucked it under his suit. Then he shook Kipper and Tom awake.

'Quick! It's the cheese hunt. They're coming out of the hall!' he whispered.

Kipper, Arthur, and Tom at the attic window

Kipper and Arthur went to the window and looked down. 'It's them I had the run in with,' said Arthur. 'But I can't see him!'

'Who do you mean?' asked Kipper.

'Snatcher!' answered Arthur.

Tom scrabbled up onto the windowsill and looked out. There was a yapping and howling as the hounds appeared. A mild panic broke out amongst the 'horses', as they did their best to avoid the hounds.

'Do you think we should send a message to the laundry?' asked Arthur.

'Yes, but let's just wait a few minutes to see what happens,' said Tom. 'Then we might be able to send more useful information.'

A large figure appeared from the door of the Cheese Hall, and the noise in the street subsided. It was Snatcher.

A riderless 'horse' walked forward, and one of the members crouched down to form a step for his leader. Snatcher closed the door, stood on the 'step', and climbed onto his mount. The hunt crowded around Snatcher, who started talking to his men. Try as they might, Arthur, Tom and Kipper could not make out his words.

A large figure appeared from the door of the Cheese Hall

'Let's get downstairs and see what Snatcher's saying,' said Tom. 'Kipper, wake up Mildred.'

Kipper reached up and poked the crow. There was a fluttering, and Mildred settled on his shoulder.

Arthur led the way downstairs. When they reached the front door, he lifted the latch very slowly and opened the door a few inches, careful not to make a sound. They could hear Snatcher addressing the group.

Snatcher closed the door, stood on the 'step', and climbed onto his mount

'The Great One is growing ever greater, and his needs must be met. We must get all the cheese we can tonight. I don't want no slacking. Anybody I catch not pulling their weight . . . ' he paused ' . . . may find themselves in "reduced circumstances" . . . Get my drift?' Snatcher's oily voice floated over the crowd.

'How much longer is we going to have to go hunting for the Great One?' came a voice.

'The time is very near! Soon we will free the Great One, and revenge will be ours!'

Evil chuckling filled the street. A shiver ran down Arthur's spine. What were these men plotting? Snatcher raised a hand.

'Quiet, my boys!' said Snatcher and the hunt calmed down. ''Tis time to wend our way.'

Snatcher kicked his horse and led off down the street. The hunt followed.

'Quick!' said Arthur. 'Let's follow them!'

'OK. Mildred, can you go back to the laundry and tell them about the hunt,' asked Tom.

As the hunt was disappearing down the street, Arthur, Tom, Kipper, and Mildred slipped out of the Nag's Head. There was a quiet flapping as Mildred disappeared. Under the cover of the shadows they began to follow the hunt down the street. Suddenly there was a shout.

'Hunt! Whoa! I've forgot me hornswoggle!' It was Snatcher.

The hunt making off down the street

'Quick!' said Tom as he looked about. 'Hide before he comes back.'

Kipper pointed back towards an alley. They turned, ran past the Cheese Hall, and into the alley.

Soon they could hear a 'horse' coming up the street. Arthur sneaked a look. Snatcher dismounted and headed for the door of the Cheese Hall. He unlocked it and disappeared inside.

Arthur sneaked a look

'Tom!' Arthur whispered. 'Can you distract the horse? I am going to see if I can get inside the Cheese Hall.'

Tom looked worried. 'It's not safe, Arthur!'

'I know. But it may be our only chance to get our friends back,' replied Arthur.

'I don't think we should let you go in there,' Kipper said, looking worried.

'Come on! There's no time to argue. I have to do this,' replied Arthur.

Tom and Kipper looked at each other for a moment, and then Tom nodded. He scuttled silently towards the 'horse', and made a very convincing bark. The 'horse' started, then Tom jumped as high as he could and bit one of the 'legs'.

'AAAAAAAH! Blinkin' hound!' came a shout from the horse, and it made off down the street.

Tom waved to Arthur, who took a last glance up at Kipper.

'Good luck, Arthur,' Kipper whispered. 'And don't worry—I'm sure Tom will think of a way for us to help you.' Arthur smiled gratefully, then ran across to the open door of the Cheese Hall. He looked into the doorway and down the passage. No one was there, but he could hear footsteps.

Tom jumped as high as he could and bit one of the 'legs'.

He ran straight through the door. Snatcher was turning into the passage. Looking around desperately, Arthur's eye fell on a very large grandfather clock, just inside the door. Arthur opened its case, jumped inside, and pulled the door to. As he pushed against the pendulum and chains, the clock made a loud clang. Snatcher stopped in front of the clock.

'That's odd. It ain't been working for years.' He gave the clock a blow with his hornswoggle, made his way through the front door, and slammed it shut.

A very large grandfather clock

The Entrance Hall

He looked about

Chapter 20

INSIDE THE CHEESE HALL

In the passage all was quiet. Then the clock started striking, and as it did, there was also a fair bit of muffled squeaking. The chimes died away and the case slowly opened. A very startled Arthur stepped out. He shook his head and blinked, then crept along to the end of the passage. Through an archway was a large entrance hall.

Arthur listened. All was silent and the place was deserted. It seemed all the Members had gone out hunting, and he would have the Cheese Hall to himself for a while. But perhaps some of them had stayed behind—he would have to be as careful as he knew how.

He looked about. There was a large marble staircase, several doors, and high up on the walls ran a painted frieze. He studied the frieze in silence. It depicted the cheeses of the world—English cheeses frolicked in the fields, cave-bound French cheeses huddled in green and blue mounds, Swiss cheeses rolled down mountainsides, Norwegian cheeses leaped from cliffs into fjords, and some Welsh cheeses huddled under a bush in the rain. There were a number of other scenes, but Arthur couldn't work out what countries and cheeses they depicted. He wondered particularly about some small tins being carried by an elephant.

Some small tins being carried by an elephant

Above the frieze were statues set in alcoves. These he took to be of heroes of the cheese world. Most of them looked very miserable, apart from one who was clutching a flaming cheese aloft. This statue of a man had a mad grin on his face. Arthur walked over to a sign on the wall below this statue and read:

Malcolm of Barnsley

1618–1649

'He lives who has seen cheese combust by its own will'

Donated by the

Lactose Paranormal Research Council

Malcolm of Barnsley

Arthur wondered what this meant. Looking around he noticed that the doors all had small plaques fixed to them. He walked to the closest door and read:

The Members' Tea and Cake Room.
Ladies' Night—February 29th 5.30–6.00p.m.
Non-members keep out!

Arthur was not sure what he was looking for so he decided to read the plaques on all the other doors as well. On the second it read—

The Chairman's Suite
Entrance by invitation only

At the third . . .

Laboratory

And at the last . . .

KEEP OUT!

I wonder? Arthur thought, and he reached for the handle, turned it, and pushed. The door creaked open to reveal a long torch-lit passageway. Arthur listened to see if he could hear anybody. From further down he could just make out a soft bubbling sound. He listened for a minute or two, and then his curiosity got the better of him. He made his way quietly down the passage.

Reaching the end of the passage, he stopped. Before him was a large hexagonal stone chamber, with an open shaft in the centre of the floor. As he stood gazing about in wonderment he noticed a large yellow banner hanging from the balcony. In the centre of the banner was a picture of a wedge of cheese, and beneath it ran the words 'R.C.G. We Shall Rise Again!' His eyes moved to the open shaft in the centre of the floor, and he realized that this was the source of the bubbling sound. He walked forward, and then recoiled. The smell of cheese was overpowering. Holding his nose and keeping a little back from the edge of the hole, he looked down. The shaft descended into total darkness, and the bubbling was coming from somewhere below.

He moved back from the hole and looked about. 'I wonder where Fish and the others are?'

Arthur noticed a small wooden door on one side of the chamber, with a sign above it that read 'Members' Changing Room'. He quietly tried the door. It was locked.

'Bother!' he muttered under his breath. 'I'll have to go back to the hall and try the other doors.'

Arthur made his way back up the passageway to the entrance hall doorway, and listened carefully. All he could hear was the bubbling behind him, so he crept out into the entrance hall and looked at the three remaining doors.

'I don't think they would keep them in a tearoom, or the chairman's suite . . . so that leaves the lab.' He tried the lab door. It opened.

Arthur found himself at the top of a flight of steps that led down into a vast hall, filled with enormous silent machines

Arthur found himself at the top of a flight of steps that led down into a vast hall, filled with enormous silent machines. Stained-glass windows high in the walls cast an eerie light over everything. Arthur looked about then listened. He could hear nothing. He decided to risk making a noise.

'Fish . . . Fish . . . are you in here?' he whispered loudly. His voice reverberated alarmingly around the hall before it died away. There was no reply.

As his eyes became accustomed to the gloom, he noticed a pale red glow in a far corner of the lab. Arthur strained his eyes. It was an illuminated sign above some door or passage. It was too far away to read.

Arthur nervously made his way down the steps, and crept along the marble pathways between the silent machinery. The smell of oil and polished brass filled the air. Arthur studied the various machines and apparatus as he passed them by. He recognized some of the machines from his grandfather's bedroom, but his grandfather's were like toys by comparison. There was a beam engine even larger than the one on the laundry, lathes and enormous drills, milling machines, rows of glass tanks filled with liquid that had metal plates hung in them, a cart with an enormous coil of metal sitting on it, and something very large with canvas sheeting tied over it.

Finally he neared the glowing sign. It hung above an archway. Through the archway was a spiral staircase, that descended to somewhere below. He looked up and read—

DUNGEON

Arthur looked back around the hall, listened for a moment, and then braced himself. It looked very dark down those steps and Arthur felt nervous about what he might find there. He swallowed and started down.

He swallowed and started down

The dungeon

Arthur reached the bottom step

Chapter 21

THE DUNGEON

Arthur reached the bottom step, and stopped. Before him
was a corridor with three cells on either side. The fronts of
five of them were made from iron bars, and each had a door
set into the bars. But the last cell on the right-hand side was
boarded up. Arthur turned to the first cell and peered inside.
Eyes stared back at him from the gloom. He could just make
out the shapes of the creatures as they quivered against the
back wall.

'Oh, poor things! They're underlings!' he said under his
breath.

There was a boxtroll, three cabbageheads, and a rare two-
legged lonely stoat. Arthur did not recognize any of them as
his friends. He tried the lock, but it was no use.

'Don't worry,' he whispered through the bars. 'I'm a

There was a boxtroll, three cabbageheads, and a rare two-legged lonely stoat

friend. I'll get you out of here if I can!' Then he turned round and peered into the cell opposite. There was just a stack of small cardboard boxes, so he walked on. As he reached the next cell, there was a flash of movement from the darkness, and suddenly snarling heads appeared between the bars and snapped at him. Arthur jumped back. They were trotting badgers.

Suddenly snarling heads appeared between the bars and snapped at him

Arthur watched them till they stopped snapping, quietened down, and finally returned to the gloom at the back of their cell. Then, shakily, he turned to inspect the cell behind him. There were three more boxtrolls. For a moment Arthur felt his heart jump, but as soon as he took a better look he realized none of them were his friends. Again he tried the lock to no avail, and again he whispered some words of reassurance before moving on to investigate the last open cell.

Three very familiar cardboard boxes were stacked on top of each other. As soon as Arthur saw what was there he stopped and called out.

Three very familiar cardboard boxes were stacked on top of each other

'Fish! Shoe! Egg!' Arthur waited for a few moments, then eventually a head slowly rose from a hole in the top box. It was Fish.

Fish gave a loud gurgle, and heads, arms, and legs sprouted from all three boxes simultaneously. The stack fell over with a clatter and was followed by a lot of moaning. Titus was standing behind where the stack had once stood. He smiled at Arthur. Arthur clutched the bars as his friends rushed forward to meet him.

Arthur clutched the bars as his friends rushed forward to meet him

'Thank God you are all right!' exclaimed Arthur. 'We have been so worried about you.'

Fish, Shoe, and Egg all gurgled excitedly, while Titus squeaked. They all reached their hands through the bars towards Arthur, and looked at him very hopefully.

'I am going to get you out of here!' Arthur said firmly. 'I promise.' He looked down at the lock. Fish followed his glance.

'I don't suppose you know where the key is, do you?' asked Arthur.

The underlings shook their heads and looked disappointed. Arthur turned round. There was no key visible anywhere, but his eye fixed on the boarded-up cell opposite.

It might be worth taking a look at that.

The underlings suddenly looked very nervous. Arthur took a step towards the boarded-up cell, but was stopped dead in his tracks. Several pairs of hands were gripping his clothes and holding him back.

'All right,' said Arthur. 'I won't go near it.'

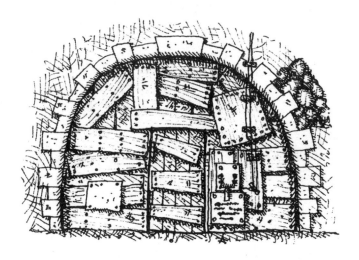

His eye fixed on the boarded-up cell

The hands holding his clothes let go. Arthur studied the front of the boarded-up cell. A large switch was fixed to the planks by its door, and underneath it, written in red paint, was—

Beware!
Dangerous Prisoner!
Put switch in upright position
BEFORE entering the cell!

'There must be something in there even worse than trotting badgers.' He turned back to the underlings. They were nodding their heads vigorously in agreement. 'What is it?' Arthur asked.

The underlings started jumping up and down, and making noises. 'Bonk! Bonk! Bonk!'

When they realized that Arthur had no idea what they meant, they gave up.

The underlings started jumping up and down,
and making noises. 'Bonk! Bonk! Bonk!'

'Well, I think I will leave it for the moment . . . I had better concentrate on getting you out of here!' The underlings looked relieved.

'I think the key must be upstairs somewhere. I'll go and see if I can find it. I will be back soon—I promise!' The boxtrolls and Titus huddled together in the cell and looked at Arthur with pleading eyes. It felt wrong to leave them alone again, but the only way he could help them was by finding the key to their cell, and his best chance of doing that was before the Members returned from the hunt.

Tearing his eyes away from them, Arthur turned and made for the steps, keeping well away from the boarded-up cell and the trotting badgers.

Arthur by the huge doors in the floor

Where would they keep the key?

Chapter 22

BACK IN THE LAB

Arthur crept up the stairs from the dungeon, and as he reached the top he checked again that no one was there.

Where would they keep the key? Arthur thought, and he started to search the lab. As he tiptoed amongst the machines he noticed some chains stretching down from the darkness to somewhere near the centre of the lab. After a while Arthur emerged from between machines, and found he was standing on a pathway that surrounded a large open area. Beyond waist-height railings were a huge set of iron doors, set in the floor. The chains that he'd seen were fixed to iron rings in the centre of the doors. High above hung a strange giant metal funnel. Its mouth pointed down towards the doors.

Arthur walked around the pathway. When he reached the far side there was a box fixed to the railings. Arthur looked at it. It was some kind of control panel. A metal tube ran down from beneath it, and through a small hole by the edge of the pathway. He peered down the hole. It was dark and very narrow, but he could just make out a pale light from somewhere deep below. Again he caught the strong smell of cheese.

There was a box fixed to the railings

I wonder what's down there? he said to himself.

He turned back to the control panel. There was an array of dials, and below them was a brass disc with a slot for a key in it. The slot was pointing to the word 'DOWN' that had been etched into the front panel. Across the panel was etched the word 'UP'. Arthur looked out across the doors, and then his eye followed the chains up towards the funnel. From the top of the funnel giant curling wires descended to the roof of what looked like an iron garden shed on stilts. This shed stood by the pathway, and overlooked the doors in the floor. Another pair of curly wires emerged from the shed roof, and led to a smaller funnel. This was fixed above the roof of a cage that stood on the floor of the lab next to the shed. Arthur looked into the empty cage. He had a bad feeling about it.

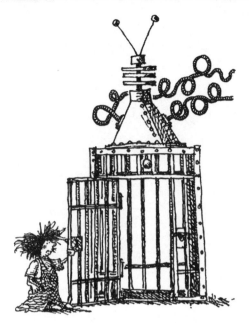

He had a bad feeling about it

There were steps leading up to a gantry that ran around the shed. Arthur was curious and made his way up them, then looked into the shed through its thick glass windows. A chair stood in front of a large console covered in buttons, levers, and switches. Behind the chair was a workbench covered in bits and pieces. There was some small machine with two funnels attached to it, some tools, a pile of cogs and springs . . . a wooden box . . . and . . . his wings.

Arthur rushed around to the door, and tried the handle. It was locked, so he went around to the back of the shed to get a better look. Yes! They were definitely his wings. And the wing spars and leatherwork had been mended. Then his heart stopped. They had taken the box to pieces!

He went around to the back of the shed to get a better look

'Oh no! What am I going to do now?' he muttered.

Arthur looked down at the floor of the lab. On a trolley close by were some tools. He rushed down and picked out a large hammer. With difficulty he lifted it, and returned to the shed. Arthur raised the hammer above his head and swung it at the window in the door.

The sound reverberated around the lab . . . and the hammer just bounced off the window! Arthur was startled. He crouched down and waited to see if the noise would bring anyone rushing in. The sound died away and nobody came. Arthur decided to try again. But again the hammer just bounced off.

'Darn it!' he muttered. 'I need to find keys!' Perhaps the keys for the shed and the keys for the cells would all be kept together somewhere.

*Arthur raised the hammer above his head
and swung it at the window in the door*

He looked about the lab. There didn't seem to be anywhere obvious that keys would be kept. Arthur climbed back down the steps, and placed the hammer back on the trolley. Then he made his way across the lab, and up the steps to the entrance hall.

For a few moments he waited to see if he could hear anybody, then crept across the entrance hall to the Chairman's Suite. It wasn't locked, and in a moment he was inside with the door closed.

The room was very dark, the only light coming from embers in a large fireplace. Arthur could just see the silhouette of a desk across the room. Carefully feeling his way, he crossed to the desk, and picked up an oil lamp which was sitting on it. Moving carefully over to the fireplace, he took a spill from the fire and lit the lamp. Suddenly Arthur felt very uneasy. The faces of generations of Snatchers stared down at him from family portraits on the walls.

Don't look at them, and you will feel better, Arthur told himself.

He turned his attention to the rest of the room. The desk was huge and very cluttered, and behind it heavy, moth-eaten velvet drapes covered the wall. In front of the fireplace were two decrepit sofas and a chaise longue. One of the sofas had an old blanket and a dirty sheet strewn over it, and next to it was a pile of dirty socks. The other sofa was a mess of horsehair and springs. Someone had cut its cloth covering away. The whole room smelt rather unpleasant.

Don't look at them, and you will feel better, Arthur told himself

The desk seemed the obvious place to look, so he walked over to it, and placed the lamp back down. He noticed an area in the centre of the desk had been cleared so a large sheet of paper could be laid out. This was held down at its corners by a paperweight, a dirty cup and saucer, and a pair of old boots. Arthur studied the sheet. It seemed to be some sort of scientific diagram, but more than that he could not tell.

Around it on the desk were stubs of old pencil, rubber bands, a broken pocket watch, the dried remains of half a sandwich, a ruler, and a broken quill . . . but no keys. Arthur decided to try the drawers. He walked around the desk and pulled open the first one.

Socks? Arthur was very surprised. The drawer was filled with socks, only a little less grubby than the pile by the sofa. Reluctantly he put his hand in and searched to see if there were any keys hidden there. When he decided there were not, he moved on.

Arthur opened the next drawer, and to his disgust he discovered it contained long johns. There was no way he was putting his hand in there. He took the ruler from the desk and used it to empty the drawer. Again there were no keys, so he put the underwear back, again using the ruler. Then he closed the drawer very firmly, dropped the ruler as hastily as he could, and shivered.

With a slight feeling of dread, he opened the next drawer. In this one he found a pink wig.

Arthur recognized it immediately—it was the wig Madame Froufrou had been wearing in the market. So there *was* a connection between her and Snatcher. But there was no time to think about that now—he had to concentrate on looking for the keys.

He lifted the wig out of the drawer, gave it a shake, and then hunted around the empty drawer. No keys!

Arthur replaced the wig, and moved on to the last drawer. This one was so full that it was hard to open, and he had to pull with all his might. When it finally sprang open, he found a great bundle of fabric crammed inside. He pulled it out and opened it up, then gave another gasp of recognition. It was Madame Froufrou's dress.

It was Madame Froufrou's dress

Things get curiouser and curiouser, Arthur thought. Then he checked the drawer for keys, and stuffed the dress back into it. It was not easy and took a certain amount of standing on to make it go back in.

Where next, Arthur wondered.

Looking about the room, he noticed a small table by one wall. There was a glass bottle on the table with some objects

in it. Arthur walked over to the table and picked up the bottle. In the bottom, amongst some straw, was a tiny piece of cheese and two very small sleeping mice . . . or very, very, very, small rats.

In the bottom, amongst some straw, was a tiny piece of cheese and two very small sleeping mice . . . or very, very, very, small rats

As he stood looking at the tiny creatures in puzzlement, a sudden noise came from outside the room. It was footsteps—and they were approaching the door. Arthur froze for a second, then ran to the drapes and flung himself desperately behind them. A moment later someone entered the room. They made their way to the desk, and sat down in the chair behind it.

'My poor feet! This blooming rain!' It was Snatcher's voice.

Arthur peeped out from behind the curtains. Snatcher had his feet up on his desk and was unlacing his wet boots. Arthur watched as Snatcher took them off and swapped them with the dry pair on the desk. Then Snatcher stood up and walked over to the fireplace. He stood by the fire and pulled back his coat. Then Arthur saw them!

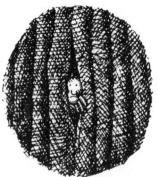

Arthur peeped out from behind the curtains

Hanging from a short piece of string attached to Snatcher's waistcoat was a large bunch of keys. After a few moments trying to warm himself, Snatcher gave up, turned, and walked out of the door, leaving it slightly ajar.

Hanging from a short piece of string attached to Snatcher's waistcoat was a large bunch of keys

Arthur crept out from behind the drapes and made his way across the room. He looked out into the hall and saw Snatcher standing in the archway facing the front door.

I have got to get those keys, thought Arthur. But how to do it—that was looking almost impossible. Then he heard a commotion from the passage.

He crept out of Snatcher's suite and made his way to the staircase

'Come on, me lads! How many cheeses did we get in the end?' Snatcher asked someone in the passage.

'Eight, I think!' came the reply.

With a sinking heart, Arthur realized that the hunt was returning, and that he needed to find a good hiding place—and quickly.

'Put the mutts in my suite,' Snatcher ordered.

Arthur looked back at the velvet drapes and thought better of it. It didn't seem a safe enough place. Then he looked at the staircase. Perhaps he could hide upstairs? He crept out of Snatcher's suite, made his way to the staircase, and started to climb as fast as he could. Behind him he heard more voices.

At the far end of the loft a pair of doors were open to the night sky

'The others made me be legs for the whole hunt!' It was Gristle.

'Stop your complaining, and get upstairs and man the cheese hoist,' Snatcher barked.

Arthur broke out into a cold sweat, and increased his pace up the stairs. As he reached the top he looked back. Gristle was just reaching the first step. Arthur rushed for the only door on the landing. In a second he was through it with the door closed.

He found himself in the roof space below the dome. Fenced pens filled with hay covered most of the floor. At the

far end of the loft a pair of doors were open to the night sky—these must be the doors that Bert had described.

He heard Gristle again. 'Oi! Master. Can you send me up some help? I'm knackered.'

Arthur felt sick. He rushed to the open doors and looked down. Far below in the street he could see huntsmen and cheese-hounds milling about.

'Oi! Snatcher! I can't lift these cheeses on me own!'

The shouting was getting closer. Arthur looked up. Above his head was a metal beam that protruded out above the street. A pulley with a rope going through it hung from the end of the beam.

The door behind him opened. Arthur held his breath and jumped for the rope.

Cross section of the Cheese Hall roof and dome

Arthur sat on the bridge of the roof and recovered his breath

Chapter 23

OUT ON THE ROOF!

He had only just made it. Arthur sat on the bridge of the roof and recovered his breath. It was still raining, and a few inches behind him was a vertical drop to the street. He did not feel happy.

Keeping his eyes straight ahead, Arthur shuffled along the roof until he reached the statues below the dome. From inside the roof he could hear muffled voices.

Then a metallic squeaking started. Arthur looked round. He could just see the pulley at the end of the metal beam. The wheel in the pulley was turning and a rope was slowly passing through it. Whatever it was lifting, it was heavy.

The plaintive bleating of cheeses grew louder.

'The poor things,' Arthur muttered, then he looked up at the dome. If he could get up there he might be able to signal to the laundry.

Without his wings he would have to climb. This made him feel very nervous. It felt so different not being able to fly. Holding on to a statue Arthur stood up slowly and started to climb. He made his way up the stonework and onto the dome. There were a few tiles missing and he found that he could use the battens beneath as steps. Soon he was hanging onto the weathervane on the plinth.

He made his way up the stonework and onto the dome

Looking across the town he could just make out the mast of the Nautical Laundry. Black specks floated around it. Arthur guessed it must be the crows. He waved but he was pretty sure they wouldn't see him. The rain grew heavier, and soon he lost sight of the crows. He looked down. Set into the dome were several small round windows. These, he thought, must act as lights for the loft. He decided to have a look and see what was going on in there.

Arthur turned round slowly, lowered himself till he found a footing, and then released his grip on the weathervane. He made his way down to a narrow strip of stonework that ran around the base of the dome. One of the windows was just a few feet from him. He eased himself along the ledge and peered in. Below he could see that the pens were now occupied by cheeses. He moved around to the far window so he could see what was happening by the hoist.

Several men were pulling something up. After a great deal of rope had been pulled in, a net came into view. More cheeses! Arthur could hear the bleating. When the net was level with the doors, one of the Members took a long pole with a hook on the end, and used it to pull the net into the loft. Then the doors were shut and the cheeses released from the net. For about a minute there was mayhem as the cheeses did all they could to evade capture. But trapped in the loft the cheeses stood no chance, and soon they were all in pens.

Several men were pulling something up

The cheeses quietened down, and the Members disappeared downstairs. Arthur decided it was too dangerous to try and get back down the hoist and, besides,

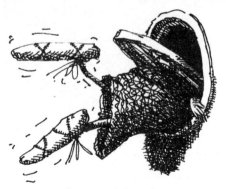

Arthur peered through it

the loft doors were shut. But he had to get back in somehow. He looked at the little window in front of him and decided to try to force it open. It gave way fairly easily, and swung open without too much noise. Arthur peered through it. Directly below him was a pen, with a good covering of hay on the floor, which Arthur thought might make a soft landing. He turned around, lowered himself through the window, and dropped. He hit the floor, just avoiding a cheese, and fell back into the hay. The cheeses in the pen started bleating noisily. Arthur sat still, hoping their noise would not bring any of the huntsmen back. But as the bleating died down he heard footsteps coming up the stairs. He groaned inwardly, but quickly covered himself in the hay and lay very still. Then he heard the door.

'Them cheeses is making a right commotion! You'd think they knew what was going to happen to them!' said a voice. It was Gristle. 'Let the cage down, and get them out the pens. Snatcher says that the Great One is going to be right hungry after they give him a good zap!'

Arthur sat still and waited for the bleating to stop

'What they going to use tonight?' asked another voice.

'Those awful trotting badgers. The sooner we cut them down to size the better!' replied Gristle. 'Did you see what they did to the Trouts?'

'Yes. Old Trout won't be able to sit down any time soon, and Trout Junior is lucky he still has a nose.'

'I am blooming glad it ain't us on lab duty tonight,' muttered Gristle. 'Anyway, they'll be done in there in about ten minutes, and so we better get on.'

Arthur peered out through the hay and saw Gristle and two other men were now standing in the loft. Gristle was standing by a pair of brass levers that stuck out of the wall.

'Move yerselves then,' ordered Gristle. 'Don't want to squash yer.'

The other men cleared a space under the centre of the dome, and Gristle pushed one of the levers down. Arthur followed the men's gaze upwards. A cage was descending from inside the very top of the dome. It clanked and shook as it moved slowly towards the floor of the loft. The cheeses were silent. The cage settled on the floor and came to rest.

'Right!' said Gristle. 'Get the cage door open, and let's get the cheeses in.'

While one of the men held the door open, Gristle and the other man grabbed cheeses from the pens and pushed them into the cage. Soon the cage was full.

Gristle and the other man grabbed cheeses and pushed them into the cage

'I do hope the Great One is hungry! Eight is an awful lot of cheese,' said the doorman.

'Don't worry, he is getting really BIG!' smirked Gristle. 'Snatcher says he will be ready real soon. All we have to do is keep up the supply of cheese and monsters.'

Arthur felt cold when he heard this. What was going on?

'Oi! Gristle! D'yer think they're ready yet?'

'The music ain't started! They 'ave to 'ave the music before the cheese goes in the pit. Otherwise it wouldn't be a Cheese Ceremony . . . would it?' Gristle replied. 'Just keep your ear out for the din.'

All was silent in the cheese loft until strange music started to waft up from somewhere below. Arthur had never heard anything like it before. It was a crazed drumming and blowing of horns. It reached a crescendo then stopped.

Gristle raised a hand then whispered, ''Ere we go!' He

pushed down the second lever. There was a loud bang and a trapdoor beneath the cage opened. The cage full of cheeses shuddered. Gristle pushed the first lever down and the cage started to disappear down through the hole.

After about thirty seconds Gristle spoke again. 'Look! The chain's gone floppy. It must have hit the fondue!'

'Let it sink slowly, then after about a minute haul it up,' whispered one of the others. 'Don't want no half-cooked cheeses hanging about!'

Arthur watched the men in silence. After a minute or so Gristle brought the cage back up. It came back through the floor . . . empty. From the bottom of the cage hung a few strings of molten cheese. Arthur felt horrified. Gristle stopped the cage, then snapped the trapdoor lever up, and the door in the floor closed.

'Done!' said Gristle. 'Now time for tea and biscuits.'

The Members trooped out of the loft and closed the door. Arthur had witnessed something awful, but he was not sure quite what.

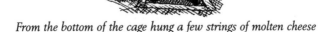

From the bottom of the cage hung a few strings of molten cheese

Kipper suddenly burst through the door with Tom on his platform

Mildred telling her news to Willbury, Marjorie, and the captain

Chapter 24

BACK AT THE SHIP

In the captain's cabin Mildred had finished telling her news to Willbury, Marjorie, and the captain, and they were all waiting rather anxiously over cups of cocoa, when Kipper suddenly burst through the door with Tom on his platform.

'He's inside!' said Kipper.

Willbury looked at Tom and Kipper. Then his face fell. 'Where's Arthur?'

'He's INSIDE!' repeated Kipper.

'Not the Cheese Hall?' said Willbury. He was met with silence. 'I don't believe it. How come Arthur is inside the Cheese Hall, and you're here? You're supposed to be looking after him.'

Tom looked rather guilty. 'After Mildred left, we started to follow them, but Snatcher came back. So we hid in the alley, and Snatcher left the door open while he went to get something . . . and Arthur says to me to distract Snatcher's horse . . . and he would sneak in . . . ' Tom paused, and looked even guiltier. 'So I did . . . '

Willbury closed his eyes and shook his head.

The captain looked very stern and took over the questioning. 'What happened then?'

The captain looked very stern and took over the questioning

Tom and Kipper both looked very upset. Kipper looked at the floor and started to speak. 'Well, Arthur rushes in, and a few moments later Snatcher comes out and locks the door. Then he gets on his horse and rides off . . . '

Tom followed on. 'So I says to Kipper that we better wait for Arthur to come out again. So we wait in the alley . . . for about an hour or so . . . ' his voice trailed off.

'Yes . . . ' said the captain.

' . . . then the hunt came back . . . ' Tom's voice quavered.

'Do you mean Arthur's trapped inside there, with Snatcher and his mob?' asked Willbury.

' Yes . . . ' Now Tom was looking at the floor too.

'What on earth do I do now?' Willbury muttered to himself. 'I am not sure he'll be able to get out of the Cheese Hall. Even if he doesn't get caught I think he's trapped.'

'It's a pity he hasn't got his wings,' added the captain. 'He might have been able to get away if he had those.'

There was a knocking from outside. The captain opened the window and two crows hopped in.

''Scuse us, captain!' said the crows. 'But we just saw something over at the Cheese Hall.' Everybody turned to look at the crows. 'We think we just saw Arthur on the roof. He's not there now but we're pretty sure it was him.'

'Can you go over there right away and see if you can find him?' asked Willbury.

'Surely,' said the crows. 'We'll go right now.'

With that the crows hopped out of the window, and flew off.

With that the crows hopped out of the window, and flew off

The Famous
BRASS ELEPHANT TEA

Inside the tearoom

He could hear distant laughing, and the chinking of crockery

Chapter 25

TEA AND CAKE

Arthur climbed out of the pen, crept across to the door at the top of the stairs, and opened it a few inches. He could hear distant laughing, and the chinking of crockery. He closed the door again.

What am I going to do, he wondered. If he went down now, he was sure to get caught.

He turned and looked at the cage that stood in the centre of the floor. It was a very sad sight. Arthur climbed back into one of the pens and lay down in the hay to think.

'I've got to get back downstairs to rescue the underlings . . . and what am I going to do about my wings? I'll never be able to put them back together without Grandfather . . . ' Arthur sat up and pulled out his doll. 'Grandfather! I've forgotten about Grandfather.'

Arthur sat up and pulled out his doll

He wound the doll, and then called his grandfather's name. He heard his voice reply.

'Arthur! Where have you been? Where are you? Are you all right?'

'I am all right, Grandfather . . . but I am in the loft above the Cheese Hall.'

'WHAT? You're in the Cheese Hall?' Grandfather sounded angry.

'Yes . . . ' said Arthur, then he explained what had happened.

'Oh, Arthur! Why can't you do what you're told? I'm very cross with you . . . and Mr Nibble. He should never have let you get into this trouble.'

'It's not his fault. He told me not to take any chances and I disobeyed him . . . and you.'

'Well, we will talk about this later!' Grandfather sounded very serious. 'But for now, we'll have to get you out of there. You say you have seen your wings?'

'Oh, Arthur! Why can't you do what you're told?'

'Yes, the spars and leatherwork have been mended, but all the workings in the box have been taken to pieces.'

'That's not a problem. If you can find a few tools I can tell you how to put them back together, if you can just find a way of getting your hands on them,' Grandfather said. 'Then you'll be able to escape!'

'If you can find a few tools I can tell you how to put them back together'

Arthur paused before he spoke again. 'I have to help the underlings escape as well.'

'Yes,' said Grandfather, 'but you'll be no use to them if you can't escape yourself. You need to get your wings fixed.'

'It might be tricky with Snatcher and the Members around . . .'

'Maybe, but everybody has to sleep.'

'What do you think they are up to?' asked Arthur.

'I am not sure . . . But I am pretty sure it's no good!' Grandfather sounded worried. 'Something strange is going on. This Great One that needs cheese . . . and they said they needed more "monsters" as they call the poor underlings . . . And those things you saw in the lab. It's all very peculiar.'

'What should I do now?' asked Arthur.

'If you hide for a while, I bet the Members will go to sleep before too long. Then get down to the lab and find a way of getting the wings. I'll guide you through rebuilding the motor.'

'All right, Grandfather. And how are you doing?'

'This damp is getting worse and all my joints are aching. About an hour ago I heard some rumbling. It sounds as if some of the caves are starting to crumble. I don't know what those damn boxtrolls think they are playing at. They are supposed to keep this place dry, and shored up.'

Arthur felt worried about Grandfather. 'Are you going to be all right?'

'I'll be fine. Anyway, you get some rest! Contact me as soon as you get hold of your wings.'

'I will, Grandfather . . . and keep warm!'

The crackling from the doll stopped and Arthur lay back in the hay. He tried to concentrate on the noise from downstairs, but soon his eyes closed and he dropped off to sleep.

He awoke with a start. Something long and yellow was pecking his nose. He sat up, and as he did two black shapes flapped up and settled on the edge of the pen.

'Sorry if we startled you.' It was a pair of crows.

'You did!' replied Arthur as he rubbed his nose. 'But I'm pleased to see you!' The crows must have flown in through the window he'd forced open.

Something long and yellow was pecking his nose

'We're from the laundry. The captain and the others are very worried about you.'

'How did you know I was here?' Arthur asked.

'We saw you on top of the dome earlier, and we reported it to the captain, and your friends. They asked us to fly over here to see if we could find you.'

'Thanks,' said Arthur. 'Can you take a message back to them for me?'

'No problem!' cawed one of the crows.

'Tell them that I've found the underlings in the dungeon under this place . . . and Snatcher and the Members have built some huge weird device . . . And they are doing really nasty things to cheeses . . . Oh! And I have found out where my wings are . . . '

'You've been busy then. Is there anything else we can do?' asked the other crow.

Arthur thought for a moment, and then listened. There was no noise from downstairs. 'Yes. Do you think you could fly down the outside of the building and check through the windows to see if Snatcher and his mob are asleep?'

'No sooner said than done! It won't take a jiffy.' The crows set off through the open window in the dome and disappeared. After about a minute they returned.

'It's all clear. We flew round the whole building and looked in every window we could. They're all asleep in a big room at the front. Looks like they've had a right feast of cake. Even that Snatcher is in there, snoring away.'

'We flew round the whole building and looked in every window'

'Good!' said Arthur. 'I'm going to try to free the underlings, and get my wings back.'

'Anything else?' asked the crows.

'No. Just tell them what I've told you . . . ' Arthur paused, ' . . . and tell them we'll all be back soon.'

The crows disappeared and Arthur set off down the stairs.

When he reached the bottom he crept across to the tearoom. As quietly as he could he opened the door. About thirty men were strewn across sofas and old armchairs, and were surrounded by the debris of an enormous feast of tea and cake. On the far side of the room in the largest armchair was slumped the sleeping Snatcher.

About thirty men were strewn across sofas and old armchairs

A cold sweat broke out on Arthur's forehead. He would have to be very, very careful. Trying not to make the slightest noise he made his way into the room and started to weave his way between the furniture, towards Snatcher. With each step he tried to avoid the abandoned teacups and plates on the floor. Slowly he got closer. The legs of one of the Members lay across his path and Arthur stepped over them. As he did the hem of his vest brushed the Member's foot.

'CAKE!'

Arthur jumped forward and turned. It was Gristle.

The hem of his vest brushed the Member's foot

' . . . just one more slice . . . I love cake . . . ' Gristle's eyes were still closed. He was talking in his sleep. Arthur closed his eyes for a moment and swallowed. He checked about the room and saw that nobody else was stirring, then made the last few steps to Snatcher.

The keyring hung on a string from Snatcher's waistcoat. There was a gentle jingling as Snatcher's enormous belly moved in and out.

Amongst a few crumbs on a cake stand that stood on the floor in front of Snatcher was a knife. Arthur picked it up, and gently took hold of the keys. He held the knife to the string and as Snatcher's belly moved the knife cut slowly into the string. The string separated and for a moment Snatcher's belly wobbled. Arthur held his breath. Snatcher snorted . . . but didn't wake. Arthur put the knife down and crept out of the room to the lab.

The knife cut slowly into the string

Once in the lab he decided that it would be better to get his wings before releasing the underlings. Grandfather was right—if he got caught himself, it would be all over. He just had to hope that Snatcher's keyring had all the keys he needed. Arthur rushed to the shed and made his way up the steps. Searching amongst the keys he found one that fitted the door. He slid it in the lock and turned. There was a satisfying clunk. He tried the handle, and the door opened. His wings were still on the bench. Arthur reached inside his suit and took out his doll.

'Grandfather! Are you there?'

'Yes, Arthur.'

'I am in the lab with the wings. Can you help me put them back together?'

'Certainly, Arthur. Can you find a small screwdriver and an adjustable spanner?'

Arthur looked about the bench and found the tools he needed. 'Yes! I've found them.'

'Good.'

Over the next hour Grandfather instructed as Arthur rebuilt the wings' motor. Occasionally Arthur looked up to check the door to the entrance hall, or would have to break

Over the next hour Grandfather instructed as Arthur rebuilt the wings' motor

off to wind up the doll when his grandfather's voice started to fade. Finally the motor was back together. Arthur smiled and thanked Grandfather.

'I think it would be a good idea if you put the wings on and wound them up . . . just in case,' said Grandfather.

'You're right,' replied Arthur as he strapped the wings on. 'I will speak to you later. I've got underlings to rescue before Snatcher wakes up!'

Arthur strapping the wings on

'Very well, Arthur,' said Grandfather. 'But make sure you call me as soon as you are out of there! And please, please try not to take any unnecessary risks.'

Arthur put the doll away and wound up his wings. Then he locked the shed and made his way back downstairs. He peered in nervously at the Members, but they were all still snoring away. Arthur prayed that they would stay asleep for long enough. Tiptoeing on, he headed back towards the dungeon.

Arthur looked down the length of the dungeon

Fish shook his head and gave him a thumbs up

Chapter 26

AN ESCAPE?

Arthur looked down the length of the dungeon and stopped in his tracks. The door of the trotting badgers' cell stood open. He glanced across to his friends' cell. The four of them were still pressed up against the bars, obviously waiting for him to come back. They looked very happy to see him. He silently pointed to the open cell door. Fish shook his head and gave him a thumbs up.

Arthur still felt wary and mouthed the words, 'HAVE THEY GONE?'

Fish nodded his head. Arthur sighed with relief, and made his way to his friends' cell. As he passed the open door he remembered what the Members had said about them in the loft. Now the trotting badgers' cell looked very empty, and he felt an odd sensation of pity as he walked past it. Then he reached his friends' cell.

The underlings ran out and hugged him

'Thank God you are still here!' said Arthur.

The underlings looked happy.

'I am going to get you out of here,' Arthur said and produced the keys. He unlocked the door, and the underlings ran out and hugged him. Arthur hugged them back.

'Now,' said Arthur. 'We had better unlock the others.'

Fish pointed to the cells with the other underlings in, and nodded.

'What about the boarded-up cell?' The underlings looked across at it, and shook their heads.

'Why not?' asked Arthur.

Again they started to jump up and down, and quietly made bonk! bonk! noises.

'I'll trust your judgement,' Arthur said, feeling a little nervous. 'It might be very dangerous to release whatever is in there.' The underlings looked relieved.

Arthur unlocked the other underlings, and his friends went into the cells to reassure the other creatures that they could trust Arthur. Soon all of them stood at the bottom of the stairs.

Arthur checked that the coast was clear

'Come on!' said Arthur. 'We have to get out of here quickly . . . but remember to keep very quiet.' The underlings nodded and set off, following Arthur.

He guided the underlings up the stairs and out through the lab to the door to the entrance hall. They stopped and Arthur opened the door just enough to check that the coast was clear. Arthur was about to lead the underlings out into the entrance hall, when there was a loud cheese bleat from the passageway to the front door. Arthur and the underlings froze. After a few seconds the door of the tearoom opened and a sleepy Gristle walked out.

A voice followed him. 'It'll be the milkman. Tell 'im to leave fifteen pints and that I will pay 'im next week.' It was Snatcher . . .

Arthur watched as Gristle disappeared down the passage. Then he heard Gristle shout.

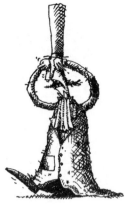

The door of the tearoom opened and a sleepy Gristle walked out

''Ave you got the keys to the front door?'

Arthur felt a lump in his throat. He looked from the archway to the passage across to the tearoom.

There was a pause then Snatcher's voice boomed from the tearoom. 'Someone's nicked me blooming keys!'

Arthur opened the door and ushered the underlings forward. 'Up the stairs! Run for your lives!' he whispered.

Just as they started to scuttle across the hall, there was a commotion from the tearoom and Snatcher stepped through the door. Arthur looked at Snatcher in horror. This might be the end of everything.

Arthur looked at Snatcher in horror

Unable to control the panic in his voice, Arthur turned to the underlings and shouted:

'RUN!'

The underlings rushed up the stairs. Arthur pushed the buttons on the front of the wing box and jumped. Thank goodness he could fly again.

'It's that blasted boy again. And he's stolen my wings!' shouted Snatcher. The other Members were now piling out into the entrance hall. They all looked up at Arthur, then at the underlings fleeing up the stairs.

'Get 'em!' screamed Snatcher as he pointed to the underlings. There was a coat stand that Arthur had not noticed before by the door of the tearoom. Snatcher grabbed a walking stick from it, and raised it to throw at the underlings. Arthur realized he still had the keys in his hand and threw them hard at Snatcher. They caught him in the face and Snatcher wailed at Arthur.

'You little swine. Just you wait till I get 'old of you!' But Arthur was already too far off the ground for Snatcher to reach.

They caught him in the face

The statue toppled over

Some of the Members had reached the stairs and were gaining on the underlings. Arthur adjusted his wing speed and flew up to one of the alcoves above the Members and grabbed hold of the statue. Then he pulled it hard. The statue toppled over. Below, the Members saw what was

The Members saw what was happening

happening and ran back down the stairs to get out of the way. The statue crashed down on the stairs.

Snatcher screamed again. 'Don't let 'im stop yer! Get those Monsters!' He grabbed another walking stick and waved it at the Members.

Arthur flew to the next statue and waited till some of the Members were brave enough to start mounting the stairs again, then he pulled on the second statue. Again there was a crash as the statue hit the stairs, and again the Members ran back to avoid it.

The underlings were just reaching the door to the loft. Arthur watched them rush through it and disappear. He came down on the landing, turned off his wings, ran through the door, and slammed it closed. As he did a walking stick clattered against the door behind him.

The underlings were standing in the loft looking scared out of their wits. Arthur looked around—they needed to barricade the door before the Members made it to the top of the stairs. His eyes fixed on the cage. He turned on his wings again, flew to the top of the cage, and unhooked it from its chain.

'Quick! Push this cage against the door,' Arthur shouted to the underlings.

The underlings obeyed and soon the cage crashed against the door. Arthur flew to the doors at the far end of the loft and pulled them open. The net was hanging from the end of the beam.

The cage crashed against the door

'Fish. Let out a bit of the rope so I can get the net into the loft!' Arthur ordered. Fish untied the rope and let a little play out. Arthur grabbed the net and pulled it back into the loft. He turned off his wings and spread the net out on the floor.

'Everybody but Fish get in the net.' The underlings looked horrified and didn't move.

'Quick!' shouted Arthur. There was a crashing as the Members threw themselves against the door. 'This is our only chance! Please get in the net.' Fish looked scared.

More crashing and shouting came from the stairway door. Reluctantly the underlings climbed into the net, and Arthur joined Fish at the rope.

As soon as the underlings were assembled in the centre of the net, Arthur and Fish pulled the rope in. There was a fearful squeaking and moaning, and the net swung out over the street.

'When you get to the ground, get out of the net and make for the canal,' Arthur called over to the underlings. He felt Fish nudge him. Fish was uncertain whether he was going to be left behind.

The net swung out over the street

'You and I are going to fly,' said Arthur.

Slowly they paid the rope out and the frightened creatures disappeared.

The crashing at the door grew louder, and Arthur and Fish let the rope out faster.

Finally the rope went limp.

'Right, Fish. Let's be off.' Fish backed away from Arthur as the cage behind them toppled over, crashing to the floor as the door flew open. Arthur grabbed Fish by the box corners and pushed him forward towards the drop to the street. As they reached the edge, he released Fish for a moment, turned the power knob on his box to full, hit both buttons, and then grabbed hold of Fish again.

For about two seconds they dropped

'Get them!' screamed a voice. The Members were racing across the loft. Arthur jumped and pushed Fish over the edge.

For about two seconds they dropped, then the wings started to beat and their descent slowed. Below them they could see the underlings running up a street in the direction of the canal, apart from the lonely stoat who was disappearing in the opposite direction looking miserable. From above screams of rage rang out.

'Stop them! Thieves! Kidnappers! Underlings! Monsters!' Then Arthur heard Snatcher's voice. 'Get downstairs and after them. They are not to get away!'

Arthur spoke to Fish. 'Fish, do you want me to put you down?'

Fish turned his head and shook it. Arthur could see that Fish was smiling.

'So you enjoy flying?'

Fish nodded, and started to gently flap his arms.

'Right then, I think we'd better catch up with the others.'

So they set off through the early morning light back to the laundry. After they had gone a few streets they heard the sound of dogs.

'They are coming after us!'

The lonely stoat disappeared in the opposite direction looking miserable

'Back to the laundry! Follow us.'

Arthur and Fish kept low as they flew

Chapter 27

ATTACK ON THE SHIP

Arthur and Fish kept low as they flew. They caught up with the underlings and Arthur shouted to them.

'Back to the laundry! Follow us.'

Arthur was surprised how fleet-footed the underlings were, but still the sound of the cheese-hounds grew louder. Soon they turned on to the canal bank and before them was the laundry. The rain had stopped and the washing was blowing in the wind. There was a shout from the deck followed by a commotion.

'Are you all right?' Arthur asked Fish. There was a happy gurgling.

The other underlings ran along the towpath and Arthur landed by the gangplank. As he landed he released Fish.

'Arthur! Fish! . . . Egg . . . Shoe . . . Titus . . . You got out!'

Arthur turned to see a very happy Willbury

Arthur turned to see a very happy Willbury standing at the top of the gangplank with Kipper, Tom, Marjorie, and the captain.

'Yes! We're all right!'

'Thank God, and well done!' Everyone looked delighted, and Kipper and Tom looked extremely relieved.

A shout came from somewhere on deck. 'Dogs ahoy!'

Arthur and Willbury turned to see the cheese-hounds rushing on to the towpath.

Arthur and Willbury turned to see the cheese-hounds rushing on to the towpath

'Quick, get the underlings aboard,' said Willbury. Fish, Shoe, Egg, and Titus led the underlings up the gangplank. The others seemed much more trusting now they could see that the four leaders knew Willbury as well as Arthur, and they followed without a murmur. Arthur ran on to the ship after them.

'Draw up the gangplank!' shouted the captain. Snatcher and his mob were now running down the towpath behind the dogs, roaring in anger. The crew hauled the gangplank up just before the first of the hounds leapt on to it.

'Load the cannon!'

'I told you, captain, we ain't got any gunpowder!'

'OK, OK! Prepare the knickers!' Crows flew down from the crow's-nest to the underwear section of the rigging, un-pegged six pairs of the largest knickers they could find, and then descended to the deck. The pirates quickly tied the knickers to various fixing points on the gunwales of the ship.

Crows with a particularly large pair of pants

From below decks came a scampering, and rats appeared carrying oddly shaped lumps, each the size of a tennis ball.

Rats appeared carrying oddly shaped lumps, each the size of a tennis ball

'What are those?' asked Arthur.

'We thought we might be attacked so Tom suggested that we make something to give the enemy a real surprise,' said the captain. 'We mixed all the gunge from the bilge pumps with glue, and then rolled it into balls. They were very sticky so we coated them in breadcrumbs and fluff. We tested one earlier . . . it's disgusting; if they hit you they burst and cover you in slime. It stinks and it is almost impossible to wash off.'

'Knickers loaded, Captain!' came the cry from the crew.

'Prepare to fire!' shouted the captain. The knickers were pulled back to form deadly catapults.

The knickers were pulled back to form deadly catapults

On the towpath everything went quiet, then a voice called out. It was Snatcher's.

'Board the laundry!'

As the cheese-hounds continued to jump up and down on the towpath, baying, the Members approached the ship. As they did the captain shouted:

'FIRE!'

'Fire!'

The twanging of six enormous pairs of knickers could be heard, followed by a whizzing, a splodging, and disgusted screams. The cheese-hounds ran back down the towpath to a safe distance. The Members looked as if they wanted to run too, but Snatcher was having none of it.

Snatcher was having none of it

'Go on, you weak-willed, yellow-bellied varmints! BOARD the laundry!' ordered Snatcher.

The captain shouted 'Fire!' again, and another volley flew over the side of the ship. More screams could be heard. This time one of the screams was Snatcher's.

'Retreat!' shouted Snatcher.

The Members didn't need telling twice. They ran back down the towpath to join the hounds, and the crew of the laundry cheered.

The Members didn't need telling twice

'I think we have got them on the run,' said the captain.

'They will think twice about attacking us again,' agreed Arthur.

'I hope you're right . . . ' said Willbury thoughtfully.

Along the towpath a meeting was being held. The group huddled around Snatcher, listening. Everybody on the Nautical Laundry watched. After a minute or so one of the Members ran off down the towpath and disappeared. Snatcher walked a little way back towards the ship, and shouted.

'You may have beaten us back, but it's not over yet!'

'Er hmm!' Arthur heard someone behind him and turned.

'Did you see Pickles and Levi?' It was the captain.

Arthur looked at the captain and could see he was waiting nervously for his reply.

'I am afraid I didn't,' said Arthur.

'No rodents at all?' asked the captain.

'Just a pair of tiny mice in Snatcher's room. And they were hardly big enough to be mice . . .'

The captain sighed, and turned away.

'Just a pair of tiny mice in Snatcher's room.'

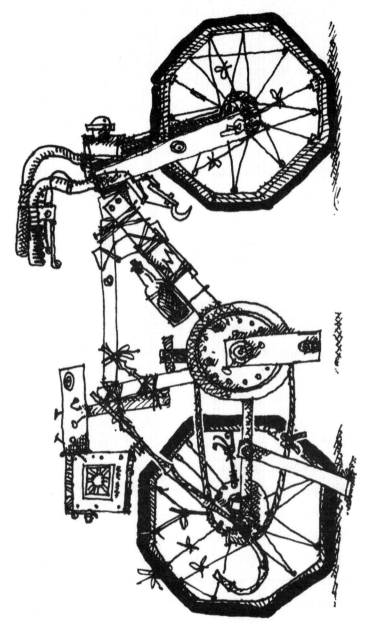

A Dodgy Tanner

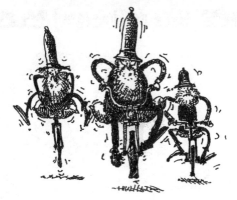

The Ratbridge Irregular Police Force on 'Dodgy Tanners'

Chapter 28

THE POLICE

The bicycles that the Ratbridge Irregular Police Force rode were known as 'Dodgy Tanners'. This was because of the shape and number of their wheels. They had two wheels the shape of thrupenny bits. If one added together two thrupenny bits, one would have sixpence, and a sixpenny coin was known as a tanner.

Penny Farthing bicycles had perfectly round wheels like the coins they were named after. Thrupenny bits were many sided. Wheels this shape did not make for the good humour of the riders. On hard surfaces such as cobbles, the policemen could be heard a long way off, as they let out little cries of pain at every turn of the wheels. Many a burglar had made an early escape because of the warning noises of an unhappy approaching rider. Some policemen even took to wearing cushions strapped to their bottoms to prevent bruising. But not all could afford padding, so the Irregulars were known locally as 'Squeakers'.

*Many a burglar had made an early escape because
of the warning noises of an unhappy approaching rider*

The Squeakers now came down the towpath as fast as they could without causing themselves too much discomfort. Emergency calls were rare, and as the Squeakers were paid by the number of incidents they attended, and arrests they made, they were in a rush to get to the scene. As they approached all fell silent.

The Chief Squeaker dismounted from his bike, unstrapped his cushion, and turned.

'Hello, hello, hello. What's going on here?'

The Chief Squeaker dismounted from his bike, and unstrapped his cushion

The Members and the pirates all looked very uneasy.

Snatcher made the first reply. 'We are being attacked by this bunch of cut-throats and robbers!'

'Attacked you say?' replied the officer.

'Yes! We were out for a peaceful stroll when these scallywags started firing at us. They need locking up!'

The sound of twenty pairs of iron handcuffs being prepared could be heard.

The sound of twenty pairs of iron handcuffs being prepared could be heard

'This sounds very serious!' replied the Chief Squeaker with a smile. 'It sounds as if a lot of arrests might need to be made!'

'That is balderdash!' called Willbury from the deck. 'We are just defending ourselves. I am a lawyer and . . .'

The Chief Squeaker raised his hand. 'A LAWYER!'

He went bright red. 'I don't think this is the sort of thing a lawyer should be mixed up in, but I expect no better. Officers, arrest that man!'

There was a rush for the ship.

'Stop!' cried Willbury. 'And a circuit judge!'

'WHOA!' cried the Chief Squeaker. 'I am very sorry, m'lud, I did not realize that you were so obviously honest. Men, arrest the party on the towpath.'

The policemen turned to the Members, still brandishing their handcuffs. But then Snatcher walked forward and spoke. 'The difference between me an 'im is CHALK and CHEESE.' Then he made a funny little sign with his hands.

Then he made a funny little sign with his hands

The police stopped in their tracks. The Chief Squeaker now spoke again in a quavering voice.

'Did you say CHALK and CHEESE?'

'Yes I did!' replied Snatcher.

'What kind of CHEESE is that?' As the Chief Squeaker spoke his hands made a number of strange gestures.

Snatcher replied, 'That would be a BIG CHEESE!' And he made the same gestures with his hands.

'Why is he doing that?' asked Arthur.

'I am not sure,' said a hesitant Willbury.

Marjorie sidled up to them. 'I think they are "Brothers"! Members of the Guilds.'

'What's that?' asked Arthur.

'Secret organizations. They are making secret signs to each other, and using code words to let each other know they are Members!'

'Why don't they just recognize each other?' Arthur asked.

'It's a very big organization, and there are lots of smaller parts of it. The police probably have their own section,' said Marjorie.

The policemen looked at each other and then fell to their knees. They then bowed their heads and whispered, 'We smell strong cheese! We smell strong cheese! It is overpowering. We respect it for it is the most flavoursome, and we are humble. What would it have us do?'

'We smell strong cheese! We smell strong cheese! It is overpowering.'

Snatcher smirked at the policemen fawning before him, then he spoke.

'I think you will find that "m'lud" might well be retired. He holds no power now—and he is harbouring a thief who has stolen a pair of mechanical wings from me. From me— A BIG CHEESE! I think that the right course of action would be to arrest the rapscallion who has stolen my wings and return them to me!'

The Chief Squeaker stood up, and turned to look at Willbury.

'Is this so, sir? You are no longer a judge?' he asked.

'Technically that is true . . . ' replied Willbury.

And before Willbury had a chance to go any further the Chief Squeaker cut in. 'Right! Drop your gangplank, sir! Any failure to do so will be seen as hindering the police in the course of their duties, and may force me to arrest you, and your entire crew.'

Willbury looked shocked. 'I think we'd better do what he says, otherwise we are going to get into real trouble.'

The pirates reluctantly lowered the gangplank.

As soon as it was lowered the Chief Squeaker shouted out, 'Arrest the boy!'

The policemen on the towpath rushed onto the ship. Kipper and the other pirates looked as if they were ready for a fight, and the policemen looked nervous.

'Hold back, crew!' said Willbury. Then he whispered to Arthur, 'Quick! Fly!'

But it was useless. Arthur had not thought to wind his wings up again, and they had no power left in them after the escape. The policemen grabbed him and snapped handcuffs around his wrists. He was then marched off the ship and the Chief Squeaker removed his wings.

The policemen grabbed him, and snapped handcuffs around his wrists

Arthur's heart sank. He thought he'd done so well to get himself and the underlings safely out of the Cheese Hall— he couldn't believe this was happening to him now. Just when he'd got his wings back, to have them taken away from him again! And for the police to be on Snatcher's side! It all seemed so unjust. But there was no point struggling now. Perhaps he'd find a way to convince the police of his innocence.

'Right! I want a couple of you to take him back to the station,' the Chief Squeaker said, addressing his men, 'while the rest of you maintain order here. Let the respectable gents on the towpath go about their lawful business, and keep a close eye on that ex-lawyer and his bunch of pirates. If any of them try to get off their ship . . . arrest them!' The Chief Squeaker winked at Snatcher.

'Here, sir!' he said as he handed the wings over. 'And if we can be of any more service to you?'

Snatcher turned the wings over in his hands, smiled, and turned to Arthur. 'I was wondering how we were going to put them back together. You have done us a service. There are a few questions I would like to ask you . . . ' Then he turned to the Chief Squeaker and spoke in a sly voice.

'I know how understaffed you are at the police station. I think it might be as well if you were to let me help you out by keeping the boy,' Snatcher smirked.

'No! You can't do that!' shouted Willbury from the deck.

'Oh yes I can!' replied the Chief Squeaker. He then placed a hand on Snatcher's shoulder.

'By the powers invested in me I now pronounce you a Temporary Gaoler Class 3. Please take custody of this criminal on behalf of the Ratbridge Police.'

Snatcher winked. 'Oh, certainly, Officer. Anything to help out the police!'

'Oi, you two! Grab him!' the new Temporary Gaoler Class 3 snapped to a couple of rather sorry looking Members.

The two approached Arthur. The older one was bandaged from waist to knee, while the younger one's nose was covered in sticking plaster.

The older one was bandaged from waist to knee,
while the younger one's nose was covered in sticking plaster.

'It's them!' Marjorie shouted from the deck. 'Those are the men who stole—'

The Chief Squeaker cut her off. 'Any more trouble from you lot, and I shall have you all locked up.'

Willbury grabbed Marjorie's arm.

'Yes. Any more trouble, and I'm sure the police will want to give us the power to administer punishment to our prisoner as well,' said Snatcher, eyeing Willbury.

'Quite right, sir,' responded the Chief Squeaker. 'It is so nice to find a co-operative member of the public like yourself.'

Snatcher then spoke to the Trouts. 'Take the boy back to the Cheese Hall!'

Arthur looked very nervously back at Willbury as he was led away. 'What am I going to do?' he cried. The thought of trying to escape from the Cheese Hall again filled him with despair. And what on earth would they do to him once they got him there?

'We will get you back!' called Willbury after him.

'I am sure your diligence will be well rewarded,' Snatcher smirked to the Chief Squeaker. 'I will arrange for some "paperwork" to be delivered to you later.'

'Oh, thank you, sir!'

The Chief Squeaker mounted his bicycle and set off down the towpath, leaving his men guarding the laundry.

The Chief Squeaker mounted his bicycle and set off down the towpath

Willbury and the crew stood in silence, watched by the policemen.

'Just when I thought things were getting better!'

muttered Willbury to himself. 'Poor Arthur—it was so brave of him to rescue the underlings and get his wings back. Now he's worse off than ever! What are we going to do?'

A Squeaker on guard

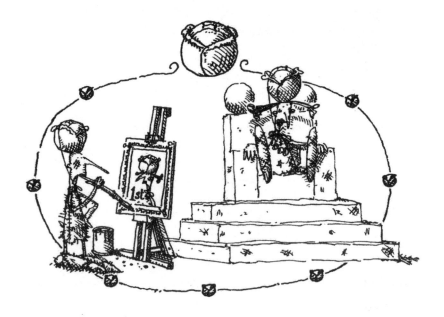

The queen very much enjoyed having her portrait painted, and would sit every two weeks for new sets of stamps. For those that couldn't read, the value of the stamp was defined by the size of cabbage she wore on her head.

*They assembled before the throne on the high
stone platform at the end of their cavern*

Chapter 29

EXODUS

Back in the Underworld, all the remaining cabbageheads had gathered together. They assembled before the throne on the high stone platform at the end of their cavern. Below them the floor of the cavern was now under several feet of water, and the level was rising very quickly.

The queen adjusted the enormous cabbage on her head, and then gave a haughty cough. She was the only cabbagehead who ever spoke louder than a whisper. 'We have brought you here today, for we have unfortunate tidings to impart. Pursuant to the ever-rising levels of ill commodious ablutive liquids, we believe sustainable brassica production ceases to be feasible. Therefore I decree that henceforth we must sojourn to an alternative affiliated venue. Hey nonny nonny, we have spoken!'

A very old cabbagehead made his way up the steps to the throne

The other cabbageheads looked at each other, confused. None of them knew what she was talking about.

Then a very old cabbagehead made his way up the steps to the throne, and whispered in the queen's ear. She gave an embarrassed nod and spoke again.

'In alternative parlance, it is too wet to grow cabbages here any more, and we'll have to find somewhere else to grow them.'

There was a lot of nervous muttering amongst the cabbageheads.

The old cabbagehead whispered in the queen's ear once more. Then she spoke again.

' 'Tis brought to one's attention that vertically positioned below dales some few leagues beyond the confines of the above populace is a sufficient aperture that we may abide. Thus we might alight and henceforth meander to yonder aperture to re establish a harmonious intergraded monarchical community, and go forth with our troglodyte agriculture.'

There was more muttering from the 'common' cabbageheads, and the old cabbagehead once more spoke to the queen. She went a deeper red.

'There is another cave not far from here where we can move to and grow cabbages,' she said rather awkwardly.

A small cabbagehead approached the throne and whispered to the old cabbagehead. He in turn whispered to the queen, and she spoke again. 'It would appear that one's subjects that are currently absent from one's realm while . . .'

The old cabbagehead gave the queen a steely gaze and she started again.

'One . . . We need someone to go and find Titus and the others, and tell them where we've gone to.'

Two younger cabbageheads raised their hands.

Two younger cabbageheads raised their hands

'Very good,' said the queen. 'Now follow one, and one's assistant,' she said indicating the old man, 'and don't forget one's seeds!'

The crowd all patted their pockets and giggled. The old cabbagehead descended the steps, and led the crowd up a tunnel away from the platform.

The queen found herself sitting alone, and feeling rather disgruntled. She surveyed her kingdom of water and bobbing cabbages one last time, and then followed.

She surveyed her kingdom of water and bobbing cabbages one last time

THE DUNGEON UNDER THE CHEESE HALL

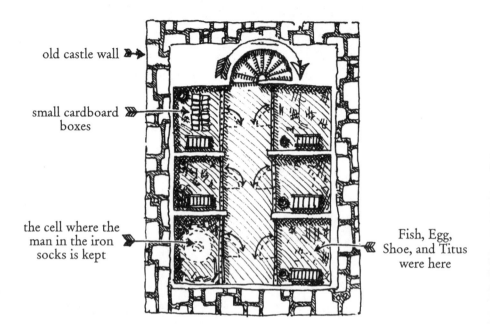

old castle wall ▶▶

small cardboard boxes ▶▶▶

the cell where the man in the iron socks is kept

Fish, Egg, Shoe, and Titus were here

The dungeon under the laboratory has a long and gruesome history, and predates the Cheese Hall by hundreds of years. It was constructed in 1247 as the dungeon/torture chamber/nursery/food cellar/rubbish tip for Ratbridge castle. In 1453 revolting peasants destroyed the castle. Eight babies and three hardened criminals survived, trapped in the dungeon for two years before they were discovered by a team of local builders who were redeveloping the site as a shoe shop. For the next hundred years the dungeon was used as a storeroom for shoes and the equipment left over from the torturing came in handy for fitting shoes to those who lied about their shoe size.

During this period a small cheese shop was built next door, and due to foul and sharp practices, became very successful. When the shoe shop failed, it was bought up by the cheese shop owner and was used as a secret workshop where date-expired labels were filed off cheeses and new forged ones applied. The cheese shop became wholesalers and gained control of the cheese trade in the area. Other cheese traders had to become members of a cheese guild (set up by the wholesalers) to be allowed to trade, and the empire expanded.

In 1712 the Cheese Hall was built and a laboratory was built behind it to further the 'science' of adulteration. The dungeon was found to be useful for the storage of those that caused any problems for the cheese guild, and long-term storage of failed experiments.

In the dungeon the Members surrounded Arthur

Chapter 30

BACK BELOW THE CHEESE HALL

In the dungeon the Members surrounded Arthur.

'What are we going to do with you, my little thief?' asked Snatcher.

'I am not the thief!' snapped Arthur.

'Oh, yes, you are! You took my wings!'

'Those were my wings. You stole them from me in the first place.'

'That is as maybe, but they are mine now. And for all the grief you've caused me, I think pretty much everything of yours is as good as mine.' Snatcher looked at Arthur then spoke again. 'Search 'im!'

The Members descended on Arthur, and emptied his pockets.

'Not much here, guv!'

Then one of the Members noticed the bump under
Arthur's shirt.

'He's got something up his jumper!'

'Get it!' ordered Snatcher.

Arthur tried to defend his doll with his cuffed hands, but
he was overpowered, and the doll pulled from him.

'What have we here?' asked Snatcher. 'The little boy has
got a little dolly!'

'Ahhhh!' scoffed the Members.

'The little boy has got a little dolly!'

Arthur looked worried and reached for the doll. Snatcher
laughed and threw it on the floor.

'By the time I've finished with you, that dolly is going to
look like your big brother.'

The Members laughed.

'What do you mean?' asked Arthur.

Snatcher laughed and threw it on the floor

'Haven't you guessed yet? Have you not realized why we are collecting big creatures and why only little creatures leave here? We is nicking their SIZE!' scoffed Snatcher.

Arthur froze. 'Size?'

'Yes!' Snatcher laughed. 'It so happens that we have come by a certain device . . . ' He stopped and winked at the Trouts, who were holding Arthur. ' . . . that can extract the size from things. All your little friends who came our way are now your even littler friends.'

Snatcher and the others now all burst out laughing.

'But what's the point in doing that?' Arthur asked.

'That is for us to know. It is part of our BIG plan.' There was more laughter. Then Snatcher's face changed, and his voice turned nasty. 'And if it was not for you, things might be progressing a lot faster. I needed them monsters you freed. Perhaps you might like to donate some of your size instead?'

Arthur did not reply.

'Yes. I thought that might shut you up. You've put a spanner in the works. Now we have to go and find a load more monsters to shrink!' snarled Snatcher. He turned to the Trouts. 'Throw him in a cell. We'll sort him out the next time we fire up the machine.' Then he smirked horribly. 'And next time I go out on a little selling trip, I am sure all the ladies will be falling over themselves to buy a miniature boy!' He looked directly at Arthur, put on a simpering face and spoke in the unmistakable tones of Madame Froufrou: 'I 'ave only one of zese little creatures, for sale to ze most fashionably rich lady of all!'

Arthur gaped. So that explained why Madame Froufrou had reminded him so strongly of Snatcher! It was just a disguise! Was this man behind everything sinister in the town?

Sniggering at the look on Arthur's face, the Trouts lifted Arthur, and threw him through the door of the cell that had contained the trotting badgers. Snatcher walked over and locked the door. Arthur noticed that the keys were now attached to his waistcoat by a heavy metal chain.

Arthur noticed that the keys were now attached
to his waistcoat by a heavy metal chain

'When are we going to fire up the machine . . . ?' asked Gristle.

'The sooner the better,' replied Snatcher. 'But there is no point doing it just for the boy, we'll get some more monsters to put in it.'

'Does that mean we have to go down . . . below?' Gristle was looking very worried.

'Don't worry, Gristle. I am sure somebody will hold your hand.' Snatcher smirked. Arthur noticed the other Members were also looking worried.

A quick cup of tea

'I think a quick cup of tea is in order,' Snatcher said, then all the Members set off up the stairs leaving Arthur alone in the dungeon.

Arthur alone in the dungeon

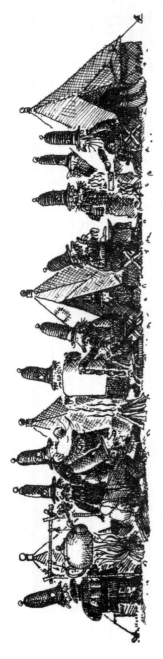

The police had set up camp on the towpath

Kipper was standing with Tom on the deck watching the Squeakers

Chapter 31

The Stand Off

Back on the laundry there was a stand off. The police had set up camp on the towpath and the crew stood about looking very glum. They were running out of food. Normally the crew would have gone shopping late on market day (to pick up bargains), but with all the excitement yesterday they had forgotten, and now they were not allowed off the ship.

Kipper was standing with Tom on the deck watching the Squeakers who were tucking into egg and bacon that they were cooking over a fire they had started on the towpath. The smell of the bacon was wafting over the side of the laundry.

'This is torture!' muttered Kipper.

'I think they must be doing it to wind us up,' replied Tom.

The Squeakers were tucking into egg and bacon
that they were cooking over a fire

The boxtrolls were also becoming uneasy. They were sniffing the air and gurgling to each other. Fish moved slowly to the top of the gangplank and stared hard at the feasting Squeakers. One of the new boxtrolls joined Fish and was whispering something to him.

'I think I can feel my energy sapping away,' said Kipper. 'If I don't get something to eat soon I shall just fade away.'

Tom looked up at Kipper's belly. 'The chance of you fading away is pretty remote. It's us rats I am worried about. We have a very high metabolic rate, you know.' Tom stopped and tugged on Kipper's arm. Fish had started to move very slowly down the gangplank towards the bank.

'What's he doing?' whispered Tom.

Kipper didn't answer and they watched as Fish reached the bank and walked nonchalantly straight past the

Squeakers. The Squeakers looked up but seemed to pay the boxtroll almost no attention at all.

'Why don't they grab him?' whispered Tom under his breath.

Kipper watched as the Squeakers returned their full attention to the egg and bacon. 'It's Townsfolk. I think it must be that they hold underlings in such low regard that they just don't notice them.'

Fish had made his way a little further down the canal bank and was now waving to the other boxtrolls on deck to join him. A small procession of boxtrolls now marched down the gangplank, past the Squeakers (who hardly gave them a second glance), and joined Fish.

A small procession of boxtrolls

'Well, blow me!' muttered Tom. 'Where do you think they are off to?'

'Off to find themselves breakfast,' said Kipper sounding very sorry for himself. 'I wish I was an underling!'

About twenty minutes later, Willbury was sitting in the captain's cabin, and Titus was playing with the miniature cabbagehead by the window, when Titus gave a squeak. Willbury turned to see him looking out of the window. Willbury got up and joined him. Back along the towpath came the boxtrolls, and they were all carrying sacks.

'Oh no!' said Willbury. 'What's going on?'

He rushed up on deck to witness the boxtrolls walk straight past the policemen and up the gangplank.

Titus looking out of the window

Marjorie was up on deck and was watching. 'Good, isn't it?'

Willbury looked baffled.

'Them Squeakers don't pay them any attention,' explained Kipper. 'So used to thinking of them as nothing, they just don't seem to notice them.'

Fish and his group of friends emptied out their sacks. There in the middle of the deck was a large pile of cake, biscuits, treacle, boiled sweets, toffee, shortbread, pasties, anchovies, pickled onions, raspberry jam, and lemonade bottles. The crew's eyes lit up, and the pile soon disappeared under a crowd of bodies.

Willbury, however, looked slightly disapproving.

Fish and his group of friends emptied out their sacks

'You know that Titus and the other cabbageheads don't like this sort of food. Didn't you think to bring anything for them?'

The boxtrolls looked a little grumpy. Shoe picked up a small sack which was still lying beside him on the floor and threw it huffily forward. Willbury reached down and emptied it out to reveal a pile of fruit and vegetables. He smiled at the sulking boxtrolls.

'Thank you, that is very thoughtful of you. I'll take these down to the store room to keep them safe for later.'

Once he returned to the deck, Willbury stood a few feet away from the mêlée, watching the crew gorge themselves on the food. Marjorie joined him. She was tucking hungrily into a doughnut. 'Aren't you hungry?' she asked.

'How could I be hungry at a time like this?' Willbury looked very downcast.

'I have a dreadful feeling that this is all my fault!' Marjorie said.

'What do you mean?' asked Willbury.

Marjorie led Willbury away from the group. 'It's my invention. I think I know what has happened to it. I had an idea, but when the Trouts turned up with Snatcher, I knew. . . I just knew.'

'The Trouts?' said Willbury, looking puzzled.

'Didn't you see the men who had hold of Arthur?' asked Marjorie.

'No, I think I must have been concentrating on Arthur rather than the men who had hold of him.'

'It was the Trouts, I swear it. They looked pretty rough, but I am sure it was them.'

'So Snatcher has your invention?'

'Yes.'

'Are you sure?'

'Yes. It's all these little creatures.'

'What do you mean?'

'The invention that was stolen from me was a resizing machine,' whispered Marjorie.

'A RESIZING MACHINE!' Willbury was flabbergasted.

'Yes, I have discovered how to take the size out of one thing and put it into another. In the wrong hands it could be very dangerous . . . and I think it has definitely got into the wrong hands . . . ' Marjorie looked mournful.

'How does this machine operate?' asked Willbury.

Willbury was flabbergasted

'It consists of two parts. If you have two things of equal size, one side of the machine drains the size out of one thing and the other part of the machine pumps the size into the other thing,' Marjorie explained.

'Do you mean it shrinks one thing and makes the other thing bigger?' asked Willbury.

'Yes . . . exactly. And Snatcher and his mob have got hold of it. I don't know quite what they are doing with it, but I bet it's something rotten.'

Willbury thought to himself for a moment, and then spoke. 'Well, we know what they're doing with it. They're shrinking the underlings!'

*'Do you mean it shrinks one thing and makes
the other thing bigger?' asked Willbury*

'Yes . . . but that's only half of it.' Marjorie paused. 'Where is all the size going?'

Willbury thought to himself then muttered, 'Oh my word! I hadn't thought of that.' Then he asked Marjorie another question.

'Why underlings?'

'It only works on living creatures. I guess they thought that nobody would notice or care if they used underlings.'

'Then I wonder why they have been blocking up the holes to the Underworld,' Willbury pondered. 'Surely that would stop the underlings coming above ground and falling into their clutches.'

'I've been thinking about that too. I think they must be blocking up the holes to help trap them in some way. Perhaps there is only one hole still open, and they lie in wait for the underlings there, knowing it is their only way to the surface . . . I don't know,' answered Marjorie.

'This is truly awful. Whatever possessed you to build a machine that could resize living creatures?'

Marjorie looked very embarrassed

'Truthfully?' Marjorie looked very embarrassed. 'I was interested in the scientific principles involved in making it. I just wanted to see if it was possible. I hadn't really worked out what it was going to be used for,' said Marjorie.

Then Willbury spoke again. 'I wonder what it is they are making bigger.'

'I don't rightly know. And I have been trying to work out how the cheese comes into it.'

'It must do somehow.' Willbury then spoke in a determined manner: 'I have a very bad feeling about this. We have to get Arthur back, and stop whatever is going on! Let's call a Council of War!'

The man in the iron socks

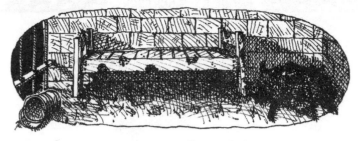

Against one wall was a bed

Chapter 32

THE MAN IN THE
IRON SOCKS

Alone in the cold dank dungeon, Arthur looked around his cell. Against one wall was a bed. It had probably not been very comfortable even before it had been used by the trotting badgers, but now it was covered with bite marks, and he thought he would just get peppered with splinters if he tried to use it. Shreds of an old blanket had been used to form a kind of nest in one corner of the cell. This did not look very inviting either.

'I bet it's full of fleas!' Arthur muttered.

The only other things in the cell were a filthy bucket, and a few strands of straw scattered about the floor. Arthur walked to the bars and looked out. About six feet away lay his doll!

If I could reach it I could speak to Grandfather and he might be able to help me, thought Arthur.

The doll lay a few feet from his grasp

He lay on the floor and reached as far as he could. If only he could get the doll back. It lay a few feet from his grasp, almost as if it had been positioned deliberately to taunt him. He looked about his cell to see if there was anything he could use to help him. There was nothing.

'This is useless!' he moaned. Feeling completely at a loss, he got up and kicked the bed against the wall in frustration. After a second or so, there came a distant dull thump in return. Arthur was puzzled.

'What was that?'

He waited for a few moments but there were no more sounds, so he kicked the bed again. There was another thump. He didn't think it was an echo, but to be sure he kicked the bed twice in rapid succession. After a couple of seconds came a 'Thump! Thump! Thump!'

'It can't be an echo then!' He kicked the bed again . . . The thumping started again, but this time it didn't stop. Arthur pulled the bed from the wall, put his ear to the stonework, and listened. The thumping was coming from the next cell. There was definitely someone—or something—in there. Then Arthur realized that the cell next to him was the boarded-up cell of which the boxtrolls had been so

frightened. He began to wish he hadn't attracted the attention of its occupant.

'Oh no! It sounds as if it's coming through!'

The thumping was getting louder and louder. Arthur looked down and noticed one of the bricks in the wall was moving out towards him.

'It is! It's coming through!' Arthur panicked. He jumped over the bed then smashed it as hard as he could against the wall, sending the brick shooting back in.

Someone shouted 'Ouch!' and the thumping stopped.

He jumped over the bed then smashed it as hard as he could against the wall

Arthur pulled the bed back again, and waited.

There was a muffled cry, an even louder thump, and, before Arthur had time to react again, the loose brick flew out of the wall and landed on the floor.

There was a slight pause, then a hand holding a stub of candle appeared through the hole. Arthur froze.

'What's all this noise about? Can't a prisoner get any sleep round here?' came a very grumpy voice. 'I'm the only one round here allowed to make a din.'

A face covered by a mask peered back

Arthur got down and peered into the hole. A face covered by a mask peered back.

'Who are you?' asked Arthur.

'I am Herbert!' came the reply. 'And who are you? You are not one of these Cheese Wallahs are you? Can't stand cheese or anything to do with it! Used to love it, but you can have too much of a good thing!'

'No. My name is Arthur,' said Arthur.

'Where you from?' said Herbert curtly. 'And what are you doing here?'

'I am from the Underworld. But I've got stuck up here in Ratbridge, and now I've been caught and put in this cell.'

'Blimey. You're in for it. I've heard what they is up to. Blooming evil! You is going to get shrunk!'

Arthur peered through the hole.

'Did you make this hole?'

'Course I did! I make lots of holes. Trouble is that when I do it makes so much noise that the Cheese Wallahs always come and fill them in again. Never seems to get me anywhere. Been trying to get out of here for years, but never been lucky. If I could get these socks off they wouldn't be able to hold me.'

'Socks?' asked Arthur.

'Yes. The Cheese Wallahs shoved me into a pair of iron socks to slow me down. They still don't dare come too close!'

'The Cheese Wallahs shoved me into a pair of iron socks to slow me down'

'Why is that?'

'They is scared of me, what with me mask and me walloper. I made me a mask out of a bit of my old boots, and a big walloper out of me bed, and if they come near me . . . wallop!'

'What's a walloper?'

'It's me big mallet! It's great for all kinds of walloping. I love it!'

'You wallop them with it?'

'I wallop everything with it!'

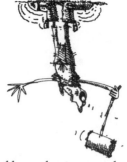

'So if I cause any trouble . . . they just turn the magnet on . . . boink!'

'I wallop everything with it! Trouble is the Cheese Wallahs got tired of it, and fixed up a way of stopping me walloping them.'

'How?'

'They stuck these socks on me and a huge electro-magnet in the ceiling above my cell, so if I cause any trouble . . . they just turn the magnet on . . . boink! I stick to the ceiling. Blooming iron socks!'

'Is that painful?' asked Arthur.

'Only when they turn the magnet off! I drops to the floor, you see . . . Bonk! But I still usually manage to wallop one or two of them.'

'Why are you locked up here?' Arthur enquired.

'Me? Can't remember much now 'cause it's been such a long, long time. Something to do with me and . . . ' Herbert's voice trailed off.

'How long have you been here?'

'Can't rightly say. But I know that I have walloped more than a hundred and thirty of them over the years!'

'A hundred and thirty!' declared Arthur.

'Well, some of them might be the same person I walloped a few times. It was much easier in the early days before they put me in the socks. These days I am lucky to get even one of them!'

'Do you know what they are up to?'

'Well, I know they are shrinking underlings what they trap and steal,' replied Herbert. 'Don't know why.'

'You say that they're trapping underlings?' asked Arthur.

'Yes, I heard them talking about it when they brought some in. They got some kind of way down into the Underworld . . . and they set traps.'

Arthur's interest was growing. 'What do you know about how they get into the Underworld?'

'Not much! But I think they must have some way down from 'ere at the Cheese Hall, 'cause it don't take 'em long.'

Arthur's mind began to whirr. If there was a route between the Cheese Hall and the Underworld then maybe there was a way for him to get back to Grandfather after all. If only he could get hold of his doll and tell Grandfather what he had learned, perhaps they could come up with a plan.

If only he could get hold of his doll and tell Grandfather what he had learned

*Snatcher climbed on to a table and took a look out
through the boards that covered the tearoom windows*

'You worry too much.'

Chapter 33

GOING DOWN!

Snatcher climbed on to a table and took a look out through the boards that covered the tearoom windows. It was raining again.

'Well, is it raining?' asked Gristle.

'No!' Snatcher lied, and climbed back down off the table.

'I still don't like it. It's getting very wet down there. Last time we were up to our knees in water.'

'You worry too much.' Snatcher chortled at the nervous-looking Members assembled before him. They didn't look convinced. 'One more load of them monsters and a few more cheeses, and all will be tickety-boo for our plans for Ratbridge.'

'The traps were nearly empty on the last two trips.'

'I know,' said Snatcher. 'Why else do yer think I got yer to grab them rats, and monsters from the shop? Now get on

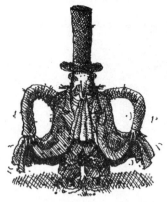

'Last time we were up to our knees in water'

with yer!' Snatcher fixed Gristle with his good eye. 'Or perhaps I could come up with a substitute for monsters . . . If you get my drift?'

Gristle turned pale. 'No . . . er . . . I'm sure we can find something in the traps.'

'Very good. Just make sure you do!' said Snatcher. 'The Great One needs 'em, and we need the Great One. Our plan relies on 'im. If you get a good haul, this will be the last time, and after that we can seal up the Underworld completely.'

'Promise?'

'Promise!'

The Members looked happier.

'All right then!' said Snatcher as he walked over to a large cupboard and opened its doors. 'First trapping party inside!'

A small group of the Members carrying sacks walked forward, and reluctantly entered the cupboard. Snatcher gave them a wink and closed the doors. Then he took hold of a bell pull next to the cupboard.

*A small group of the Members carrying sacks walked
forward, and reluctantly entered the cupboard*

'Going down!' he giggled, and pulled the bell pull. There
was a grinding noise, then muffled screams that faded away.
After a couple of seconds there was a distant splash, followed
by a bell ping.

'Maybe it is a little wet,' Snatcher smirked. Then he
waited for a few seconds before pulling the bell pull again.
After a few more seconds there was another ping, and
Snatcher opened the doors. The cupboard was empty, apart
from two inches of dirty water that ran out onto the carpet.

'Second trapping party, please,' ordered Snatcher.

The Members looked very, very nervous and shuffled
backwards.

*The cupboard was empty, apart from two inches
of dirty water that ran out onto the carpet*

'Second trapping party, PLEASE!' Snatcher snapped.

Reluctantly, the remaining group walked into the cupboard.

'Not you, Gristle!' Snatcher said. 'You can go down on the last load with me.' He closed the cupboard and sent the Members on their way. Then he turned to Gristle and took a banknote out of his pocket. 'But first I want you to pop down the shops quick and get me a pair of wellies.'

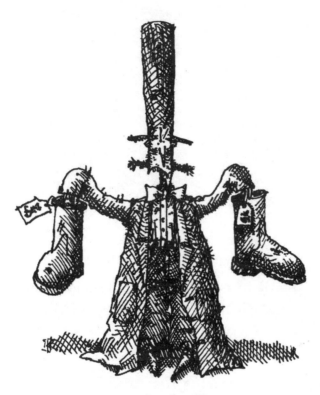

Gristle with wellies

Kipper and Tom disturb the meeting in the hold

Willbury, Marjorie, and the captain sat behind an ironing board

Chapter 34

THE COUNCIL OF WAR

It was early evening and it was raining . . . again. In the hold of the laundry all the dirty clothes had been pushed to one end to make space for the Council of War. Willbury, Marjorie, and the captain sat behind an ironing board, facing the crew and underlings. Even Match and the miniature cabbagehead and fresh-water sea-cow were there. The fresh-water sea-cow had been adopted by some of the crew and was swimming about in a small barrel on wheels amongst her new guardians, who kept sneaking her lumps of cucumber. The only people missing were Kipper, Tom . . . and Arthur.

Willbury looked about, and then turned to the captain. 'Where are Kipper and Tom?'

'We needed someone to act as watch on deck, and as it was raining, I gave them the duty as punishment. They should never have let Arthur go into the Cheese Hall alone.'

The fresh-water sea-cow had been adopted by some of the crew

'Oh . . . all right . . . Well, I think we'd better call the meeting to order, and get started.' Willbury stood up, and the hold fell quiet.

'My friends, we have a number of problems. Firstly, we have to get Arthur back from the Cheese Guild and return him to his grandfather. And secondly, I think we must find out what Snatcher is up to, and put an end to it.' Willbury paused. 'I have some disturbing new information. Snatcher, we think, is in possession of a new invention.'

Marjorie looked uncomfortable and stared at the floor.

'It is a machine that resizes things!'

There were gasps from the crowd.

'Yes! I believe it is Snatcher and his mob that are responsible for the tininess of our tiny friends.'

Match and the little cabbagehead who were standing on a stepladder amongst the underlings squeaked, and they all turned to look.

'We don't know what he is doing with the size he takes from the creatures—but I think we can be pretty certain that whatever it is, we're not going to like it. We have to get into the Cheese Hall. Does anybody have any ideas?'

Match and the little cabbagehead were standing on a stepladder

Willbury looked around expectantly, but there was no reply.
The meeting in the hold had been almost silent for two
minutes, and Willbury was trying to decide what to do next,
when Tom and Kipper suddenly burst through the door,
drenched from the rain on deck.

'Willbury!' cried Tom as he and Kipper scanned the
surprised faces. 'We've just spotted some cabbageheads on
the towpath! Two of them! What should we do?'

'We've just spotted some cabbageheads on the towpath!'

'Hmm,' said Willbury. 'I wonder where they have come
from—all the cabbageheads from the Cheese Hall are down
here with us, aren't they, Titus?'

Titus nodded, looking excited.

'Then I think you had better go up and see what's happening, Titus.'

Titus stood and made his way quickly past Tom and Kipper and up the stairs to the deck. Tom and Kipper followed, along with the other cabbageheads and Willbury.

As soon as he reached the deck, Titus ran to the side of the ship and disappeared down the gangplank.

He ran past the Squeakers and along the towpath till he approached the shadows where Tom and Kipper had seen the cabbageheads. The others watched from the deck as shapes in the shadows approached Titus and seemed to be having a conversation. Then Titus turned back towards the laundry, followed by two other cabbageheads. They looked very nervous and were holding hands. Titus led them past the Squeakers, who ignored them completely, and up the gangplank.

Titus turned back towards the laundry, followed by two other cabbageheads

As soon as they reached the deck the cabbageheads all ran to meet each other, hugged, and started whispering. After a few minutes the huddle broke up, and Titus came over to

The cabbageheads all ran to meet each other

Willbury, looking quite agitated. Willbury leant over to allow Titus to whisper in his ear. When Titus had finished whispering, Willbury stood upright and spoke.

'Oh dear me! The cabbageheads have all fled from their home. It seems that the water level underground has driven them out.'

'How did they get up here if the holes are all blocked?' asked Kipper.

Willbury looked puzzled. 'That is an excellent question. I . . . or rather Titus . . . shall have to ask them.'

Titus scampered over to where the cabbageheads stood, and they formed another huddle. After a few moments he returned and whispered in Willbury's ear again. Willbury turned back towards the others with an expression of surprise on his face.

'They came up through the rabbit women's tunnels. Arthur told me about the tunnels, but he didn't know quite where they were. Apparently they come up in the woods just outside town.'

Kipper smiled. 'Well, that's how we get into the Cheese Hall then. We get under the town and burrow up!'

Tom and Willbury turned to look at Kipper.

'They came up through the rabbit women's tunnels'

'You're right, Kipper! You're not as green as you are— No, that would not be very apppropriate,' said Willbury. 'Titus, would your friends show us the way?'

Titus returned to the new cabbageheads and whispered to them. They nodded.

' . . . But how do we get off the boat?' asked Tom. He looked across at the Squeakers, who were still drinking tea and looking very wet and grumpy. Any attempt to get off this laundry by the crew was going to be noticed.

'I just don't know . . . ' said Willbury. 'Why don't we go back down to the meeting, tell them about the tunnels, and get out of this rain? There has to be a way to get past the Squeakers.'

The Squeakers were still drinking tea and looking very wet and grumpy

Tom and Kipper looked sheepish. 'We are supposed to stay up here and keep watch.'

Willbury smiled. 'I don't think anybody is going to attack us in this rain. Why don't you come down with us?'

They went below. Willbury returned to his chair, and the others found space amongst the underlings. The captain and the others looked quizzically at the newcomers.

Willbury spoke. 'Gentlemen, the cabbageheads who have joined us have just come up from the Underworld. They have found tunnels that are not blocked, which come up just outside the town walls, in the woods. Kipper has suggested that we use these tunnels to get under the town and burrow up into the Cheese Hall.'

There were murmurings of approval, and Willbury turned and smiled at Kipper.

'It's going to take a lot of burrowing,' said Bert.

'Yes . . . yes, it is,' said Willbury. 'I think we'll need as many hands and paws as we can muster. Volunteers?'

A sea of hands and paws went up, and was followed by a cheer.

'Good. But we have a major problem. How do we get off the laundry?' asked Willbury.

'We could jump over the side and tie up the Squeakers, then throw them in the drink!' said Bert.

'We could jump over the side and tie up the Squeakers, then throw them in the drink!'

There was another cheer.

'I don't think so, Bert. There are rather a lot of policemen, and they might win in a fight. Even if they didn't, if even one of them got away, he could warn the Cheese Guild we were coming.'

They all sat and thought.

'Boxtrolls!' Kipper cried.

'What do you mean, boxtrolls?' asked Willbury with a puzzled look on his face.

'Seeing that the boxtrolls and cabbageheads can get on and off the ship, we dress up as boxtrolls. Then the Squeakers won't pay any attention to us.'

'You don't think the Squeakers might notice we're not real boxtrolls?' asked the captain.

'Well, they're not too bright,' said Tom.

'And if the disguises were good then I think we might get away with it,' smiled Willbury.

'Don't you think that they'd notice if there was no one left on the ship?' asked the captain.

'I think that we might be able to get around that,' said Marjorie. 'Leave it to me.'

Soon everybody was busy. In a storeroom, where the crew kept all the things that they would put out for recycling, were a lot of folded up cardboard boxes. Under the guidance of Fish and the other boxtrolls, the crew prepared these. They found that economy Stainpurge boxes were just about the right size for humans, and that luxury 'Blotch-b-white' boxes fitted the rats. Meanwhile the rats set about making troll teeth out of the vegetables and fruit, while Marjorie was seen constructing dummies and some strange rigging device out of ropes and laundry. By late that evening everybody was below decks and ready. Fish and the other boxtrolls were very happy having so many new 'boxtrolls' about, and were chortling to themselves.

Willbury raised his hands and shushed the crowd. Then he spoke. 'Arr arware bawaee waaee.'

Soon everybody was busy

'Whaa?' came the reply.

Willbury took out his new orange-peel teeth.

'I said, is everybody ready?' There was a lot of nodding and giggling. 'Well then, I think it may be best if we leave the laundry in ones and twos, then meet up by the West Gate. If we take a rope ladder we can use it to climb down from the town wall.'

Tom found a rope ladder and Kipper stowed it inside his new box. With his new parsnip teeth Kipper looked like Fish's bigger brother.

'Is your distraction ready?' Willbury asked Marjorie.

Marjorie nodded. 'I have arranged a party . . . powered by the beam engine, for the policemen to watch. It's going to take a few minutes to really get going, but I don't see why we can't start sneaking off. It should stop them noticing that the ship is empty.'

The captain and Willbury organized everybody and handed out candles. These would be needed in the dark tunnels. Then they led the first group up onto the deck.

Marjorie followed them up the stairs. The 'boxtrolls' then started to make their way down the gangplank in small groups, and walked straight past the policemen.

On deck Marjorie adjusted the beam engine and the flywheel started to turn. She'd piped some of the steam from the boiler to a small harmonium and the crows had agreed to stay behind, as they were not very good at burrowing, and play the instrument. As their beaks hit the keys, steam and a great deal of noise started to come from the back of the keyboard. The crows were delighted. Before long terrible tunes could be heard up and down the towpath. The Squeakers covered their ears and moaned.

As their beaks hit the keys, steam and a great deal of noise started to come from the back of the keyboard

'It's working!' said Marjorie.

She pulled a handle on the side of the beam engine and a number of ropes fixed to pulleys tightened. Strange cloth figures appeared, and started to dance about the deck. The Squeakers were straining their necks to see the dancers but they were obviously unwilling to get too close to the awful noise, and did not approach the boat. More boxtrolls made their way up on deck and sauntered past the police, unnoticed. After half an hour only Marjorie and Willbury were left on board.

Strange cloth figures appeared, and started to dance about the deck

'This is really ingenious, Marjorie. I hope it will give us the time we need!' Willbury said.

Marjorie looked a little sad. 'It's the least I can do to help. I still feel terrible that my invention has caused so much trouble. I'll do anything to put things right.'

'You mustn't blame yourself,' said Willbury kindly. 'You had no way of knowing what would happen. All we can do is

to do our best to thwart these awful people, and stop whatever it is they're up to. Now, I think it's time for us to go. How long will this dancing, and "music" last?'

'Well, if the crows can keep stoking the boiler, it could go on all night.' Marjorie smiled.

'I don't think that will be very popular with the locals!' said Willbury.

'You never know. The crows might get better!' Marjorie chuckled. They put their teeth in and set off.

The West Gate

When Willbury and Marjorie arrived at the
West Gate, Tom rushed up to meet them

Chapter 35

Up and Under!

When Willbury and Marjorie arrived at the West Gate, Tom rushed up to meet them, and snatched his teeth out of his mouth so he could talk.

'Quick! Bert has just seen town guards. They're coming round on their patrol, and they'll be here in a minute.'

Willbury took out his boxtroll teeth. 'They won't bother us if we are dressed as boxtrolls, will they?'

'Yes they will! They're not like the police—they're always on the lookout for boxtrolls. They know who's responsible for "borrowing" things. They hate them!' replied Tom.

'Let's get over the wall then,' suggested Willbury.

Tom looked up at the town wall. 'How?'

Willbury followed his gaze. 'Oh my. We didn't work that out, did we!'

'We've got to do something,' Tom said urgently.

'I ah . . . ah.' Willbury started to panic. Then he felt a tapping on his box. It was Fish.

Fish pointed at the real boxtrolls who were settling themselves outside a sweetshop that stood next to the wall. They crouched down, then pulled their heads and arms inside the boxes. All that was left was what appeared to be a pile of boxes outside the shop. Fish led Willbury over to the shop and indicated to him to do the same.

'Fish wants us to pretend to be boxes. Quick! Do as he says!' Willbury whispered to the others.

With the help of Fish they assembled themselves in a stack outside the shop. Fish settled down beside them, and the cabbageheads hid behind the stack. Footsteps approached.

Fish pointed at the real boxtrolls who were settling themselves outside a sweetshop

'An' I sez to 'er, if our girl Sonya did that to . . . 'Ello? What we got here?' said a voice.

'Looks like someone has made a late delivery to the sweetshop,' said the second. 'They wasn't 'ere an hour ago.'

The two guards approached the boxes. One of them rubbed his chin and looked about.

The two guards approached the boxes

'I am rather partial to sweets. Mind you, "Stainpurge" doesn't sound that tasty. Still, you never know . . . Do yer think anyone is going to miss one of these boxes?'

'No! Course not! There must be at least twenty or thirty of them and if one goes missing that's only five per cent! You must expect five per cent natural wastage when you leave something lying about, don't you think?'

'Oh, I should think so! Do you think that if we got a cart, then maybe twenty or thirty per cent natural wastage might be acceptable?'

'I should think that if we got my brother Big Alf's wagon, then almost a hundred per cent natural wastage might occur!'

'You stay here and I'll get the wagon!'

Off went one of the guards while the other kept watch on the stack of boxes. After a few minutes there was a clattering of wheels. A large, high wagon appeared, stopped by the wall, and the guard jumped down. With difficulty the two of them managed to lift the boxes onto the wagon. When their backs were turned the cabbageheads jumped up, and hid amongst the boxes now on the wagon. When the guards had finished they stopped for a breather.

A large, high wagon appeared

A head popped out of one of the larger boxes and looked about. It was Willbury. He saw that the top of the town wall was just inches above him, and he smiled. A hand came out from the side of his box, and removed his troll teeth.

'RIGHT! Everybody over the wall!' he shouted.

The two guards looked round and fainted at the sight of a cart-load of boxes all standing up at the same time.

They all clambered on to the top of the wall from the cart, and Kipper got out the rope ladder, hooked it to the top of the wall, and lowered it over the other side. Climbing down

*The two guards looked round and fainted at the sight
of a cart-load of boxes all standing up at the same time.*

dressed in a cardboard box was not easy and several of the pirates ended up dropping off the ladder and crumpling their boxes. This distressed the real boxtrolls.

When everybody was down, Titus whispered in Willbury's ear.

'We'll follow our cabbagehead friends—they'll lead us to the rabbit women's tunnels,' said Willbury. The party set off following the new cabbageheads. It made a strange sight, with the moon casting long shadows across the landscape.

Soon they were in the woods. The new cabbageheads wandered about a bit before they found an old oak tree. They ran to its base and pulled back some undergrowth to reveal a large hole between the tree's roots. Everybody gathered round as the new cabbageheads whispered to Titus. Titus then whispered to Willbury and after some moments Willbury spoke to the group.

'This is the entrance to the rabbit women's tunnels. Our new cabbagehead friends don't want to go any further.' Willbury smiled at the cabbageheads. 'They are rather frightened of what's happening down there, and want to catch up with the other cabbageheads who are apparently making their way to a new cave in the hills. I think it is totally understandable. We don't really know what we are going to find down there.'

They ran to its base and pulled back some undergrowth
to reveal a large hole between the tree's roots

There were some nervous murmurings from the crowd.

'Yes, I think we should thank them for bringing us this far.'

The new cabbageheads looked rather chuffed, and gave a little bow. Titus approached Willbury again. When he'd finished Willbury spoke.

'Titus says that the cabbageheads that Arthur freed are going to go with them, but that he himself would like to stay with us for the moment and help to find Arthur.' Willbury turned to Titus. 'You are very brave, Titus.'

The murmurings in the crowd grew louder, and Titus took Fish's hand. The other cabbageheads took one last look at the hole, waved and disappeared rapidly into the woods.

The other cabbageheads disappeared rapidly into the woods

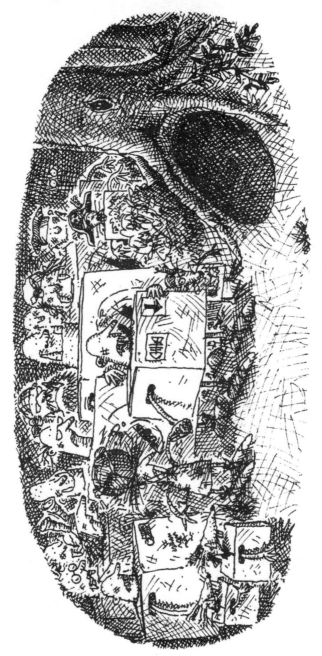

The strange party stood around the hole

The captain lit his candle

Chapter 36

THE RABBIT WOMEN

The strange party stood around the hole. It was much, much larger than a rabbit hole, but it would still be a tight fit for a large pirate dressed in a stiff cardboard box. There was an air of trepidation among the group—if the cabbageheads were so frightened of what they would find down the hole, was it really a place that the rest of them wanted to go?

'Who is going to lead the way?' asked Willbury.

There was a pause. Then Fish and Titus put up their free hands.

'Very well,' said Willbury. 'Everybody get out your candles.'

The captain walked over to the hole, produced a box of matches, and lit his candle.

'Right then, me hearties!' he said. 'Form an orderly queue!'

Everybody got in line, with Fish and Titus at the front, followed by Willbury, Tom, Kipper, and Marjorie. Then, one by one, each member of the queue took a light from the captain's candle and disappeared down the hole. Some of the larger pirates took quite a bit of shoving to get them into the hole, but they were all able to manage it without damaging their boxes.

Once underground the tunnel opened out, and even Kipper could stand up and move about with ease. There was a warm earthy smell in the passage.

The procession set off. After a few hundred yards Fish held up a hand, and the procession ground to a stop. Fish turned to Willbury and put his finger to his lips. Then Titus whispered something to Willbury, and Willbury turned to Kipper and Tom.

Even Kipper could stand up and move about with ease

'Fish wants us all to be quiet, and Titus wants us to put our teeth in. Pass it along.'

The message passed down the line, and soon all that could be heard was the sound of teeth being put in. Fish and Titus put their candles down and disappeared into the darkness.

'Aat oo ooh iiink aaye rrr oooht ooo?' Kipper whispered.
'Iiierrrt!' snapped Tom.

After a minute or two, they heard voices from somewhere
ahead. The voices grew louder and small green lights
appeared. Before long Willbury could make out Fish, Titus,
and some other shapes coming towards them.

As they got closer, the candlelight revealed that Fish and
Titus had returned with two rabbit women. The women
were both dressed in knitted one-piece suits, with long ears,
and they carried glass jars full of glow-worms.

The women were both dressed in knitted one-piece suits,
with long ears, and they carried glass jars full of glow-worms

They marched up to Willbury and smiled.

One of them, in a grey suit, spoke. 'Your friend Titus has
told us that you'd like us to guide you through our tunnels
so you can get under Ratbridge?'

Willbury nodded.

Then the other, who was dressed in brown, spoke. 'We'll
show you the way but you'll have to be very careful.'

Willbury nodded again, and the rabbit women smiled.
Then the one in brown gave Kipper a funny look.

'You look rather big for a boxtroll.' Then she looked down at Tom. 'And you look rather small?'

Titus trotted over to her and whispered.

'What's he say, Coco?' asked the rabbit woman in the grey suit.

'Well, Fen, he says they're a different type of boxtroll . . . just visiting.'

'Well, that explains it!'

'I suppose so. But I think they need to see a dentist.'

Willbury blushed.

'Come this way, please, and please remember to be careful!' The rabbit women led the way.

After a short walk the tunnel became lighter, and Willbury could hear more voices. They rounded a bend and were confronted by a wooden door. In the centre of the door was a notice.

A wooden door

Please close the door after you.
Remember
There are trotting badgers about, and
we don't want to lose any of the old folks!

'Mind where you walk!' warned Coco, and then she opened the door.

Through the door was a large, low cavern. Hundreds of jam jars, filled with glow-worms, were tied to roots that hung from the ceiling, and a pale green light fell on the scene below. There were small groups of rabbit women working at looms and spinning wheels, and tending raised vegetable beds. All around them were thousands of rabbits. By each group of workers sat a rabbit woman reading aloud.

There were small groups of rabbit women working at looms and spinning wheels, and tending raised vegetable beds

Fen turned and spoke. 'Please be very careful not to step on our parents. They are not very bright, but we do love them.'

As the group carefully made their way through the door and into the cavern, Willbury noticed Marjorie was grinning from ear to ear despite her vegetable teeth. She was obviously very impressed by the rabbit women. As Fen closed the door behind them after shooshing some rabbits away, Marjorie made her way to Willbury, and furtively removed her teeth.

'They're fantastic,' she whispered. 'Just who are they?'

Willbury checked to see that nobody was watching and slipped his teeth out. 'The story I heard was that they were abandoned babies or little girls that fell down rabbit holes. The rabbits took them in and brought them up as their own. It seems to make sense. I guess as they grew up they took charge and now look after the rabbits.'

Despite the working rabbit women not seeming to pay any attention to the visitors, Willbury and Marjorie both quickly put their teeth back in.

Coco pointed to the vegetable plots. 'We can grow most things here, but we avoid greens. Sometimes the old folks manage to burrow into the plots, and if they eat greens it doesn't agree with them.'

Fen noticed Willbury looking at the readers.

'We are very fond of books. You can learn nearly everything from them that rabbits can't teach you.'

Willbury was dying to take his teeth out again and ask questions, but he didn't want to give away that he was not a boxtroll. So as they were led through the cavern he listened and tried to make out what was being read. There were some passages from *The Country Housewife's Garden*, some Greek, mathematics, and even bits of *Tristram Shandy* and Jane Austen.

These rabbit women are very well educated! he thought.

The procession reached a door at the far side of the cavern and their guides led them through it and then closed it behind them.

'We are very fond of books. You can learn nearly everything from them that rabbits can't teach you.'

'We do have to be so careful as we have a real problem with trotting badgers. Last month someone left this door open, and Madeline's step-parents escaped and were eaten. It was very upsetting,' said Coco.

'It's all to do with the size of the tunnels,' added Fen. 'We had no idea when we made them bigger that it would allow the trotting badgers to get down them.'

They followed the rabbit women through a maze of passages till finally they reached one that tilted down at a steep angle. The passage emerged in a stone cave and the rabbit women halted. The floor of the cave was awash with water.

Coco held her jar aloft

Coco held her jar aloft.

'It's getting higher!' said Fen.

'Yes, but it will have to rise a good deal further before it gets close to our burrows. It's the cabbageheads and you boxtrolls that I am worried about.' Coco gave them a concerned look. Then she pointed into the darkness.

'At the other end of this cave is a tunnel that takes you under the town. I am sure Titus and your friend Fish can lead you from here.'

Willbury smiled through his vegetable teeth and bowed in thanks. The others followed his lead.

'No problem. And good luck,' said Coco, and she and Fen turned back up the passage and disappeared. When they had gone Willbury held up his candle, looked towards the other end of the cave, and took out his teeth.

'Fish and Titus, are you all right leading us from here?'

Fish took a very long smell at the air, smiled, and then nodded.

A rabbit woman gardening underground

Herbert and Arthur

'Do you think you could lend me your walloper?'

Chapter 37

THE DOLL

Back in the dungeon, Arthur was determined to find a way
of escaping.

'Do you think you could lend me your walloper?' he
asked the hole in the wall.

'You! Borrow my walloper! I should think not!' snapped
Herbert. 'Anyway, what do you want it for?'

Arthur pleaded. 'A doll that I need is in the corridor
outside the cell and I can't reach it. I need something to help
me get it back.'

'Well, you can't borrow my walloper,' replied Herbert.

'Have you got anything else I could use?' asked Arthur.

'Might have!' Herbert was not an easy man. 'What's in it
for me?'

Arthur thought for a moment. 'If I can get the doll, it
might help me find a way out of here. And if I get out, I'll see
if I can get you out as well.'

There was silence for a few moments then Herbert replied, 'Is a bit of string any good?'

Arthur looked across at the doll. 'It might be. How long is it?'

'About six feet.'

'That ought to do it.'

'Well, how much do you want to borrow?'

'Enough!' snapped Arthur in frustration.

'Well, would two feet do?'

'No!' barked Arthur. 'If you want to get out of here why don't you just lend me all of it?'

'Oh, all right! But don't get funny with me. It is my string!' came back a very grudging voice.

There was a scuffling in the cell beyond the hole and a ball of hairy string appeared

There was a scuffling in the cell beyond the hole and a ball of hairy string appeared. Arthur took it and said, 'Thank you.' Then he unwound it, tied a lasso in one end, and walked over to the bars. After a few attempts he managed to get the lasso around one of the doll's arms and hoist it into the cell.

'I've got it!' he cried.

'Can I have my string back?' came a worried voice from the hole.

*After a few attempts he managed to get the lasso around
one of the doll's arms and hoist it into the cell*

Arthur un-knotted the lasso, rolled up the string, and held it out towards the hole. Herbert's hand darted out and snatched it from him.

Arthur sat on the edge of his bed, and wound the handle on the doll.

'Grandfather! Grandfather! Are you there?' he called.

There was a popping, some static noise, and then he heard what he was hoping for.

'Arthur, where are you?'

'I am locked up in a cell below the Cheese Hall.'

'WHAT!' cried Grandfather. 'They caught you?'

'No,' said Arthur. 'I escaped . . . but the police handed me over to Snatcher. He accused me of stealing the wings from him!'

'Archibald Snatcher!' Grandfather sounded angry. 'He's up to his old tricks again.'

'I am sorry, Grandfather.'

'You're not to blame. With that shyster involved nobody is safe,' his grandfather said. 'We have to get you out of there . . . and soon. Are you on your own?'

'Well, almost. There is a man called Herbert in the next cell.'

'Pardon? Did you say a man called Herbert?' asked Grandfather, sounding astonished.

'Yes!' said Arthur.

'Ask him if his nickname is Parsley!'

Arthur leant down to the hole and spoke. 'Is your nickname Parsley?'

'Don't you know it's rude to call your elders by their nicknames?' came the voice from the hole.

'That's him all right,' came Grandfather's voice. 'Arthur, can you let me speak to Herbert?'

Arthur held the doll out close to the hole, and he saw the masked eyes staring at it.

Arthur held the doll out close to the hole,
and he saw the masked eyes staring at it

'What are you doing there, Parsley?'

There was a silence from the hole, then Herbert's voice asked in a quizzical tone, 'Is that you, William?'

'Yes!'

'What are you doing talking out of a doll?'

'I will tell you later, but you . . . Oh, Herbert, I can't believe it's you. Are you all right? Have you been in that dungeon for all these years?'

'I . . . ' Herbert's voice trailed off. 'I . . . can't remember . . . '

'Herbert. Have you been in here all these years?'

'I am not sure. I am not even sure where I know you from . . . William . . . '

'Oh, Herbert. Don't you remember what happened?'

'No. Not really. My mind is so fuzzy.'

'Don't you remember the fight?'

'No . . . just something vaguely about you, me, and . . . Archibald Snatcher . . . it's all very confused.'

'Maybe if I remind you?' came Grandfather's voice.

'Maybe . . . ' muttered Herbert.

Arthur's grandfather paused for a moment. 'Arthur, you should listen to this too. It's time you heard the truth about why we live underground.'

'My mind is so fuzzy'

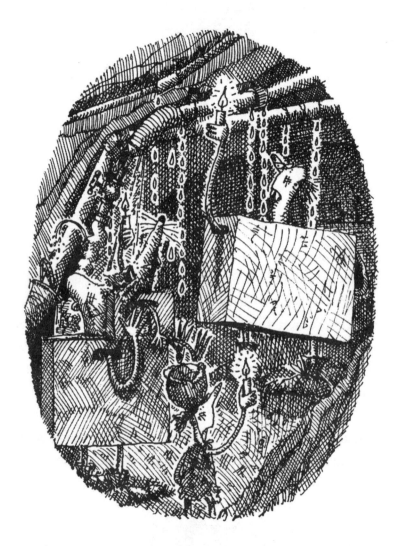

Something was wrong

*Fish and the other real boxtrolls had a way of walking
with their feet a few inches up either wall to avoid the water*

Chapter 38

WET!

Several inches of water ran down the tunnels as the procession made its way under the town. Fish and the other real boxtrolls had a way of walking with their feet a few inches up either wall to avoid the water, but even so it dripped down from the ceiling onto their boxes. Willbury and the others were getting very, very wet, and the rats were complaining as the water came up well over the bottom of their boxes.

Tom came to a stop and took out his teeth. 'It's not the water that I hate,' said Tom. 'It's the feeling of the soggy cardboard rubbing on my legs. It feels really horrid, like old wellies.'

'It's the feeling of the soggy cardboard rubbing on my legs'

Rats with dripping boxes were lifted, and carried aloft

'We can do something about that,' said Willbury, taking out his teeth. Then he shouted the order: 'Large boxtrolls please pick up small boxtrolls and carry them till it gets drier. And you can remove your teeth till further notice.'

All down the line teeth were removed and rats with dripping boxes were lifted and carried aloft.

'Thanks!' said Tom to Willbury.

The tunnels slowly rose up towards the town, but remained very wet. The real boxtrolls were now in familiar territory, and they didn't need their candles. Fish kept rushing ahead into the darkness and returning excitedly. After a few of these forays he seemed to grow pensive.

'Have you noticed pipes up on the roof?' asked Tom.

Willbury held up his candle to look. There were pipes . . . and most of them were leaking. Something was wrong.

The tunnel levelled out, and Fish led them to an area of what looked like very old cellars. They went in and turned a corner to see an iron ladder fixed to a wall in front of them. The ladder disappeared up into darkness. Fish signalled to them to stop, then went up the ladder followed by the other

real boxtrolls. After a few minutes a distressed-looking Fish returned alone.

Willbury spoke. 'What is it, Fish?'

Fish signalled to them to follow him up the ladder.

The group silently followed Fish and after a short climb they came up through a hole on to a dry floor. Wherever they were it was big, as the light from their candles faded into darkness around them. There was a loud click, and above them a light came on. Shoe was standing on top of a huge pile of nuts and bolts, and holding a chain fixed to some kind of glass ball. The light from the ball flooded the cavern. Everywhere there were machine tools, half built pumps, broken bicycles, bits of wire, tools, and pieces of metal of every shape, colour, and description. The place was an Aladdin's cave of engineering scrap.

Shoe was standing on top of a huge pile of nuts and bolts,
and holding a chain fixed to some kind of glass ball

'This is the boxtrolls' nest!' exclaimed Willbury.

The boxtrolls nodded.

Marjorie was staring up at the glowing glass ball. 'They've got electric light! Fancy that. I thought it might be possible one day.'

Willbury looked about. 'Where are the other boxtrolls?'

The real boxtrolls looked very sad and unhappy.

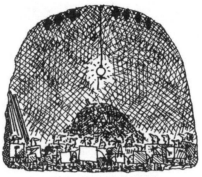

The place was an Aladdin's cave of engineering scrap.

Kipper looked at them and whispered, ' . . . I think Snatcher has taken them . . . '

Willbury took this in, then replied. 'That may be it. But it would mean that he must have been capturing them somehow . . . and down here!'

Fish turned to the boxtrolls that Arthur had freed. They just nodded.

Willbury spoke to them very gently. 'You were captured down here?'

The boxtrolls nodded again, pointed back down the hole, and started burbling.

'Could you show us the way up to the Cheese Hall?'

They shook their heads and mumbled.

Titus whispered to Willbury, then Willbury turned to the others. 'Snatcher and his mob put them in sacks after they were captured. But they think he has some sort of mechanical elevator, with an entrance down here somewhere. They say it shot them up to the Cheese Hall as fast as a rocket.'

'They say it shot them up to the Cheese Hall as fast as a rocket'

'Do you think we could find it?' asked Tom.

The boxtrolls looked unsure, and Titus whispered again to Willbury.

'Titus says that this place is such a warren that the elevator could be hidden anywhere.'

Everybody looked very glum.

Then Willbury spoke again. 'I think we should split up and search for the elevator. It shouldn't take long with so many of us. We'll meet up here in an hour?'

It was agreed, and they split up into small groups and set off. Willbury stayed with Fish, Titus, Tom, and Kipper, while Marjorie teamed up with Shoe, Egg, and some other boxtrolls. As they waited for their turn to descend the ladder, Willbury spoke to his group.

'There is something else I want to do before we start looking for the elevator. I've got to find Arthur's grandfather. I am very concerned, as he must be running out of food.'

Fish perked up and raised a hand.

'Do you know where he lives?' asked Willbury. Fish burbled something and Titus whispered something to Willbury.

'You say you have heard that there are some humans living in a cave off one of the large caverns?'

Fish nodded.

'Do you think you can lead us there?' Fish looked a little unsure, then nodded again.

'Well, let's try that!' said Willbury. And off they set back down the ladder.

And off they set back down the ladder

The Evil Crime

'Don't you remember burning a hole in my mum's carpet with the toy steam engine we tried to build?'

Chapter 39
THE TELLING

In the cell in the dungeon Arthur listened as Grandfather started to talk. 'Herbert. Do you remember growing up?'

'No.' Herbert sounded very sad.

'What? You don't remember anything? Don't you remember the Glue Lane Technical School for the Poor?'

'Not really . . . I do remember the name . . . You're going to have to remind me.'

'Herbert, we grew up in the same street! We played together, got measles together, got in trouble together . . . and got our ears clipped together. Don't you remember burning a hole in my mum's carpet with the toy steam engine we tried to build?'

There was a pause. 'Was the carpet a rather odd green colour?'

'Yes! Yes it was!'

'I do remember something . . . '

*'Do you remember us sinking in the canal up to our
waists when we tried to cross it when it was frozen?'*

'Do you remember us sinking in the canal up to our
waists when we tried to cross it when it was frozen?'

'And the ice was so thin in the middle that it cracked and
your dad had to pull us out?'

'Yes!'

' . . . It is coming back to me . . . remind me more,'
Herbert said.

'Do you remember Tuesday mornings with the smell of
the brewery? And cold nights in winter when the smell of
the tannery filled the streets?'

'I loved the smell of the brewery, but the tannery smelt
awful!'

'You are not wrong there!'

At first Arthur somehow felt that it was not his place to
be involved in the conversation, but now he asked a
question.

'I know there is a tannery, but a brewery?'

'Not any more. It went the same time as the Cheese
Industry . . . with the pollution.'

'What happened?'

'Ratbridge was founded on the cheese, but when new industries came to the town, the smoke and waste they produced poisoned the water supply and a lot of countryside around here. It got so bad that the local cheeses were decreed unfit to eat, and the cheese industry collapsed. The Cheese Barons went bankrupt overnight.'

'The Cheese Barons went bankrupt overnight'

'I think I remember that . . . ' Herbert said. 'Ain't that the reason that Archibald Snatcher turned up at the Poor School?'

'Yes,' replied Grandfather. 'His father was partly responsible for the ban.'

'Why?' asked Arthur.

'He ran a mill that had always produced really dodgy cheese. They used all kinds of evil processes. One of their tricks was to boil down cheese rinds, extract the oil, and then inject it into immature cheeses. It was illegal . . . and cruel, but they had got away with it. What they didn't realize was that as the pollution got worse, making cheese oil was concentrating the poisons. Finally they got sued when they produced the cheese that poisoned the Duchess of

Snookworth . . . and it was her husband who got the ban brought in. Archibald's dad lost his fortune and couldn't afford to have dear Archibald privately tutored any more.'

'Oh, I remember Snatcher turning up at school now!' Herbert's memory was coming back. 'He didn't take his fall from Ratbridge society well. Hateful little snob!'

'One of their tricks was to boil down cheese rinds, extract the oil, and then inject it into immature cheeses'

Grandfather continued. 'Herbert and I were in our third year at school when Archibald turned up. He had spent his whole life being waited on hand and foot, so poverty came as a bit of a shock to him. He hated the school, and everybody in it . . . including us!'

'Why?' asked Arthur.

'He thought it was his rightful place to do what he wanted, and never lift a finger . . . but we didn't play that game,' said Herbert. 'He loathed us and everybody else. He seemed to think that Ratbridge had done him out of his rightful fortune, and his resentment turned to cheating and stealing.'

Grandfather went on, 'But, oh, he was cunning! Over the next few years Archibald took every opportunity that came his way to advance himself back towards his "rightful place". Smarming up to the teachers, borrowing work, a little blackmail, some bullying, and extortion. When it came to the final exam results it was no surprise that he got the highest results . . . '

'When it came to the final exam results it was no surprise that he got the highest results . . . '

'Because he stole them!' interjected Herbert.

'On the strength of a bit of blackmail, and his stolen results, he got a scholarship to Oxford. And that was the last we heard of him for a few years, till . . . ' Grandfather's voice sounded bitter. 'Do you remember now, Herbert, what happened?'

'At the inn?' Herbert replied, slowly.

'Yes, at the inn.'

'Yes . . . some of it is coming back.'

'What did happen?' asked Arthur.

'Herbert and I had just set up as freelance inventors and engineers. We worked in the factories for years, but we had managed to save up enough to start a small workshop, and the work was coming in . . . Then one lunchtime we went to the Nag's Head. We were just setting about a couple of large pasties when we heard a raised voice at the next table. I looked over, and there sat Mr Archibald Snatcher flanked by a couple of heavies.

' "Are you calling me a cheat, sir?" he said to a red-faced man across the table from him.

' "Yes, sir, I am," said the red-faced man. "It is not possible to have a hand of cards containing seven aces!"

' "It is, sir, for I am very lucky!" Archibald said.

' "Well, today, sir, your luck has run out!" And the man at the other end of the table reached inside his pocket. Thinking he was going for a gun, one of the heavies also reached for his pocket, and in an instant the bar cleared, leaving just Herbert and me watching the altercation.'

'It is not possible to have a hand of cards containing seven aces!'

'Oh, yes!' broke in Herbert. 'The man took out a note-pad and asked for Snatcher's name and address. He wanted to report him to the police . . . But he didn't notice that one of Snatcher's men had taken out a catapult . . . '

Herbert fell silent again, and Grandfather continued.

'That's right,' he said. 'And that's when Snatcher gave the order to the heavy with the catapult . . .

'And that's when Snatcher gave the order to the heavy with the catapult . . . '

' "Administer the treatment!" he said. There was a blur and something green whizzed across the table and struck the red-faced man in the mouth. The man went pale and slumped to the floor. Then we caught the smell. Oil of Brussels!'

'What's Oil of Brussels?' asked Arthur.

'It is poison distilled from sprouts. It is very fast acting, and often lethal. Later I found out they had shot a small wad of cotton soaked in it down the man's throat,' replied Grandfather.

'It is poison distilled from sprouts. It is very fast acting, and often lethal.'

'Awful!' added Herbert.

Grandfather went on, 'Then there was the sound of police whistles outside, and Snatcher saw us.'

' "Oh, look! A couple of old school friends," he said. Then he reached inside a pocket and threw something to me. The very moment I caught it, the bar door swung open, and a group of Squeakers ran in and saw the man slumped on the floor. Then Snatcher stood up, and pointed at me.

'Then he reached inside a pocket and threw something to me'

' "It was him, officer! He has just poisoned that man. Look! He is still holding the evidence." I looked down . . . and in my hand was a bottle of Oil of Brussels.

' "Arrest that man!" shouted one of the Squeakers, and they rushed to get me. So I panicked and made a run for it straight through the back door to the street. The Squeakers followed me, but I was quite fit in those days and I managed to shake them off and climbed down a drain . . . '

'I managed to shake them off and climbed down a drain . . . '

'I remember!' cried Herbert. 'You ran out of the door with the Squeakers after you, then . . . ' He paused for a long time, and then whispered, ' . . . everything went green . . . and I woke up here.'

'Everything went green . . . '

'How do you think you got here?' Arthur asked him.

'They must have knocked me out or something, then kidnapped me . . . ' muttered Herbert.

'I knew you had disappeared, because that night I came up out of the drain and found posters up for our arrest for attempted murder. I just didn't know where you had gone. I grabbed some food from a garden, then went back underground to avoid being caught. I knew I would never be safe above ground again unless I could find you as a witness to the truth.'

'Attempted murder? So the man wasn't dead?' asked Arthur.

'No, he survived, but he suffered from permanent memory loss of the event, due to the poison and trauma.'

'That's why everything went green. They must have had some more Oil of Brussels and smothered me with it. That's why me memory is so bad!' said Herbert sounding furious. 'And I guess we've both been prisoners of sorts ever since . . . '

'Yes . . . Yes . . . it is true,' replied Grandfather. 'Mr Archibald Snatcher has a lot to answer for.'

'So can you help us, William?' Herbert started to ask. But before Grandfather could reply, Arthur heard footsteps coming down the steps to the dungeon.

'Quick! Someone is coming. I'll speak to you later, Grandfather.' He tucked the doll inside his suit, pushed the stone back in its hole and pushed the bed against the wall. The footsteps approached, and a Member appeared carrying a bowl in one hand and a cudgel in the other.

'The guv sent me down 'ere with some nosh for you.' He put the plate down, took a key from his pocket, and unlocked the door to Arthur's cell. Then he slid the plate into the cell with his foot and closed and locked the door.

'Take your time, boy! I got to wait for the plate, but I'm in no hurry. They ain't going to be back from the traps for ages.' He sat down, leant against the bars of the cell opposite, and started to watch Arthur eat.

*The footsteps approached, and a Member appeared carrying
a bowl in one hand and a cudgel in the other*

They saw a small window in a wall of rock ahead

'It's rhubarb! We must be getting close!'

Chapter 40

A Glimmer at the End of the Tunnel

Fish led the way, and as they walked water washed around their feet. The water level seemed to be rising all the time. Then a smell gently wafted into their noses. It was sweet and vaguely familiar. Something about it reminded Willbury of jam. They'd not eaten for a long time and the smell was almost too much to bear.

Willbury stopped. 'That's it! It's rhubarb! We must be getting close!'

After a few bends in the pathway, a light became visible. Over the rush of water they could just hear music. Then they saw a small window in a wall of rock ahead. As they got closer, the music grew louder, and next to the window a door became visible. They reached the door and Willbury knocked.

The music stopped, there was some muttering, and the door swung open to reveal a short stocky old man with a huge beard and glasses. He looked very damp.

'My word! You're big for a boxtroll!' Grandfather said.

Willbury had completely forgotten he was in disguise and was rather suprised.

'My word! You're big for a boxtroll!'

'I am not a boxtroll!'

'Well, you will do until a boxtroll comes along. I have something I need you to help me with—urgently!'

'Of course, we will do anything we can to help. I have spoken to you before, sir. I am Willbury Nibble.'

'Oh! I thought you were a lawyer, not a boxtroll! It just shows that you shouldn't jump to conclusions. But I am pleased to meet you anyway,' said Grandfather, looking surprised.

'It's a disguise,' said Willbury. 'I *am* a lawyer. And I'm afraid I have some rather bad news for you about Arthur.'

'I spoke to him just a little while ago,' said Grandfather. 'He managed to call me from the dungeon at the Cheese Hall. We have to do something to help him before it's too late.'

'That is why we are here,' said Willbury. 'We believe there is a way up into the Cheese Hall from the Underworld. If only we can find it, we can make our way up into the Hall and help Arthur escape.'

'I see,' said Grandfather thoughtfully. 'I don't know of any such way—but there may be one . . . I also have an idea of how to help Arthur—but I can't do it on my own. I've been hoping for some underlings to come along and help me, but they seem few and far between these days. But perhaps you and your friends can make it work.'

'Of course we will do anything we can. Arthur is our friend and we all want to get him back as soon as we can.'

'Well, do come in,' Grandfather said, taking a step back and gesturing Willbury into his home. 'And bring your friends.'

'Thank you!' said Willbury, and they followed Grandfather in.

'The more the merrier!' said Grandfather. 'If you all like stewed rhubarb I think I might have just enough to go round. Please help yourselves,' he said, pointing to a saucepan on an old range. 'Then I would appreciate it if you would come through to the back room. I need some help.'

There was a cheer and they set about serving up the rhubarb. Very soon it was all gone and they followed

Grandfather into the back room of the cave. There were puddles on the floor and water was dripping from the ceiling.

'If you all like stewed rhubarb I think I might have just enough to go round.'

The small room was about the most crowded Willbury had ever seen. At its centre was a brass bedstead. This was covered in a beautiful patchwork quilt. Surrounding the bed was a huge hotch-potch of wires, rods, cogs, pulleys, and other things that Willbury couldn't identify.

'Er . . . What is it?' he asked.

'It's something I have been working on for years. It's finished, but I am too frail to operate it. I just spoke to Arthur and he desperately needs help. I think this is the only way we may be able to get him out of his situation.'

Grandfather explained his machine.

'It sounds amazing!' declared Willbury. 'I only wish Marjorie was here to see it . . . But I certainly think we can help—obviously we need real muscle and some brains here,' he continued, smiling at Kipper and Tom. 'And I know just the pirate and rat for the job!'

Grandfather followed Willbury's gaze. 'Are you sure, Mr Nibble?'

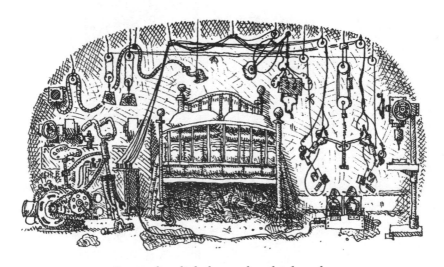

Surrounding the bed was a huge hotch-potch of wires, rods, cogs, pulleys, and other things

Arthur in the dungeon

He used his fingers to scrape it off the surface of the bowl

Chapter 41

THE KEYS

Arthur was very hungry and even though the cold porridge in his bowl was almost solid, he tried to eat it. He'd not been given a spoon so he used his fingers to scrape it off the surface of the bowl. It was a very slow process. As he ate his gaoler slowly drifted off to sleep.

'I give up!' Arthur muttered eventually. 'I think I'd rather starve.'

He looked over at the gaoler, who was now fast asleep and starting to snore. Arthur coughed loudly, but the gaoler didn't stir. Encouraged by this, he put the plate down slowly on the floor, reached under his suit, and retrieved his doll. Glancing nervously at the sleeping gaoler, he quietly wound the handle, and whispered into the doll.

'Grandfather! Keep your voice down! There's one of Snatcher's mob just outside the cell . . . asleep.'

'What's he doing there?' came a quiet voice from the doll.

The gaoler didn't stir

'He just brought me some food.'

'Did he have to unlock your cell?'

'Yes . . . Why?'

'So he's got a key?

'Yes.'

'Well, this might just be our lucky day. Where's the key?'

'It's in his right-hand coat pocket,' Arthur whispered. 'But how are we going to get it off him? He's right across the corridor, and there is no way I can reach him.'

'Listen, Arthur. I have a plan, but you need to do exactly as I say. I want you to wind up the doll till you hear it ping . . . then give the handle a few more turns until you feel the clockwork can't take any more. But be very careful and don't break the spring!'

Arthur carefully did what he was told, and wound it very gently till there was a ping. The noise made him jump, and he turned to check it hadn't disturbed the sleeping gaoler.

Then he carefully wound the handle a few more times until he felt it couldn't go any further.

Arthur wound it very gently till there was a ping

'OK, I've wound it up.'

'Right,' said Grandfather. 'Reach out of your cell as far as you can, and stand the doll up, facing towards the pocket with the keys in.'

Arthur was puzzled, but did what he was told.

In Grandfather's bedroom underground, Kipper and Tom were ready. Kipper sat on a bicycle that had had its back wheel removed and replaced with some kind of complicated pump. But Tom was involved in something far more complicated. He was at the centre of a web of levers and wires that stretched out from all over the room. And on his head were a pair of goggles far too large for him. Fixed over the lens of the goggles was a box with wires sprouting from it.

Grandfather turned away from the strange trumpet mouth he had been speaking into, and spoke directly to Tom and Kipper. 'I am really not sure if this is going to work. Can

*Kipper sat on a bicycle that had had its back wheel removed
and replaced with some kind of complicated pump*

you please get ready . . . and remember what I said to you.
You have to work together!'

'Working together is what we do best,' replied Tom from
behind the goggles.

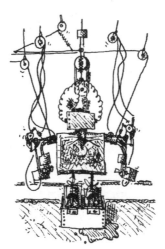

Tom was at the centre of a web of levers and wires

Kipper began to pedal and soon a humming started to
come from the pump, and the levers and wires attached to
Tom went taut.

High above in the dungeon, Arthur stood by the bars and stared down at the doll . . . Something was happening! Arthur heard the ping, and then a slow ticking. The doll's eyes lit up, and cast two small pools of light towards the coat pocket. Then the doll started shaking and fell over.

The doll started shaking and fell over

In Grandfather's bedroom Kipper was working the pedals as hard as he could, and Tom was cursing.

'What's the matter?' asked Grandfather.

'It's fallen over,' said Tom.

'What can you see through the goggles?' asked Grandfather.

'Just the gaoler's boots, at the moment,' replied Tom.

'Use the levers to move the doll's arms. They should be able to help you get it upright again,' instructed Grandfather.

Tom carefully started to move the levers. After a few moments he spoke.

'The doll must be moving! I can see all of the gaoler now.'

'Try moving your legs. The doll should copy your movements.'

Tom felt the wires pull as he started to bend his legs.

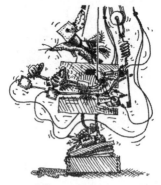

Tom carefully started to move the levers

Arthur watched the doll in amazement as it now started to move its arms. It seemed to be trying to get up on its own!

The doll's legs now moved as well and it managed to stand again. Then its wings unfolded. Suddenly Arthur understood.

'Faster!' Grandfather shouted at Kipper. 'Pedal faster! We need all the power we can get.'

Kipper was already sweating, but did all he could to increase his speed.

'I don't know if I can keep this up for very long. Please be as quick as you can, Tom.'

'All right, all right!' said Tom, from behind the goggles. 'I'll go as fast as I can, but it's pretty difficult operating this doll. You just concentrate on pedalling!'

Tom adjusted a knob at the end of one of the levers strapped to his arm.

The doll started shaking as its wings began to beat, then it slowly rose from the floor. Arthur watched as it wobbled and tried to keep upright. The lights from the doll's eyes flicked around the dungeon.

Its wings began to beat, then it slowly rose from the floor

The doll began to fly more steadily. Then it moved slowly across the corridor towards the gaoler. As it reached him, it slowed to a wobbly hover over the pocket.

'Oh my Gawd! I feel sick!' barked Tom. He moved his feet to try and steady the doll. 'That's it! I can see the pocket. But we need to lose height! How do I do that?'

'Kipper, you gently ease off the power,' ordered Grandfather. 'Tom, you will have to tell him when you start to fall, and when he needs to increase his pedalling.'

Kipper looked up at him and nodded his head. 'I shall enjoy easing off!'

The doll steadily descended till it was just an inch or so above the pocket.

'Steady, Kipper, steady!' whispered Tom. He moved the levers in his hands very slowly and the doll moved forward till its arms entered the pocket.

'A little more power, Kipper!' said Tom, and he started to manipulate the levers attached to his arms, concentrating as hard as he could. For a few moments there was silence as he struggled to make the precise movements he needed. Then, suddenly, he gave a triumphant shout.

'Got them! Now, Kipper, give it everything you've got!'

Kipper began pedalling ever more furiously, wheezing and panting with the effort.

The doll rose and the keys lifted from the pocket. Tom shifted the controls and the doll turned towards Arthur's cell.

'Please, get this done as quick as you can, or I am going to pass out,' moaned Kipper.

'Stop complaining, Kipper!' snapped Tom.

'Oh my Gawd! Something is happening!' said Kipper in a panic.

'Shut up and pedal!' shouted Tom.

William and Willbury were more concerned. Smoke was starting to rise from where the pedals joined the pump.

'Quick! Get the keys to the cell!' Grandfather shouted.

'What's happening?' asked Kipper. 'I'm going as fast as I can.'

There was a crunching noise, and the pedals seized.

'It's bust!' shouted Grandfather. 'Quick, before it dies!'

Smoke was starting to rise from where the pedals joined the pump

In the cell, Arthur had watched mesmerized as the doll had retrieved the keys. Now he stood horrified and helpless as it started to fall towards the floor. Tom pushed both of the levers in his hands forwards as far as they would go, and the doll tilted forward and dropped into a dive. As it neared the floor Tom pulled the levers back and the doll pulled out of the dive and rushed towards the cell door. Arthur stared in horror. If only it could keep going until it got to him—but it didn't look as if it was going to make it.

Now he stood horrified and helpless as it started to fall towards the floor

The doll hit the ground about two feet from the cell. In Grandfather's cave, Tom made one last frantic effort with the levers. Just as it hit the floor, the doll let go of the keys and seemed to propel them desperately towards Arthur. They slid across the floor and through the bars. Arthur picked them up, then reached through. He could just stretch far enough to retrieve the motionless doll.

'Grandfather! Grandfather! I've got the keys!' Arthur whispered in delight, but no one heard him. The doll was dead.

They slid across the floor, and through the bars

Very wet and miserable!

Snatcher and the other Members had been wading around for hours

Chapter 42

THE TRAPS

Snatcher and the other Members had been wading around for hours, and were very wet and miserable. First they'd checked the traps close to the elevator, but when they'd found nothing in them, they'd had to go further afield to check their other traps. Water was everywhere, running over the floor, running down the walls, and gushing from the ceiling. And the sound of it was so loud they had to shout to make themselves heard.

'Maybe we already got all the monsters down 'ere,' shouted Gristle.

'Well, you remember what I said. You don't want to find yourself in reduced circumstances do yer?' Snatcher replied.

'I think we should check the traps near the elevator again then . . . ' Gristle replied.

They made their way back towards the elevator. As they approached one of the traps Gristle smiled.

"Ere, guv. We got some!'

''Ere, guv. We got some!' and he pointed to a large net full of boxtrolls.

'My word, we struck it lucky. And some of them is big 'uns!'

Over the next few minutes they lowered the net and bundled their haul into sacks. Then they set off to check the next trap leaving a trail of vegetable teeth floating in the water. To Snatcher's delight and surprise, the next trap was also full of boxtrolls.

'Cor! You can never have enough size!' he shouted as he rubbed his hands together. 'Get them down, boys! I'm starting to enjoy this!'

The members bagged up the boxtrolls and moved on. At each trap they found more.

'This is blooming marvellous!' Snatcher chuckled. Gristle had never seen him so happy. 'Makes you wonder where they all bin hidin'—we ain't seen so many for weeks! Right lucky for us, but unlucky for them . . . and Ratbridge!'

'Ain't we got enough now?' asked Gristle, struggling under the weight of a sack.

'Oh, go on. Let's just check one more trap. It ain't going to hurt.'

'It's killing my back,' complained Gristle.

'That ain't nothing to what it's going to do to Ratbridge!' chuckled Snatcher.

'Ain't we got enough now?' asked Gristle,
struggling under the weight of a sack

The Underworld

'No,' replied Grandfather, looking rather glum

Chapter 43

DEEP WATER

Willbury looked at Grandfather and sighed. 'I guess we don't know if Arthur got the keys.'

'No,' replied Grandfather, looking rather glum.

Just then Fish rushed into the room with Titus following behind. Fish started gabbling to Willbury.

'I don't understand,' said Willbury. 'I will have to get Titus to translate.'

He bent over and listened to Titus. Slowly he turned pale.

'Fish says that the water is starting to bring down the tunnel roofs. We had better get out of here quick.' Willbury paused for a moment. 'I think we should get back to the boxtroll nest to see if the others have found the elevator.'

Then he turned to Grandfather. 'You had better come with us.'

Kipper and Fish took Grandfather's arms

'Anything to get out of this damp. My bones are killing me,' said Grandfather.

Kipper and Fish took Grandfather's arms and led him out of the bedroom, with the others following. When they reached the living room Grandfather looked around.

'I shall rather miss this place,' he muttered.

'We better be quick or God knows what's going to happen,' urged Willbury.

Willbury grabbed a lantern and they set off towards the boxtroll nest as fast as they could through the water, which was starting to turn to a brown muddy soup.

When they reached a junction in one of the passages they had used to get to Grandfather's they had to stop. The tunnel ahead was flooded.

'What do we do now?' asked Willbury. 'We can't go back.'

Grandfather looked worriedly towards Fish. 'Do you know another route?'

The tunnel ahead was flooded

Fish thought for a moment then pointed to a side passage rather nervously. It too was flooded, but the roof of the passage was somewhat higher than the tunnel ahead.

Fish started to whimper.

'What's the matter, Fish?' asked Willbury.

Titus tugged on Willbury's cuff, and Willbury leant down to listen to him.

'Oh, dear!' muttered Willbury.

'What is it?' asked Grandfather.

'Fish is scared. It's the idea of having to swim. Boxtrolls loathe swimming. It is bad enough that they get their boxes wet . . . but swimming.'

Kipper waded towards Fish and smiled. 'How about I hold you up as high as I can so you can keep dry?'

Fish did not look convinced. In the distance there was another rumble and the sound of rushing water grew louder.

'Right, Fish. Close your eyes.' And before Fish could protest Kipper picked him up, and swung him above his head.

'Any room for a small one?' Tom asked hopefully.

'Go on, then, climb on board,' said Kipper, raising his eyebrows. Tom scrambled up to join Fish, then Kipper

Kipper carrying Fish, Tom, and Titus

turned to Titus. 'You may as well hitch a ride. One more is not going to hurt.'

Titus looked at the passage ahead, then with Willbury's assistance struggled up to join Tom and Fish.

Willbury looked concerned. 'I think I can manage with Grandfather, but the lamp?'

'I can take that,' said Tom, and Willbury passed the lamp to him.

'Do you think you will be all right, Kipper . . . carrying that lot?' asked Willbury.

'With all the exercise I get carrying washing?' he said and winked at Willbury.

Kipper turned and waded into the tunnel ahead and Willbury followed with Grandfather.

The water was very cold and Willbury felt his box go soggy as he hauled Grandfather through the water.

Kipper turned and waded into the tunnel ahead
and Willbury followed with Grandfather

'Are you all right?' asked Willbury.

'I could do with a warm bath, but don't worry,' said Grandfather quietly, then he smiled.

Soon the water grew less deep as the passage angled upwards and they made their way to a point where the water became shallow.

'Do you mind if I have a breather,' puffed Grandfather.

'Let's climb up on that rock for a few minutes and rest,' said Willbury pointing to a large flat rock that was still above water. Everybody climbed up, looking forward to sitting down for a moment. But before they could even catch their breath, there was a twang, and they found themselves hanging in a net from the ceiling.

'No!' cried Willbury. 'It's one of Snatcher's traps.'

There was nothing they could do but hang there and wait. Wet and miserable, they huddled in silence, too dejected even to talk. It was a few minutes before lights started to appear.

'You keep quiet and pretend to be boxtrolls,' Grandfather whispered to Willbury, Kipper, and Tom. 'I think they'll be taken in, even though you're not wearing your teeth any more. I'll have to take my chances.'

They fell silent as the Members approached.

Willbury saw Snatcher grinning from ear to ear.

'This one's full too!' he called back to the struggling Members. 'Sack this lot up, me lads, and we'll call it a day.'

The net was lowered onto the rock and the quarry inspected. There was a cry from one of the Members. ''Ere, guv. There's an old man in here with the monsters!'

'Well I never,' said Snatcher, leaning over Grandfather. 'If it ain't me old school friend William Trubshaw!' Then he grinned. 'So this is where you've been hiding all these years. It's typical of you to be mixed up with all these wretched underlings.'

'If it ain't me old school friend William Trubshaw!'

'Archibald Snatcher,' hissed Grandfather. Some of the Members close by heard this and giggled under their breath when they realized that Archibald was Snatcher's first name. Snatcher turned round and fixed them with a steely gaze.

'You think Archibald is funny, do you?' They fell silent. 'Shove him in a sack like the rest of them.'

Then he leaned over Grandfather again. 'You just wait till I get you back to the lab! By the time I've finished with you, you'll be wishing you were doing time for attempted murder instead!'

Members returning with their quarry by 'Cupboard'

Tea and cake

Chapter 44

THE SHAFT!

Snatcher stood by the open cupboard doors watching as the last of the Members dragged their wet sacks into the tearoom. Flashes of lightning threw shafts of light through the cracks in the boards over the windows and across the floor. Outside the rain fell hard on the streets of Ratbridge.

'Take 'em straight down the lab and chain 'em to the railings. It'll make it easier for sticking 'em in the "Extractor" . . . Then we'll 'ave a quick cup of tea and some cake.'

The Members picked up the struggling sacks and hiked them off to the lab. There they emptied the sacks out, chained the contents to the railing as ordered, and returned to the tearoom.

Willbury looked around the railing, and recognized all his fellow prisoners. There were the crew of the laundry, Marjorie and the boxtrolls Arthur had rescued, Fish, Shoe, Egg, and Titus, and finally Grandfather. Everybody looked rather battered and very miserable. The ones that had dressed up as boxtrolls now had broken or missing vegetable teeth.

Willbury noticed that Marjorie was anxiously studying the large funnel that hung above them.

Willbury looked around the railing, and recognized all his fellow prisoners

'What is that thing, Marjorie?' he whispered.

Marjorie looked very forlorn. 'They have done it! They've built a copy of my machine . . . only much, much bigger.'

'I thought you said it had two funnels?'

Marjorie pointed. 'See the small one over there, on top of the cage by the shed?'

'Yes,' replied Willbury.

'I think that is where they put the underlings to shrink them,' said Marjorie.

'And the big funnel up there?' asked Willbury.

Marjorie looked at the large doors in the floor. 'I'm not sure . . . '

They heard footsteps approaching from the entrance hall and they put their teeth back in. The duck stick appeared followed by Snatcher and the Members, all wearing their ceremonial robes. Snatcher made his way across to the control shed, climbed up the steps, went in, and then spoke through a trumpet device.

The duck stick appeared followed by Snatcher and the Members

'Tonight, gentlemen, we have a special show. Not only do we have enough monsters to finish our project, but also as a finale we shall for the first time use the machine to extract the size from humans. Please get the first boxtroll ready.'

Several of the Members descended on the boxtrolls. Marjorie was the nearest, and so they seized on her, unchaining her and pulling her across the room. She wailed and put up a good fight, but it wasn't long before the Members had her inside the cage with the door shut. The underlings were howling in despair. Willbury could stand it no longer.

It wasn't long before the Members had her inside the cage with the door shut

'Stop! This is inhuman.'

The Members turned to look. Snatcher came out of the control shed, and slowly walked down to where Willbury was chained.

'Human? What do you boxtrolls know about human?' Then he paused, and eyed up Willbury. 'Well, maybe you are a little more human than I thought!'

He put his good eye up very close to Willbury.

'I know you! You are that Willbury Nibble, that lawyer we've had so much trouble with. We've got your little friend locked up downstairs. I think I'll have him brought up so you can get shrunk together.'

Willbury froze. If Arthur had escaped then Snatcher had not found out yet! If he hadn't then the longer he stayed away from this machine the better. Either way, delaying Snatcher from sending someone down to get him was a good thing. He decided to change the subject.

He put his good eye up very close to Willbury

'This machine of yours is rather impressive. What are you using it for?'

'Wouldn't you like to know?' Snatcher grinned.

'It's not as if I can do anything about it. I'm sure your plan must be rather good.'

Snatcher puffed up a little as his vanity took over. 'You're right! You and your friends have already had your fate sealed so there can be no harm in telling you my plan. We are going to reclaim our rightful place as the overlords of Ratbridge. The Cheese Barons shall rule again!' And he laughed madly.

'So how are you going to do that?'

'This is what is going to allow us to do it. We are creating a Monster!' Snatcher paused for dramatic effect. 'And in part it's going to be with your help.' Snatcher laughed again. 'You know we have been shrinking your friends . . . well, have you wondered where the size goes?'

Willbury tried not to look worried.

'AH! You have! Well, I can tell you . . . the size is being put into a very special friend of mine, and as he gets bigger, he becomes more and more unstoppable!' Snatcher was now looking power crazed.

Snatcher was now looking power crazed

'Oh!' said Willbury. 'Your special friend . . . do we get to meet him?'

'Yes. Very shortly!'

'And . . . where does cheese come into all of this?' asked Willbury.

'The cheese! Cheese is central to it. To aid our monster's growth we have been force-feeding him a fondue of molten cheese. It goes down very well.' Snatcher guffawed. 'A DEEP WELL!' And he laughed at his own evil joke.

'Well, well,' said Willbury.

'Very droll, Mr Nibble. We have a heated pit that we drop cheeses into. This is piped directly to . . . the Great One. Right down his throat. I think 'e rather likes it.'

Willbury was horrified. What sort of monster could they possibly have created? 'So what happens now?' he said, playing for time.

'The boxtroll in the cage is about to donate some size to the Great One, and after that the rest of you is going to do the same. Then when you is all shrunk, and the Great One is finally the size we want, it's time to unleash him. Boy! Are we going to have fun! I hate this town!'

Snatcher turned and called for a ladder. Soon he was on the top of the shed waving his duck stick wildly in the air.

Soon he was on the top of the shed waving his duck stick wildly in the air

'To your places, gentlemen, we are about to start!'

The Members moved to positions around the lab tending different machines, and under Snatcher's feet, in the shed, sat Gristle at the controls. Great whooshes of sound filled the air as the beam engine started to move, then generators started to hum, and power surged through the sizing machine.

'Open the hatches!' Snatcher yelled above the noise.

Trout junior operated a winch in the roof that wound in the chains connected to the doors, while Trout senior took his place by the control panel on the rails and inserted a key. Soon the chains were groaning under the strain as they tried to lift the doors.

'More power, Little Trout!' shouted Snatcher.

Slowly the doors lifted and revealed a tiled shaft.

'Bring up the Great One!' screamed Snatcher.

Trout senior took his place by the control panel on the rails and inserted a key

Trout senior turned the key in the panel and a great creaking came from below. The Members stared towards the open shaft from their various stations, and everybody chained to the railings pulled back.

The creaking grew loud, and there was another sound, a hissing, sluggish breathing. It grew louder, as whatever it was rose up the shaft. Willbury and the others strained on their chains but it was no good. Their chains were fast.

Snatcher moved to the front of the shed roof and started to peer down the shaft. From his high vantage point he could see whatever was coming. He looked up at Willbury and laughed in a menacing way.

'You are about to meet my creation, Nibble. For all your meddling, it's done you no good. See what I am about to unleash on the world!'

Everybody chained to the railings pulled back

A huge bloated creature, larger than an elephant

What looked like a huge jelly covered in filthy grey matted carpet started to emerge from the shaft

Chapter 45

THE GREAT ONE!

What looked like a huge jelly covered in filthy grey matted carpet started to emerge from the shaft. As it did the smell of fetid cheese engulfed the lab.

Higher the great grey jelly rose, wobbling as it came. Something very long and rope-like was attached to one side of it, and on the other side . . .

Willbury stared as a pair of hairy door-sized ears came into view. 'It really is a monster . . . '

The ears were followed by great, red, dinner-plate sized eyes. They swivelled about wildly.

Willbury stared as a pair of hairy door-sized ears came into view

'No, it couldn't be!' cried Tom.

Still the creature rose. Its snout, bent and hairy, appeared.

Tom was jibbering. 'No! It can't be. It just can't!'

There was a loud clunk and the platform stopped as it reached the top of the shaft. Before them in all its glory was the Great One. A huge bloated creature, larger than an elephant.

'What is it?' wept Willbury

'I . . . I . . . I think it's a rat,' moaned Tom. 'And I think it's . . . Framley.'

'YES! What was once Framley is now . . . the Great One!' cried Snatcher. 'Once just nasty . . . Now made monstrous by the hand of man!' Snatcher broke into hysterical laughter for a few seconds, then he stopped, and turned to look directly at Tom.

'I'd been looking for someone really nasty, and when I saw dear sweet Framley in action I realized what a perfect subject he would make.'

'I . . . I . . . I think it's a rat,' moaned Tom. 'And I think it's . . . Framley.'

Tom was looking ill as his gaze darted between the Great One and Snatcher.

'Now you will witness the fulfilment of my dream.' Snatcher stamped on the roof of the shed and shouted. 'Extract the size!'

Snatcher stamped on the roof of the shed

At the controls in the shed, Gristle threw a lever.

Willbury blinked as there was a flash of blue light from the cage. He realized he could no longer see Marjorie. Then he heard another cry from Snatcher.

'Gristle! Give the Great One what he needs!'

There was another flash, but this time from the large funnel above, and the Great One wobbled.

Snatcher called out another order. 'Next, please! I think we will have the boy from the dungeon.'

'No!' screamed Willbury and Grandfather, as one of the Members set off in the direction of the dungeon.

'Oh yes! You'll enjoy watching!' laughed Snatcher, then he called after the disappearing Member, 'And can you bring back one of those shoeboxes down there. We need something to put all our friends in.'

'You're going to pay for this!' Willbury shouted.

'Quiet!' replied Snatcher. 'Or I'll turn up the voltage and you'll all be reduced to the size of ants!'

Willbury fell silent.

Snatcher spoke again. 'Get the little creature out of the cage.'

Willbury watched as Trout senior left his post by the railings, opened the door of the cage and groped about the floor inside. Then he stood up with something in his hands.

'What shall I do with it?'

'Perhaps Mr Nibble would like to be reunited with his friend?' Snatcher joked. 'Show him to the lawyer.'

Trout senior walked around to where Willbury was chained and held out his hands.

Standing there was a new tiny Marjorie, about seven inches high, and looking very unhappy.

Standing there was a new tiny Marjorie,
about seven inches high, and looking very unhappy

'Are you all right?' asked Willbury.

'Yes!' came a squeak. Marjorie looked startled by the new sound of her own voice. Then she squeaked again. 'I should never have built the prototype! I just never foresaw the consequences.'

Trout senior looked surprised at the little talking boxtroll in his hands, and lifted it up to take a closer look. Just as Trout realized who it was, Marjorie kicked him right in the eye. Trout screamed and dropped Marjorie on the floor, where she ran under one of the machines.

'Get back to your post!' Snatcher ordered Trout. 'We'll let the hounds find it later.'

Trout skulked off. Willbury looked about to see if he could see where Marjorie had gone, but he couldn't see her anywhere.

'Please, please find somewhere safe to hide,' Willbury muttered to himself. 'I couldn't bear it if you were eaten.'

'Now where is that blooming kid?' boomed Snatcher, as he looked towards the dungeon.

Trout screamed, and dropped Marjorie on the floor,
where she ran under one of the machines

A struggling Arthur appeared, being held by the scruff of his under-suit

There'd been quite a lot of noise from the dungeon

Chapter 46

THE NEXT VICTIM!

There'd been quite a lot of noise from the dungeon, before Snatcher heard heavy footsteps coming up the stairs. A struggling Arthur appeared, being held by the scruff of his under-suit. His captor was rather shorter than Snatcher remembered.

'Oi!' shouted Snatcher. 'You've forgotten the shoebox. Bring the boy here, then go and get it.'

As the Member led Arthur through the machines, loud metallic footsteps reverberated around the lab. Snatcher looked puzzled.

Grandfather and Willbury watched in despair as Arthur appeared by the pathway. Arthur and the Member froze at the sight of the Great One, and Willbury and the others chained to the railings.

'Come on! Come on! We haven't got all night. Get a move on!' ordered Snatcher.

The Member guided Arthur along the pathway towards the shed. As they passed, Arthur was looking worried, but winked, and Grandfather noticed the Member was wearing a mask and was holding something under his ceremonial robes. They stopped on the pathway before the shed.

'What you waiting for?' snapped Snatcher. 'Shove him in the cage, and go and get a shoebox.'

'No,' snapped the Member. 'Get your own shoebox.'

Snatcher was gobsmacked. No Member had ever answered him back.

'What!' he screamed. 'Me! Get my own shoebox?'

'Yes, Archibald!' replied the Member. 'Get your own shoebox!'

Snatcher went red with rage, and almost fell off the roof.

'You . . . ' Snatcher screamed, as he waved his duck stick at the truculent Member, 'are Expelled!'

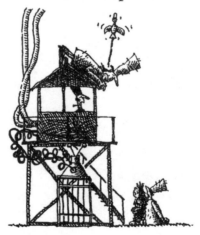

Snatcher went red with rage, and almost fell off the roof

Suddenly the Member released his grip on Arthur, and threw off his hat and robe. Standing by Arthur was Herbert in his iron boots . . . with his walloper.

The Members froze and Snatcher went very pale.

'Oh my God, he's out! Get him!' ordered Snatcher.

The Members didn't move.

'Get him!' screamed Snatcher. Still the Members held back as they'd all had experience of the walloper, and weren't willing to get within range.

Snatcher was starting to panic. ' . . . all right! . . . all right! . . . Break out the weapons!'

The Members rushed towards a large cabinet on a wall of the lab.

Grandfather shouted to Herbert. 'Smash the railings!'

Herbert looked back at Grandfather and grinned. Then he raised the walloper and brought it down hard.

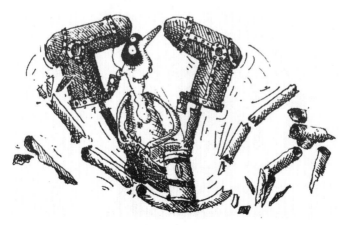

Then he raised the walloper and brought it down hard

There was an enormous crash as a section of the railing shattered. The blow was so hard that the Great One started to wobble violently, and let out an awful low moaning. Some of the boxtrolls were freed, and Herbert moved on to the next section. There was another blow and the Great One let out a huge bellow.

'Faster!' screamed Snatcher at the Members, who'd reached the cupboard, and were fiddling with the keys.

With two more blows all the railings lay shattered, and the prisoners freed. Willbury watched as Arthur ran to his grandfather, and hugged him. Willbury smiled for a moment, then turned and shouted to Herbert.

Willbury watched as Arthur ran to his grandfather, and hugged him

'Could you bash a hole in the wall so we can get out of here?'

Herbert looked serious. 'Where I wallop is me own business!' Then he winked at Willbury, and made for the wall opposite the cupboard where the Members were now arming themselves with blunderbusses.

Snatcher screamed, 'They're going to get away! Open fire!'

Willbury heard the first shot, and bits of broken cutlery flew over his head

Willbury heard the first shot, and bits of broken cutlery flew over his head. The Members didn't yet have clear sight of the escaping prisoners, as there were so many machines in the way.

'Follow me!' Willbury shouted. 'Kipper, can you help Arthur get Grandfather out of here?'

Kipper saluted, and ran to where Arthur was helping Grandfather. They took him by both arms, and set off after Willbury.

Herbert reached the outer wall and set about creating an exit. Within seconds a large hole appeared. He turned back to see Willbury approaching followed by the others.

Herbert reached the outer wall and set about creating an exit

Willbury guided the escapees through the hole

'Would you like it any bigger?'

'No,' smiled Willbury. 'I think it is big enough. An elephant could get through it.'

Snatcher was getting frantic, and dancing about on the roof of the shed in rage.

'They're escaping! Shoot them!'

Volleys of marbles, nails, bits of china, even old boiled sweets, clattered against the wall of the lab as Willbury guided the escapees through the hole.

'Make for the laundry!' he shouted.

The last out were Kipper, Arthur, and Grandfather. As soon as they were in the street Willbury turned to Herbert.

'Can you bring down the wall?' Willbury asked.

'A pleasure!' Herbert took a good long look at the wall, and swung his walloper.

There was a dull thump, and for a moment Willbury thought it hadn't worked. Then, cracks ran up the wall and a low rumbling started.

'Let's get out of here!' shouted Willbury.

Masonry crashed down as the wall collapsed, sending out huge clouds of dust.

As the dust settled all that could be heard was the sound of rain and distant iron socks on cobbles.

Iron socks on cobbles

*Willbury and Herbert caught up with Kipper and Arthur just
as they were helping Grandfather up the gangplank*

Tom and the captain came forward to meet them

Chapter 47

HOW ARE WE GOING TO FIX IT?

Willbury and Herbert caught up with Kipper and Arthur just as they were helping Grandfather up the gangplank. The Squeakers had gone, the dummies on deck had stopped dancing, but the crows were still very happily playing the harmonium. They hadn't got much better.

Reaching the deck they were greeted by the sight of all the other escapees. Tom and the captain came forward to meet them.

'Is everybody all right?' Willbury asked.

'I think so,' Arthur smiled. 'But where is Marjorie?'

Willbury looked glum. 'I forgot about her in the rush. I think she must still be trying to hide somewhere in the lab.'

'What are we going to do then?' asked Arthur.

'I think we will have to go back and get her.' Willbury

sounded a little reluctant. 'We also have to try to save Ratbridge from Snatcher and Framley.'

'How are we going to do that?' asked the captain.

'I don't think we have any choice but to take them on, and the sooner we do, the less damage they will have had time to do to the town.'

'We better be quick about it then,' said the captain. 'I don't really know how we take on Framley now he's so monstrously big, but I suppose we do have to try.' He turned to the crew and gave the order. 'OK! Gather all the weapons you can find!'

'Can we take off these stupid boxes?' asked Bert.

Fish, who was close by, looked very offended.

'I'm sorry,' apologized Bert, 'but damp cardboard . . . it chafes my legs!'

'OK. Everybody get changed!' ordered the captain.

Kipper raised a hand. 'May I keep my box on?'

'Oh! . . . If you really want to!' replied the captain. Fish smiled at Kipper who smiled back.

'And would you get me out of these darn socks?' pleaded Herbert.

Kipper went and found a cold chisel. He held it against the hinges of the boots, and with two careful blows of Herbert's walloper the socks were off.

Willbury looked at Herbert's feet. 'I think you had better go and wash those in the canal . . . And, Kipper, can you see if you can find some tin snips. Herbert needs to cut his toenails.'

He held it against the hinges of the boots

Shortly afterwards, when Herbert and Kipper returned, everybody was ready.

'Do you need shoes?' asked Willbury.

'Nah! After years in those socks, me feet are as hard as granite! And by the way you need some new tin snips.'

'And by the way you need some new tin snips'

'Herbert,' said the captain. 'I think we would like you to lead the assault.'

There was a cheer, and Herbert smiled.

Then Mildred came forward. 'Is there any chance us crows could come too? We could play you all into battle.'

Everybody went quiet, and then the captain spoke. 'I think it would be a good idea if you gave us a rousing send off, but somebody has to have the important job of looking after, and er . . . ' The captain paused and raised an eyebrow. ' . . . entertaining Grandfather and the miniature underlings.'

There was another cheer. The crows returned to the keyboard and started to try to play a march.

The crows returned to the keyboard and started to try to play a march

Arthur turned to his grandfather. 'Do you realize that now that Herbert is free, you have a witness to what happened? We could clear your name . . . And live above ground.'

'Yes, Arthur, maybe we could. But first we need to worry about Archibald Snatcher and whatever it is he's up to.' He smiled for a moment, and then he looked more serious. 'I'm not going to stop you from going back with the others to the Cheese Hall, but please think about it.'

Arthur looked him squarely in the face. 'I think I have to go back. I am not sure what's going to happen but I need to be there.'

'All right, Arthur, but . . . '

'I will be careful!' Arthur smiled. 'I haven't come this far to . . . well, you know?'

'Yes, I know,' said Grandfather, and he winked. 'Go on. Off with you!'

Arthur looked him squarely in the face

'Careful now, we don't want to hurt Baby'

A smile spread over Snatcher's face

Chapter 48

LET'S HIT THE TOWN!

As the clouds of dust settled, a smile spread over Snatcher's face. There was a huge hole in the wall of the lab.

'I was wondering how we were going to get the Great One out of here.' Then he snapped out an order. 'Ready the armour!'

Some Members ran to a corner of the lab and pulled dustsheets from a strangely shaped heap. Beneath the covers was a set of iron war armour. It looked like a cross between a giant snail shell and an old riveted boiler. A cannon was fixed above a small platform on either side, and on top in the centre of the back was another platform for the Great One's master to ride into battle upon.

Beneath the covers was a set of iron war armour

Inside the shed Gristle fiddled with some levers, and a crane moved across the floor to the armour. A hook was lowered from the crane, the Members attached it to the armour, and the armour was lifted from the floor. The crane moved towards the Great One.

'Careful now, Gristle, we don't want to hurt Baby.'

The armour slowly lowered, and the Members manoeuvred it over the rat. Snatcher climbed down from the shed and inspected the armour for fit.

'It's a bit loose around the edges,' Snatcher muttered. 'We really did need the extra size from those wretched underlings.'

Then he turned and cried, 'Gristle, could you lift the armour off for a moment . . . and could the Trouts please go into the cage, and check that the extractor funnel is correctly positioned . . . I am not sure it's working properly . . . '

The armour was lifted off, and the Trouts made their way into the cage. Snatcher followed, but stopped outside the door. Then in a blink, Snatcher snapped the door closed, and locked it.

'Shrink 'em, Gristle!'

The Trouts looked horrified. 'But Masterrrrrrrrrrrrr . . . '

There was a flash from above the cage, and the Trouts' cries grew higher and higher pitched, until only an indecipherable squeaking could be heard. Then there was another larger flash from the funnel and Framley wobbled again.

'That should do it!' said a satisfied Snatcher. 'Can we try the armour for size again?'

When the armour was back on the rat, Snatcher inspected it for fit again. 'Marvellous!' he chuckled. 'I knew he'd grow into it.'

The Great One now looked fearsome. The Members took the ladder from the shed and put it up to the platform on the back of the rat. Snatcher climbed up, and a couple of the Members climbed onto the platforms on either side.

Snatcher climbed up

'Right, me lads. Gather round.'

The Members assembled, and Snatcher spoke from his seat, perched high on top of the rat.

'Members of the new Cheese Guild, the time is here!'

There was a loud cheer.

'The Great One is ready, and Ratbridge is going to pay!'

There was an even louder cheer.

'Yes, my brothers! We shall use our Leviathan to overthrow those that have held us down for so long. First we shall remove their government, then destroy the banks, smash their factories, and return Ratbridge to follow an open free trade in cheesy products!'

There was a silence, and then Gristle raised a hand. 'Eh . . . what do you mean?'

'We're going to use the big rat to clobber them what done us down, blow up the council offices, rob the bank, knock down the factories, and then start flogging dodgy cheese again!' Snatcher replied.

There was an enormous cheer.

The Members followed carrying their blunderbusses

'Right! Let's hit the town!' shouted Snatcher, and he took hold of a pair of reins that had been fixed to the mouth of the Great One, and pulled hard. Slowly his war machine rose and turned towards the broken wall. The Members followed carrying their blunderbusses.

'I've been looking forward to this.' Snatcher smiled to himself.

'Right, what's the plan?' asked the captain

Herbert leading the way with his newly fresh feet

Chapter 49

ATTACK ON THE CHEESE HALL

Herbert led the way through the streets of Ratbridge. The sun was rising and was just breaking through under the dark storm clouds, and their footsteps were mixed with the rumble of thunder and rainfall. As Willbury surveyed the little army, he wondered about their selection of weapons. Some of the pirates carried large pants, and were accompanied by rats carrying the notorious gunge balls. This he understood, but the others . . .

The boxtrolls had selected screwdrivers and adjustable spanners, Titus had found a small trowel and a bucket full of gravel, and the other pirates and rats seemed to have grabbed anything that was handy—mops, buckets, old fishing rods, in fact anything that took their fancy. Willbury carried an umbrella that was keeping him dry, and that he thought might be useful in a fight, while Arthur walked by his side carrying the doll.

The thunder drew closer as they stood in front of the Cheese Hall in the rain.

'Right, what's the plan?' asked the captain.

Kipper smiled. 'Perhaps Herbert could "open" the front door for us, and we could creep in that way and surprise them?'

'I don't think there will be much surprise after the noise of Herbert walloping down the door,' said Arthur.

'If we wait for a flash of lightning, count a few seconds, then Herbert wallops the door, the thunder will mask the sound of the wallop,' suggested Tom.

'That is a very intelligent idea!' Willbury agreed, and smiled at Tom.

They waited for a minute or so until the next flash came. Willbury held up a finger, counted for a few seconds, then gave the signal to Herbert. At the very moment the walloper struck the door, a loud clap of thunder filled the street. The front door was reduced to matchsticks and everybody waited to see if the Members were going to come rushing out to meet them. After another minute there was still no sign of them.

'I think we got away with it,' said Kipper.

'Right! Get the mobile knickers ready,' ordered the captain.

Pairs of pirates stretched knickers between them, rats loaded them with the gunge balls, and each pair of pirates was joined by a third pirate who stretched the knickers back ready for firing.

'Everybody keep quiet and follow the knickers,' ordered the captain.

Slowly, the pirates with the loaded knickers made their way up the passageway towards the entrance hall and the others followed. As they reached the archway to the hall, one of the leading pirates peeked round the corner, and signalled that nobody was there. The little army made its way into the entrance hall.

Slowly, the pirates with the loaded knickers made their way up the passageway towards the entrance hall

'Prepare yourselves,' whispered the captain. 'I think Herbert should wallop the lab door, and then we let off a volley of knickers . . . ' But before he could finish, the lab door started to creak open and everybody froze.

Around the bottom of the door a tiny person appeared. It was Marjorie.

'I wondered when you were going to get here,' she squeaked. 'But you're too late. They've gone!'

There was a mixture of surprise, relief, and worry.

Around the bottom of the door a tiny person appeared

'Thank God you are all right,' said Willbury to Marjorie.

'I am not hurt, but all right is not exactly how I feel,' squeaked a sad-looking Marjorie. 'Six inches tall . . . ' Her voice trailed off.

'Well, I am not sure we can do anything about that right now,' said Willbury sympathetically. 'I think we'd better stop Snatcher and the Members before they cause too much destruction. Do you know where they have gone?'

'They've taken the rat to wreak their revenge on the town. First they're going to destroy the Town Hall, then rob the bank, and after that they are going to destroy all the factories!' squeaked Marjorie.

Everybody looked shocked.

'We've got to stop them!' cried Willbury.

'But how?' asked Arthur.

'Knickers and a good walloping!' suggested Herbert.

The crew of the laundry gave a cheer.

'I don't think even that could stop them now,' Marjorie said to Herbert. 'They have equipped the rat with some really heavy iron armour and cannons. And from what I can see, that rat is vicious and afraid of nothing now he's enormous. It's going to take something really powerful to stop them now.'

Everybody fell silent, then after a few moments Arthur spoke.

'Did you say "iron armour"?'

'Yes,' replied Marjorie.

'The same stuff that Herbert's boots were made of?'

'Yes. Why?' Marjorie asked.

'I am not sure if it would work, but I have an idea,' Arthur explained. 'There is a powerful electromagnet somewhere above the roof of Herbert's cell. When they wanted to stop him from attacking them, the Members would turn it on, and Herbert's boots would stick him to the ceiling. Couldn't we use that?'

Marjorie's eyes lit up. 'If it was powerful enough, it might work.'

Willbury looked perplexed, and turned to Arthur. 'I don't understand.'

'Don't you see? We could use the electromagnet!' said Arthur. 'If Framley is wearing iron armour, we could turn on the magnet, and pull him back here.'

'Yes . . . But is the magnet powerful enough?' asked Willbury.

'We could use the electromagnet!'

Marjorie smiled. 'It will be by the time I'm finished with it!'
Everybody cheered.

'Where was your cell?' Marjorie squeaked to Herbert.

'Just below us somewhere,' replied Herbert.

'Could you pick me up and show me approximately
where?' Marjorie asked him. 'If we can find the spot just
above your cell, we should be able to find the magnet.'

Herbert carefully picked up Marjorie and looked towards
the stairs to the dungeon. Then he made towards a space
behind the beam engine.

Arthur and the others followed. As Herbert rounded a
corner, Marjorie let out a squeak.

'Here it is!'

There was a very large coil of wire on a cart.

Willbury looked puzzled. 'Are you sure? It's just a large
coil of wire.'

'YUP! That's what it is until you put electricity through
it,' Marjorie squeaked with glee. 'Now all we have to do is
put enough electricity through it to give that rat a surprise!'

There was a very large coil of wire on a cart

'What do you want us to do?' asked the captain.

'Well, when we turn it on, we have to make sure the rat comes to the magnet, rather than the magnet going to the rat. If we make sure there is something really solid between the coil and the rat, that should stop it moving,' squeaked Marjorie.

'How about the end wall of the lab . . . and it is closest to the Town Hall,' suggested Arthur.

'Good idea,' said Marjorie.

'What about all the machinery in here?' asked Willbury. 'Won't the coil be attracted to that?'

'Mmmmmm! You have got a point. We'll have to fix the magnet to the wall. Some of the loose parts of machinery might fly towards it, but the heavy stuff is fixed down firmly, I think.'

Fish made a gurgling noise, and Titus came forward to whisper to Willbury.

Willbury spoke. 'Titus says the boxtrolls are very good at that sort of thing and would like to help.'

'Very good!' Marjorie squeaked, turning to the boxtrolls. 'You lot move the coil and fix it to the wall.'

The boxtrolls smiled, and Shoe made a burbling noise.

Titus whispered to Willbury, and Willbury passed on the question to Marjorie.

'I don't really understand, but they would like to know if you would like them to rewire the cabling so you can have the switch up here rather than down in the dungeon.'

'Bless me! That would be grand,' squeaked Marjorie. 'Could we have the switch in the control shed, please? And wire the coil directly to the generators?'

Shoe nodded, and the boxtrolls set to work. Then Marjorie turned to the captain.

'We need as much power as possible if we are going to stop that rat,' squeaked Marjorie. 'Do you think your crew could stoke up the boiler as fast as you can? The beam engine that powers the generators will have to be running flat out.'

'Be our pleasure!' said the captain. 'We know all about stoking boilers.'

So the crew of the Nautical Laundry set to stoking the boiler of the beam engine. The boiler was still hot, so it

didn't take long before the great arm of the beam engine was pumping up and down, and the flywheel was spinning again.

Marjorie asked Willbury to carry her up to the shed, and Arthur and Titus accompanied them. As they entered Willbury looked about. On the bench at the back of the shed were Arthur's wings and the strange device with two small funnels.

The strange device with two small funnels

Willbury pointed to it. 'Is that yours?'

Marjorie looked rather awkward. 'Yes . . . Yes, it is.'

Arthur was not paying any attention to them as he was checking his wings.

'At least they haven't had time to take them apart again,' he muttered to himself.

Willbury put Marjorie down on the control panel. She took a few moments to study the controls, then pointed to one of the dials.

'That shows the pressure in the steam boiler.' Then she pointed to a lever. 'And that lever engages the generators. Arthur, could you swing it to the upright position, please?'

Arthur obliged. As soon as he did, a gentle whirring started and built to a loud hum that filled the whole lab. A needle in another large dial in the control panel started to climb.

Arthur thought for a moment then asked Marjorie a question. 'How did they make the magnet work when the beam engine wasn't running?'

'Arthur, you really are as sharp as a knife.' Marjorie smiled. 'You saw all those glass tanks?'

'Yes,' replied Arthur.

'Those are batteries. They store power, but not enough for what we want. That's why I asked the boxtrolls to wire the coil directly to the generators,' answered Marjorie. 'Now all we have to do is wait until the needle hits the red.'

'Are you sure that's safe?' asked Willbury.

'Er . . . no,' confessed Marjorie. 'But it should be all right . . . for a bit . . . '

The stokers were doing their work well; the beam engine kept increasing in speed and the generators hummed louder. Soon the needle reached the red.

'Arthur, can you tell the boxtrolls to stand clear of the magnetic coil, please?' asked Marjorie.

Arthur leant out of the door and shouted to the boxtrolls. 'We are going to turn the magnet on. Stand clear!'

Arthur was surprised that the boxtrolls immediately dropped all their tools and ran to the other end of the lab as fast as their legs could carry them. He turned to Marjorie.

'They're clear!'

'Well then,' Marjorie squeaked to Arthur. 'Would you like to throw the switch?'

Arthur looked a little uncertain.

'Don't worry. What can happen?' smiled Marjorie.

Arthur paused for a moment, and then threw the switch.

Every piece of loose metal in the lab flew towards the magnet. Tools, nuts and bolts, pieces of machinery, the door handle of the lab, bits of chain, and several enamelled mugs and plates whizzed past fearful heads, as they made the most direct way to the magnet, where they formed a jumble on the surface of the coil.

'Strong, isn't it?' Marjorie smiled.

'Strong, isn't it?'

At the head of the procession rode Snatcher high on the back of Framley. Following were the other Members, carrying an assortment of blunderbusses and other weapons, and behind them ran the cheese-hounds.

Shutters were thrown open by the townsfolk to see what all the commotion was

Chapter 50

MAGNETISM!

Ratbridge was a strange town and had seen some very strange and fearful sights during its history, but none as strange and fearful as that which made its way through its streets now.

At the head of the procession rode Snatcher high on the back of Framley. Following were the other Members, carrying an assortment of blunderbusses and other weapons, and behind them ran the cheese-hounds. Sparks flew out from below Framley's belly as his armour grated on the cobbles of the streets. The noise drew people from their beds, and as the procession approached, shutters were thrown open by the townsfolk to see what all the commotion was. Very quickly the shutters were closed and bolted again.

Very quickly the shutters were closed and bolted again

Encouraged by the obvious fear they were generating, Snatcher chuckled to himself. He hadn't felt this good for years . . . or ever! Life felt wonderful.

'Just wait till I get to the Town Hall!' he giggled. Looking ahead his eyes fixed on a rank of shops. About halfway down the rank was a shuttered shop frontage with the three balls of the pawnbroker's sign hanging above it.

'I wonder . . . ?' he muttered to himself.

As Framley drew level with the shop front Snatcher pulled hard on the reins attached to Framley's jaws. The Great One stopped. Snatcher turned to the Members who had come to a sudden halt behind him. And spoke.

'I am sorry, lads, but I can't resist it!' He then pulled on Framley's reins and aimed the rat at the front of the shop. 'Go on, my beauty! Let's see what you can do.'

For a moment the rat didn't move, then realizing just how big he was and just how small the shop looked, he raised his head and swung it at the front of the shop.

The shop did not put up much of a fight. Within a fraction of a second the shutters and windows gave way and the contents of the windows spilled out. The Members let out a mighty cheer and ran forward to gather up the treasures now strewn across the street.

'This is going to be so easy!' shouted Snatcher. 'Help yourselves, boys, there is going to be plenty more where that came from.'

Snatcher pulled on the reins and set the mighty rat off

The shop did not put up much of a fight

again towards the market square. As they made their way through the streets he set Framley upon several more unfortunate shops that took his fancy, and each in turn was reduced to a wreck in seconds.

Finally they arrived at the market square, and crossed it to arrive outside the Town Hall. Snatcher brought the procession to a halt, and turned to the Members.

'This is where the real fun begins, lads! Prepare to charge!' Snatcher shouted.

Gristle, who had made his way to the side of the Great One, now spoke up. 'Can't we use the cannons? I likes a bang. Please, please let's use the cannons.'

Snatcher looked down at Gristle and smiled. 'Oh all right, Gristle. As you have been so good. We'll use the cannons.'

Then Snatcher gave the order. 'Prepare to fire!'

The Members who were standing on the platforms on the sides of the rat took out boxes of matches, and the other Members levelled their weapons at the front of the Town Hall.

'Ready ... Fire!' Snatcher cried, as he brought down his arm.

There was a roar of cannons and blunderbusses ... but then something very strange happened that seemed to defy the laws of nature. The cannon balls, and the nuts and bolts that the Members had fired, hurtled towards the Town Hall, then very rapidly slowed ... stopped ... and turned back towards the Members.

A Member with a box of matches

'Duck!!!' screamed Snatcher. The Members hit the floor as the missiles whizzed over their heads and continued back across the market square in the direction of the Cheese Hall. Everybody looked very baffled.

'Prepare to fire!' Snatcher screamed again.

The Members tried to follow orders but now their guns and ammunition seemed to want to go home, and were pulling the Members back towards the Cheese Hall.

'Master . . . ' cried a very frightened Gristle. 'Something weird is 'appenin' . . . '

The Members hit the floor as the missiles whizzed over their heads

Their guns and ammunition seemed to want to go home

'Stand firm!' ordered Snatcher, but the terrified Members were now letting go of their blunderbusses, and untying their ammunition bags from their belts to avoid being dragged across the square.

'Load the cannons!' cried Snatcher. The two Members on either side of the rat unstrapped cannon balls from the platform floors, but before they could load them into the cannons found themselves dragged off the platforms, and disappeared across the square, screaming.

'It's a curse!' cried one of the Members.

'Run!' cried another. And the Members ran in all directions.

Across Ratbridge many people were just getting up, and might well have been very frightened by the noise of the blunderbusses and cannons, if it were not for the thunder, and the fact they had problems of their own. In every household, objects were coming to life.

Saucepans and cutlery had suddenly decided to stick to walls, and cooking ranges and iron bedsteads were going for walks. Several ladies who had slept in their steel reinforced corsets now found themselves irresistibly drawn to join the saucepans and cutlery. One man who had invested in an

expensive set of metal false teeth found himself hanging on as tightly as he could to the kitchen table to avoid being dragged through the house, while outside in the street, dogs with studded collars found themselves sliding through the mud towards the Cheese Hall.

Snatcher looked completely flummoxed. A cart, riderless bicycles, garden furniture, and several old barrels were all making their way at high speed across the market square. Snatcher looked down at the head of the great rat.

Snatcher looked completely flummoxed

'It's down to us, Framley! Attack!' And Snatcher pointed towards the Town Hall.

The Great One let out a low moan.

'Come on, my horrid!' cried Snatcher.

Framley seemed very perturbed. His legs were scrabbling on the wet cobbles, but he and Snatcher were not moving forward . . . in fact, they were starting to slip backwards . . .

Inside the lab Arthur and the others were feeling a little nervous about the strange noises that were coming from outside. They seemed to conform to a pattern. All seemed to start with a distant whizzing or clattering that grew louder very quickly, then stopped suddenly with thwonk, thud, or similar.

'Do you think we'd better go and have a look at what's happening?' Arthur asked Tom.

'I think we know what's happening, Arthur. For the time being I think we'd better stay safely in here. If the metal doesn't get us, I think there are going to be some very angry people out there,' Tom replied and then winked.

Snatcher turned around to see the last of the cannon balls break from their lashings and fly off across the square. The rat was picking up speed, despite desperately trying to cling on to the cobbles with its claws. There was a horrible scraping and grinding as the armour slid across the market square.

'Oh, my poor horrid!' Snatcher muttered. Framley just let out a mournful whimper.

On the way to the Town Hall Snatcher had taken what he thought was the most direct route, but he now discovered that there was an even shorter route back . . . a straight line.

As the armoured rat reached the edge of the market square, it was not a street that they met but a cobbler's shop. Snatcher could see what was going to happen and crouched down on the back of the ever-accelerating rat and hung on.

The shop, like most of the buildings in Ratbridge, was badly built, and put up little opposition.

There was a crashing and they disappeared through the shop frontage, leaving a large armoured-rat-shaped hole. In the apartment above the shop where the cobbler lived, there was much surprise as a screaming crouched man on a small railed platform came through the wall, moved rapidly across the room, and out through the back wall. The Great One then slid across the muddy back garden till it reached the next building, and disappeared again.

There was much surprise as a screaming crouched man on a small railed platform came through the wall and moved rapidly across the room

The armour protected Framley as they smashed through badly-built building after badly-built building, but Snatcher was getting rather bruised. And all the time they were picking up speed.

Finally, with a great deal of splintering and crashing of masonry, Framley broke from a cake shop across the road from the lab, shot across the street, and hit the lab wall in a puff of flour and cake crumbs.

The building shook.

'I think someone's arrived!' Marjorie squeaked, then Herbert giggled.

Willbury spoke to Arthur. 'Can you get up to one of the windows and see what's happened?'

Arthur ran down to the floor of the lab and found a wooden stepladder, placed it below a window near the magnet, and climbed up. After a few moments he turned and shouted.

'It's Snatcher and the rat! And they both look really angry . . . '

'We'd better keep them there then,' replied Willbury.

Arthur took another look out of the window. 'I'm not sure you want to do that!'

'Why?' shouted Willbury.

'Because Framley is being squashed by his armour. He could burst at any moment!'

'Can we just reduce the strength of the magnet, Marjorie?' asked Willbury.

Marjorie looked unsure. The stokers were still very enthusiastic, and the generators were spinning faster and faster.

'The circuit is either on or off. The only way we can ease the power off the magnet is to slow down the generators, and that's going to take a few minutes even if we stop stoking the boiler and let off some steam . . . !'

'Framley is being squashed by his armour. He could burst at any moment!'

'Quick!' shouted a very worried-looking Arthur. 'Framley looks like he could blow any second . . . '

Willbury turned to Marjorie. 'Well?'

'We could turn the current off for a few seconds . . . ' Marjorie suggested.

'Do it!' snapped Willbury.

'Herbert! Can you lift me up so I can turn off the switch?' Marjorie squeaked.

Herbert lifted Marjorie to the switch and she tried to grab it. The switch was red hot and Marjorie jumped back.

'Let me try!' shouted Herbert. And he leant forward and again pulled back from the red-hot switch.

'I can't! It's too hot.'

Marjorie jumped back

Willbury wrapped a handkerchief around his hand and tried. It was useless . . . with all the current the switch had fused solid.

'We have to get everybody out of here!' cried Willbury. 'An explosion could bring down the rest of the lab.'

Willbury grabbed Marjorie and ran out of the shed followed by Herbert and Titus, and then he shouted from the top of the stairs.

'Everybody out! Run for your lives! Don't use the hole in the wall! It's too close to the rat! Use the door to the entrance hall.'

Willbury, Titus, the stokers, and boxtrolls all ran for the entrance hall, but as Willbury reached the door he turned to see Arthur making for the shed.

'Arthur! What are you doing?' he shouted.

'I've got to get my wings,' Arthur shouted back.

Arthur ran up the steps to the shed and in through the door. He grabbed his wings and hastily strapped them on. Then he grabbed Marjorie's prototype from the bench, and made for the door. As soon as he was outside he wound the handle on the wings' motor as fast as he could. He had never wound it as fast in his life.

Over the noise of the machines in the lab he heard Willbury calling him from the door to the hallway.

'Arthur! Arthur!'

Arthur turned to see the last of the underlings and laundry crew disappearing out of the door past Willbury.

Arthur adjusted the knob on the front of the box, pressed both buttons, and jumped.

Arthur adjusted the knob on the front of the box,
pressed both buttons and jumped

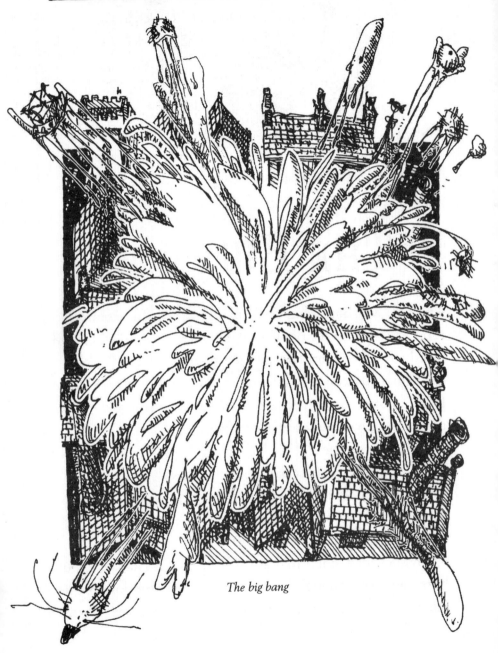

The big bang

The day was not going well for Snatcher

Chapter 51

THE BIG BANG

The day was not going well for Snatcher. His attempt to return himself to his rightful social position seemed to have failed; the Members had all run away; he'd been dragged through a number of buildings; and now it was raining water from above and small metal objects from every other direction. How could things get worse?

Beneath him the iron shell that had protected the giant rat was now looking rather battered and flimsy. The Great One was being squeezed and was bulging out round the edges of the armour like a squashed balloon.

Then it happened.

Framley had not eaten since he'd had his last dose of 'size', and even though he was extremely uncomfortable he felt rather hungry. There on the ground right beneath his head, in the midst of a pile of rubble and cake crumbs, was a

*There on the ground right beneath his head,
in the midst of a pile of rubble and cake crumbs, was a cream bun*

cream bun. It was not a large cream bun, but it would do until he could get more cheese. He reached down, snapped up the bun, and swallowed. What followed was disastrous.

A clap like thunder broke as Framley burst and everything went yellow!

A cream bun

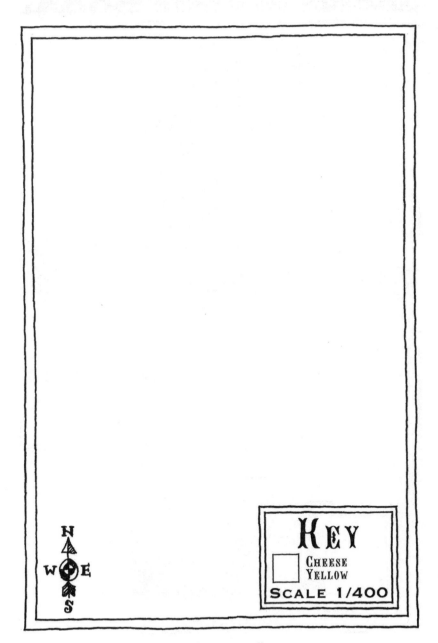

Everything went yellow!

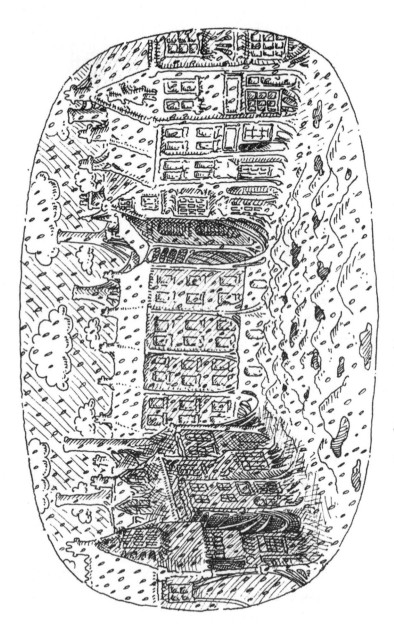

Everything was covered in a smooth film of elastic cheese

The two mice in the bottle

Chapter 52

SKINNED!

Arthur flew straight towards the lab door where Willbury stood waiting. When Willbury was sure Arthur was coming, he turned and ran. Arthur followed.

Just as Arthur was about halfway across the entrance hall, he remembered the two mice in the bottle. He turned and landed by the door of Snatcher's suite, ran in, grabbed the bottle from the table, ran back out of the door, and then across the hall through the archway. As he ran down the passageway to the front door he was hit by a blast from behind.

The blast shot him through the door, and as he saw the front windows of the inn approaching rapidly, he felt someone grab him out of the air and pull him to the ground. Then he felt himself covered by something thick and very sticky, and everything went silent.

Arthur tried to stand up. He was under some kind of soft elastic yellow tent. With a slight struggle, he freed his hands, and then with one finger he managed to poke a hole through the yellow skin. With a little difficulty he stretched the hole until he could step out of it. Strands of cheese hung from his wings.

With one finger he managed to poke a hole through the yellow skin

He was standing in a shiny yellow street. Arthur looked about. Everything was covered in the smooth film of elastic cheese. He turned towards where the Cheese Hall had once stood. Now there was just a low, shiny, yellow mound. The buildings around the Cheese Hall all now had yellow frontages, but didn't seem to be damaged (apart from the bakery).

Then Arthur remembered the others. He looked about on the ground close to where he stood. Odd shapes were wiggling under the cheese skin, and some were just starting to break through the film. Close to where he stood was the form of Willbury, laid flat with outstretched arms. Arthur ran and started to peel the cheese film away from his friend.

'Willbury . . . Willbury . . . Are you all right?' Arthur cried.

Arthur tore at the cheese

A muffled grunting came through the skin. Arthur tore at the cheese and soon he had Willbury freed.

'Thank you, Arthur!' said Willbury as he tried to disentangle cheese strands from his wig. 'We'd better help get everybody else out.' Then he stopped.

'Have you seen Marjorie?'

'No!' replied Arthur. 'When did you last see her?'

'I think I let go of her when I grabbed you.'

They looked down at the smooth film that covered the cobbles. Arthur couldn't see any shape that could be Marjorie, and then he turned towards the inn. In the middle of the front door was a perfectly formed moulding of their friend.

'Look!' cried Arthur, pointing at the door. Willbury ran over and unpeeled her.

She gave a splutter. 'I hate cheese!'

A perfectly formed moulding of Marjorie

Within a few minutes, everybody was unpeeled and had gathered together. They all looked rather shocked, but happy, apart from the captain and the boxtrolls. The boxtrolls' boxes were now so damaged by the rain and the blast that they were embarrassed to be seen in them.

Arthur remembered the bottle and ran to where it lay, still under the cheese. He broke through and saw that the bottle was smashed. Close by, the bodies of the two tiny mice lay on the ground.

'Captain! Quick, over here!' Arthur called.

The captain rushed over and looked.

'I think it's Pickles and Levi!'

'You're right . . . I would recognize them any size,' said the captain. 'But they're not moving . . . '

The captain picked them up and looked at them very closely

The captain picked them up and looked at them very closely. 'They are not quite the right shape though . . . sort of swollen up around the belly . . . and there seem to be strands of cheese around their mouths.' His eyes lit up. 'And they're breathing!'

Levi and Pickles started to move and let out little groans.

'They must have gorged themselves on the cheese,' the captain said, smiling, and then carefully placed them both in his pocket.

'What do you think has happened to Snatcher and Framley?' asked Arthur.

'I think we can guess what has happened to Framley,' said Willbury, surveying the cheese. 'But Snatcher? I think we'd better go and look for him.'

Willbury led the group over the mound that had once been the Cheese Hall, towards the place where the back wall of the lab had stood. Large pools of water were now collecting on the surface of the cheese. They reached the street on the far side of the mound, and started to look about for signs of Snatcher.

Willbury led the group over the mound that had once been the Cheese Hall

After about half an hour, they were just about to give up when a new noise started. It was a low rumble and they could feel it under their feet. Beneath the town, the water had been doing its work. The foundations below the Cheese Hall had been almost completely washed away and, combined with the shock from the explosion, it was just too much. The rumbling grew louder and the earth began to shake. Arthur turned towards the mound and noticed ripples running over the surface of the pools of water.

'Look, Willbury! Look at the water!' Everybody turned to stare.

'Quick!' shouted Willbury. 'Get back from the mound!'

The rumbling was growing louder, and they could see that the mound was starting to shake.

Having retreated quickly, they just stood and stared as there was a huge cracking noise and the mound suddenly disappeared.

'Look, Willbury! Look at the water!'

In the same moment, all across the town, the iron plates covering the holes to the Underworld were blown high into the air, and in the woods the trotting badgers were shot out of their tunnels, and were last seen flying over the next county. Fortunately for the rabbit women, the doors they had constructed to keep the rabbits in were very well built, and saved them from the blast.

Quiet returned and everybody moved forward to look down the hole. It was some twenty or thirty feet deep and lined with the skin of cheese. Water was washing about in the bottom.

'It's a big hole!' said Kipper. 'If it was blue it would look like a swimming pool.'

'What's a swimming pool?' asked Arthur.

Willbury smiled. 'I think we had better get back to the ship to see if your grandfather and the others are all right. Kipper can show you what a swimming pool is later.'

'It's a big hole!' said Kipper

Then Willbury noticed how forlorn the boxtrolls looked.

'I am sure we can find a few new boxes; if not I shall have you some made!' The boxtrolls beamed, as they had never had brand new boxes.

'It's all very well for them,' said Marjorie. 'But what about me, and the other shrunken creatures?'

'Hang on a minute!' said Arthur, remembering the prototype. He rushed back around the edge of the hole to where it lay under the cheese skin. After a few seconds he managed to break through the skin and retrieve Marjorie's machine. Arthur lifted it up carefully, and then ran back to where the others stood.

As he arrived back at the group he heard Marjorie squeak with delight. 'Oh, Arthur, thank you, you've got my sizer!'

Willbury took the sizer from Arthur, and gave it a long look, and then spoke. 'I don't want to disappoint you, Marjorie, but where do you suggest we get your size back from now that Framley is no more?'

Marjorie looked glum. 'I hadn't thought of that . . . '

'There must be somewhere to get it from,' said Arthur.

'Where do you suggest we get your size back from now?'

'Maybe,' said Willbury. 'We'll have to think.'

As they set off for the ship the townsfolk were just arriving to find out what all the commotion was. They formed small, very puzzled, silent groups that gawped at the newly decorated hole and buildings. The underlings had been through so much that now even Titus held his cabbage up in a very un-cabbagehead way, and walked straight past them.

What nobody noticed was that high above, just under the gables of the bakery, was what looked like a ship's figurehead of a very angry man wearing a top hat. The figurehead started to slide slowly down the wall.

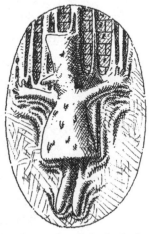

The figurehead started to slide slowly down the wall

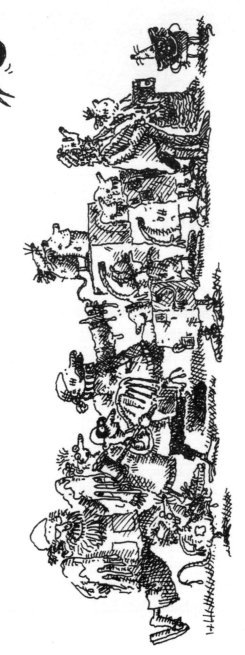

She swooped down to meet them

They saw a crow flying towards them

Chapter 53

REPAIRING THE DAMAGE

Weary, and covered with bits of sticky cheese, but feeling proud and relieved, the group began to make its way back to the laundry. As they did so, the rain stopped, and they saw a crow flying towards them. It was Mildred. She swooped down to meet them, and circled a few feet above their heads.

'What's happened?' she cawed. 'We heard an explosion and a big crunch a little while later.'

Everybody smiled, and Willbury spoke. 'We got Marjorie and Levi and Pickles back, and we stopped Snatcher.'

'Is everybody all right?' asked Mildred.

'I think so!' said Kipper. 'Well . . . Marjorie, Levi, and Pickles are still little . . . '

Marjorie gave an unhappy squeak.

'And Framley blew up!' added Arthur.

'That was the explosion you heard,' said Tom. 'We are not sure about Snatcher. He disappeared.'

'How did Framley explode?' Mildred asked.

'It's a long story,' said Willbury. 'I think it best if we get back to the ship, then everybody can hear it.'

'I'll fly back and tell them you're coming,' said Mildred.

Arthur had an idea. 'If you'll wait a moment I'll join you.'

Mildred looked surprised, and watched as Arthur stopped and wound the box on his front. After a minute or so they heard the ping, and Arthur unfolded his wings.

'Cor! Like your wings,' said Mildred. 'What are those bits that look like cheese on them?'

'Cheese!' giggled Kipper.

'What are those bits that look like cheese on them?'

Arthur crouched down, jumped, and pressed a button. Mildred flapped out of the way as Arthur rose up to join her.

'We'll see you in a few minutes!' Willbury called after Arthur. 'And get the cocoa on!'

Arthur followed Mildred up above the rooftops and back towards the laundry. The streets were filling with people and many of them turned to stare up at Arthur as he flew over.

'Ain't they seen anybody fly before?' cawed Mildred.

They were joined by the other crows

Arthur smiled. It was magnificent flying over the town by day, and with all the rain there had been the air was clean and clear. As they approached the laundry, they were joined by the other crows. Arthur spotted Grandfather below, on the deck, and waved. Grandfather waved back and Arthur could see him smiling.

'Get the cocoa on!' said Arthur as he touched the deck. 'The others will be back any minute.'

Grandfather came forward and gave him a hug.

'It's good to see you in one piece!'

'Not bad to see you either!' chirped Arthur.

Grandfather released him. 'We had better get the cocoa on. The milkman has been, and there's plenty of hot water as the boiler was on all night.' Grandfather chuckled.

'We'll get the stuff,' cawed Mildred. 'Give us a hand, Arthur.'

She led the way below decks to the galley, and they returned just in time to see the others returning. Soon everybody was sitting on deck grinning, swapping stories, and drinking cocoa out of buckets. Even Marjorie seemed happier, and was fiddling with her prototype.

Then they heard a whistle from along the towpath, and everybody turned to look. It was the Squeakers.

'Goodness, will we never be given any peace?' sighed Willbury. He stood up and walked to the top of the gangplank to meet them, and everybody followed.

The Squeakers dismounted from their bicycles and took out truncheons and handcuffs. The Chief Squeaker approached the bottom of the gangplank carrying a large sheaf of papers. When he reached the gangplank he stopped, raised the papers in front of him, and spoke.

'I hereby arrest all presently residing upon this ship, formally known as the Ratbridge Nautical Laundry, under sections . . . ' He paused and shuffled through his papers. '. . . C35 . . . D11 . . . Y322 . . . T14 . . . W24a . . . W24b . . . Q56 . . . of the Ratbridge penal code. I also charge you with . . .' And he looked at his papers again, 'riotously destroying a grade six public building, escaping custody, playing music without licence, causing a disturbance between the hours of 11 p.m. and 6.30 a.m. . . . and about fourteen other charges . . . '

Willbury raised a hand. 'I think, sir, that it ill behoves one who has assisted in kidnap and wrongful imprisonment, handled stolen goods, aided in a plot for the destruction of the official offices of this town, been a member of an illegal organization, connived with those who have been illegally hunting cheese and have been experimenting on animals without a licence . . . to cast the first stone.'

'I hereby arrest all presently residing upon this ship'

The Chief Squeaker looked puzzled. 'What do you mean?'

'I will explain it in court!' snapped Willbury. 'And while we're at it, I have another case to talk to you about.' He turned and waved Grandfather and Herbert forward.

'Do you remember a case many years ago where a man was poisoned with Oil of Brussels in a local hostelry?' said Willbury, addressing the Chief Squeaker.

'Yes. I'd just joined the police, and it was the first crime scene I ever attended. Very nasty case. We chased the assailant but he disappeared,' the Chief Squeaker replied.

'Well, do you remember that one of the witnesses also disappeared?'

'Yes—Archibald Snatcher said he had gone home for tea . . .'

'I think, sir, that it ill behoves one. . .'

'Was it not lunchtime? And was this not the man?' Willbury pointed to Herbert.

Herbert grinned, and the Chief Squeaker gave him a funny look.

'It could be . . .'

'I am telling you it was. This man was knocked unconscious and imprisoned by your good friend Archibald Snatcher, and has languished in a miserable cell under the Cheese Hall ever since, to stop him from giving true evidence.' Willbury paused for a moment and fixed the Chief Squeaker with his gaze. 'It was Archibald Snatcher who was responsible for the poisoning. Yes! That very same Archibald Snatcher, whom we all witnessed you investing with legal powers to justify a kidnapping and aiding in the theft of a pair of mechanical wings. I intend to sue whatever remains of the Cheese Guild on behalf of my clients here, for compensation, and I am sure the full story will come out.'

The Chief Squeaker went very pale. 'Umm . . . Er . . . I think there might have been a misunderstanding . . .' He lowered his papers. 'Didn't you say you had retired?'

'I was retired but I now feel that it is my duty to return to the law,' replied Willbury.

'Oh!' muttered the Chief Squeaker and then turned to the other Squeakers. 'Back to the nick . . . Quick!'

Everybody on the deck of the ship cheered as they watched the Squeakers disappear down the towpath.

'You're rather good at this law thing,' Arthur said to Willbury.

Willbury grinned, and turned to Grandfather. 'I think it's going to be safe for you to set up home above ground now if you would like to.'

'Thank you,' said Grandfather, and he shook Willbury's hand.

Everybody on the deck of the ship cheered

The deck of the Ratbridge Nautical Laundry

Chapter 54

HOME

On deck everybody had finished their cocoa, and with the Squeakers sent off with their tails between their legs, there was an air of relaxation. Some of the crew were disappearing below deck to get cleaned up, while others were snoozing in the morning sun. Willbury wandered across to Arthur and whispered quietly to him.

'I think that your grandfather is very tired. It would be a good idea if he had a rest and time to recover. Why don't you and Herbert take him down to the captain's cabin, and look after him, while I get a few things sorted out.'

'All right,' replied Arthur as he turned and looked fondly at his grandfather. Then Arthur turned back to Willbury looking a little worried. 'I don't like to ask this but I am worried about where we are going to live, and—'

Willbury cut him off. 'You are not to worry about that.

I have an idea. You concentrate on looking after Grandfather. I am sure he has missed you and it would be good for both of you to catch up.'

Arthur smiled and walked over to where Grandfather and Herbert were chatting.

'Willbury says we're to get you down to the captain's cabin so you can have a rest, Grandfather.'

'Oh, all right. If I have to! I am feeling much better though, now that it's stopped raining and my bones have had time to dry out.'

'Come on!' chuckled Arthur, as he and Herbert helped Grandfather to his feet and then across the deck to the stairs down to the cabin.

He and Herbert helped Grandfather to his feet then across the deck

For the rest of the day Arthur sat by Grandfather, listening to stories of Herbert's and Grandfather's youth. There didn't seem to be anything wrong with Herbert's memory now as story after story unfolded, and Arthur could hardly bear to tear himself away from them, but they kept needing fresh top ups of cocoa and biscuits from the galley.

There were tales of learning to ride bicycles, disastrous experiments, of pet frogs and engineering projects.

By late afternoon they were all growing sleepy, when Grandfather turned and spoke to Arthur.

'I am glad we have come above ground. I loved every moment I spent living in the Underworld with you, but it's not the best place for a child to grow up in. You need sunlight, and you need friends. And now you are going to have both.'

Arthur smiled, and a quiet calm settled on the cabin.

About seven o'clock there was a knock on the cabin door and Arthur, Grandfather, and Herbert awoke to see Kipper's face, smiling and covered in splashes of paint.

'If you would like to come through, Willbury has called a meeting in the hold, and would like you all to attend.'

'Why have you got paint all over you?' asked Arthur.

'You'll just have to wait and see,' replied Kipper, as he turned and disappeared out of the door.

Herbert and Arthur went to help Grandfather up but before they got to him he had stood up on his own.

'Come on, then,' said Grandfather, 'what are you waiting for, let's get to the meeting.' And he set off. Herbert and Arthur grinned at each other then followed.

When they arrived in the hold Willbury was sitting behind the ironing board with the captain. In front of him lay the prototype resizing machine and Arthur noticed Marjorie almost hidden behind it.

Willbury saw Grandfather walking by himself and smiled. 'Would you like to join me here, Grandfather? There is a spare chair.'

Grandfather nodded and made his way to the chair while Arthur and Herbert joined Kipper, to sit amongst the boxtrolls. Arthur noticed that quite a few of the pirates and rats also had splodges of paint on them and that they were smiling at him. Then Willbury spoke again.

Splodges of paint

'My dear friends, there are a number of important issues to resolve, and I think it best if I outline them, then we discuss how they might be solved.' He turned to Grandfather. 'I have already taken the liberty of asking my landlady if she would rent the vacant rooms above my shop to you and Arthur. She agreed and this afternoon I had Kipper lead a working party to clean and repaint the rooms. There is even a small boxroom that Herbert could use till he gets his own place. Kipper tells me he has sorted out some basic furniture, so you are welcome to move in any time you like.'

Grandfather smiled from ear to ear and called to Arthur, 'What do you think?'

'Yes, please!' answered Arthur with a huge grin. Kipper and Fish both patted him on the back.

There was a roar of approval from the meeting and then Grandfather spoke. 'I want to thank you from the bottom of my heart . . . but how are we to pay the rent? I don't have a job and I haven't got any savings.'

'You're not to worry about that. I have filed a claim for compensation, on your and Herbert's behalf, this afternoon with the clerk of Ratbridge courts, against Snatcher and the Cheese Guild. Until it comes to court, if Arthur helps out with chores, I'll sort out the rent.'

'I have filed a claim for compensation, on your and Herbert's behalf, this afternoon with the clerk of Ratbridge courts'

There was another cheer. Willbury raised a hand and spoke again. 'Now we come to our friends the underlings.' He turned to where the underlings sat.

'The problem of the entrances to the Underworld has been solved, but . . . ' He paused, 'at the moment most of the Underworld is flooded. Does anybody have any suggestions?'

Marjorie stood up on the table and squeaked, 'Easy!'

Willbury looked startled. 'Yes?'

'We already have a beam engine on this laundry. Pumping water is what they were built for. All we have to do is drop a pipe down into the Underworld and pump out the water.'

'I might be being stupid,' said Willbury, 'but where are we going to pump the water to?'

Marjorie looked flummoxed.

Marjorie looked flummoxed

Kipper raised a hand. 'How about the hole where the Cheese Hall was? That cheese seems to be pretty waterproof and would stop it leaking back into the Underworld.'

'Would it work?' Willbury asked Marjorie.

Marjorie thought for a moment. 'I think so . . . and once the underground becomes drier the boxtrolls could repair their drainage system to stop it flooding again.'

The boxtrolls made gurgles of agreement.

Kipper raised a hand again. 'Can I help them?'

'I see no reason why not,' Willbury said and turned to the captain, who was nodding in agreement. Kipper smiled.

'Well, that just leaves us with one last problem. Size! We have our friends here who have been reduced in size, but we know there are many others, and some in the hands of those

who just treat them as pets. We have to get them back, and we have to work out where to get the size to put them right. Does anybody have any suggestions?'

'How about we find the Members what ran away, and suck the size out of them?' Bert suggested. There were cheers from the pirates and rats.

Willbury stood silently until the cheers died away. 'I'm sorry but I'll not countenance revenge shrinkings. We must not lower ourselves to that. No, we must find another way. Does anybody have any other suggestions?'

'Couldn't we use vegetables to suck the size from?' asked Tom.

Titus looked shocked, as Marjorie raised a hand to speak. 'It doesn't work. You have to use living creatures. If you used vegetables it would be very dangerous and you might end up with some strange results.'

'What, like half trotting badger, half potato?' asked Kipper.

'Yes,' replied Marjorie.

'Might be an improvement,' suggested Tom.

Half trotting badger, half potato

'I think we have to stick with getting the size from creatures,' said Willbury. 'But I am really not sure how.'

'Couldn't we all donate a little bit of size?' asked Grandfather.

'You could, but with all the creatures we have to resize it would leave you all pretty tiny if it were to make any difference,' replied Marjorie rather sadly.

'Well, let's think on it,' said Willbury. 'And there is the issue of how we get the other underlings back to resize them in the first place. They're in homes all over the town and we simply don't know where they are. If we do find them and just steal them back we are going to start another whole round of trouble, and with the court case coming up that is the last thing I want.'

The hold fell silent and everybody looked rather glum. After a few minutes Willbury spoke again.

'Let's get some rest. It has been a tiring few days, and I am sure we'll think better after some sleep. We can all meet up here tomorrow morning to start pumping out the underground. Marjorie, will you take charge of that?'

Marjorie nodded.

'Could those that are coming back to the shop meet me up on deck?' said Willbury.

The meeting broke up, and a few minutes later Arthur found himself on deck with the boxtrolls, Titus and the tiny cabbagehead, Grandfather, Herbert, Marjorie, and Willbury.

'Are we taking the little sea-cow with us?' asked Arthur.

'No, she is staying here for the moment. The crew have grown very fond of her,' Willbury replied.

They set off, and soon arrived at the shop. Willbury opened the front door and stopped in his tracks.

Willbury opened the front door and stopped in his tracks

'Oh, my word!' he exclaimed.

Before them was the shop but now it was cleaner and tidier than Willbury could possibly have ever imagined. The walls and ceiling had been given a fresh coat of white paint, the old bookshelves had been righted and repaired, and were tidily stacked with all his books, the floorboards had been swept and polished, and against one wall stacked soap boxes formed open-fronted storage spaces into which the rest of Willbury's loose possessions had been neatly piled up. His bed was freshly made and some extra blankets were neatly folded at the foot of the bed.

There was a popping noise and Willbury turned towards the fireplace. He smiled. In front of the fire was his old

*Before them was the shop but now it was cleaner
and tidier than Willbury could possibly have ever imagined*

armchair . . . and it also had been repaired.

Willbury turned round. 'Welcome home! Would you like to come in?'

The little group walked into the shop and Willbury closed the door, then took a key off his keyring and handed it to Grandfather.

'This is a spare key to the front door. Please feel free to wander through here whenever you like.' Then he turned to Fish.

'Would you like to show our friends their new home?'

Fish smiled at Arthur and led them through the door at the back of the shop into the hallway. Now it was Fish's turn for a surprise. Where once the hallway had been dark and dingy, it was now bright and clean. A lit ship's lantern hung from the ceiling, and every surface was painted white. Fish was just about to lead them up the stairs when he noticed there was something different about the back room as well. He ran down the hall and gave a gurgle. Arthur, Grandfather, and Herbert followed.

The back room looked like a new ironmonger's shop.

Cubby-holed shelving made from cardboard now covered the walls, and all the nuts and bolts that had been on the floor had been sorted and placed in different labelled holes.

Fish let out a whistle, then stopped still when he noticed a stack of folded . . . clean . . . brand new . . . cardboard boxes on the floor. After a few seconds he walked forward slowly, and bent down to stroke the top box. Then he turned and let out an enormous gurgling cry.

He walked forward slowly, and bent down to stroke the top box

There was a scrabbling of feet from the shop and the other boxtrolls rushed past Arthur, stopped, and hooted at the sight of the boxes. The boxtrolls looked from the new boxes to each other then to Arthur, Grandfather, and Herbert.

Fish came forward and gently shooed Arthur, Grandfather, and Herbert out of the room and closed the door. As soon as the door was shut, there was a frantic tearing of cardboard, and whooping, followed by some chewing noises, then the door opened again. Fish and the other boxtrolls were wearing the new boxes and were grinning from ear to ear.

Wearing new boxes and grinning from ear to ear

Fish swaggered along the hall and marched up the stairs, waving for Grandfather, Arthur, and Herbert to follow. As they reached the top of the stairs Arthur ran ahead. There were three doors. He opened the first one and there was a tiny room with a hammock and another cardboard box. But this time the cardboard box had been tipped upside down to form a table. On it was a small vase of flowers and a cake.

'Is this my room?' he called over his shoulder.

'No, that is the boxroom for Herbert.' Arthur smiled and opened the next door. There he saw a brass bed, and to his surprise, tools laid out on a workbench.

'Is THIS my room?' he asked.

'No!' came Willbury's voice. 'It's Grandfather's.'

'Is THIS my room?'

Grandfather walked past Arthur and smiled. 'I do hope so.' He walked forward, looked at the bench, then sat on the edge of the bed and smiled a huge smile.

Arthur then turned to the last door. 'Then this MUST be my room!' He opened the door.

The room was a little smaller than Grandfather's and was painted completely white, including the floor. There was a cardboard box table like in the smaller room, but there were also some shelves. On the top shelf, lying on its side, was a large bottle. And inside the bottle was a model of the Ratbridge Nautical Laundry—complete with tiny washing. Arthur ran forward to look at it, and noticed a small plaque fixed to the bottle. Engraved on the plaque were the words, 'To Arthur from the R.N.L.'. Arthur beamed and turned to the others standing behind him.

Inside the bottle was a model of the Ratbridge Nautical Laundry

Herbert spoke. 'Kipper had been making it since they arrived in Ratbridge, and when he heard that you had lost all your toys, he decided you would make a good home for it.'

Arthur felt very touched. 'I shall treasure it always.'

Then Arthur looked about the room again. There was a hammock hung from corner to corner. Arthur jumped into

He was holding his doll

it and lay down. It felt very comfortable apart from a bump behind his neck. He reached his hand round and retrieved whatever was causing the discomfort. To his surprise he found he was holding his doll. Arthur was confused. He checked to see if he had another doll under his suit, but discovered it was not there.

He swung himself out of the hammock and ran next door to his grandfather.

'My doll? It was in . . . ah . . . my room!'

'Where else did you expect to find it?'

'I don't understand?'

'I think you dropped it when you were caught in the explosion. Tom found it and knew that it was broken . . . so he brought it to me. My eyesight is not so good these days and I asked Marjorie if she could fix it this afternoon.'

Arthur smiled and held up the doll.

'I'm afraid that it will never fly again, but you will be able to speak to me through it in a few weeks after I have got to grips with these new tools.'

They smiled at each other, and Grandfather spoke again. 'I think we are going to be happy here.'

'Cocoa!' came a call from downstairs.

'Yes . . . yes we are,' said Arthur.

They smiled at each other

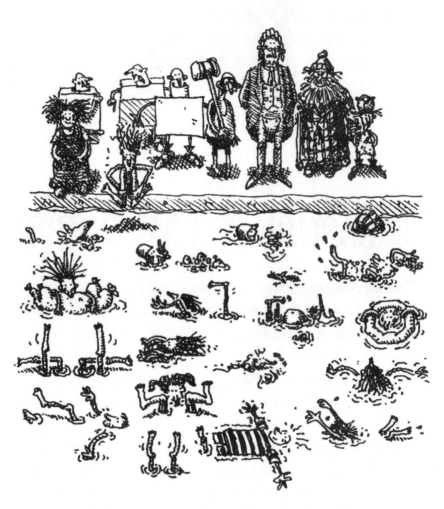

Children swimming in Grandfather and Herbert's hole

Arthur helps with the pumping out of the Underworld

Chapter 55

MEASURE FOR MEASURE

The next few weeks were very busy for Arthur. Grandfather thought it would be a good education for him to help with all the work that had to be done, so each morning Arthur would set out for the laundry and help out. Some days, under the guidance of Marjorie, he would help the crew of the laundry pump out the Underworld, and on other days he would work with the boxtrolls as they rebuilt the underground drainage system. He enjoyed these days most as Kipper and Tom worked with the boxtrolls. Kipper still wore his battered cardboard box and now had learnt to 'speak' boxtroll. This made him very useful and happy.

While Arthur worked during the day, Willbury, Herbert, and Grandfather spent their time preparing the compensation case against Snatcher and the Cheese Guild. When the day of the trial came, neither Snatcher, nor any

Member of the Cheese Guild, turned up to defend themselves, and the court awarded the hole in the ground to Herbert and Grandfather (as it was the only property that Snatcher and the Cheese Guild owned).

That evening after dinner, everybody who lived in the shop went for a gentle walk to view Grandfather and Herbert's hole. As they approached it they noticed local children swimming in it.

'I think you are going to have to fence off your hole,' said Willbury. 'What would happen if a child got into difficulty?'

Herbert and Grandfather looked at the swimmers rather glumly.

'Seems a pity. I suppose we could pay one of the pirates to keep an eye on the kids . . . But where would we get the money to pay him?' said Grandfather. 'We still have not got even enough money to pay you rent.'

'Why don't you charge for admission?' asked Willbury.

Herbert and Grandfather agreed this would be a good idea, and Willbury advised them that it would still be a good idea to put up a fence, to stop any accidents. They all trooped off to the laundry and were greeted with friendly cries.

'Is the captain about?' Willbury asked Mildred, who had flown down to meet them.

'Yes! He's down in his cabin. You know the way.'

They made their way below decks and knocked on the cabin door.

There sat Tom with the captain's hat on, behind a huge heap of laundry slips

'Come in!' came a familiar voice.

Willbury opened the door and there sat Tom with the captain's hat on, behind a huge heap of laundry slips.

'What are you doing here?' asked Willbury.

Tom smiled. 'I got voted captain last Friday. It's rather nice but I am looking forward to next Friday. I can't stand the paperwork. Anyway, what can I do for you?'

Willbury explained and it was agreed that in exchange for half the profits the laundry would provide lifeguard cover every day between six a.m. and eight p.m., and that they would also help erect the fence around the pool. It was also agreed that any spare hot water left over from the laundry would be piped into the pool.

Soon the 'Ratbridge Lido' (as the pool became known) was the main attraction in the town. Children would swim there by day, and in the evening when it wasn't raining the fashionable women would parade along its shores, while the pirates would have raft races. Herbert, who enjoyed swimming very much, taught Arthur how to swim and once the water became warm, Grandfather could be found taking a dip most days.

The pirates would have raft races

All this time the question of the shrunken creatures had not been solved, but then something happened.

A Frenchwoman arrived in Ratbridge and found work in one of the cafés that had sprung up around the Lido. She immediately became the centre of attention for the fashionable women, as she was from 'Pari'.

For days the ladies spent their time plucking up courage to ask her questions about the latest fashions till finally one Ms Hawkins could bear it no longer and stormed into the café.

'May I ask you about the Pari fashions, my dear?' Ms Hawkins asked.

'Certainly. What do you want to know?' replied the Frenchwoman.

'Is it true that hexagonal buttocks are going to be the rage this year?' said Ms Hawkins knowingly.

'*Quel horreur!* What is it with zee Ratbridge ladies and their fascination for ridiculous buttocks?'

Ms Hawkins dropped her pet boxtroll and fainted. When she recovered she went straight round to her friend who wrote the fashion articles for the *Ratbridge Weekly Gazette*, and the following Friday a special edition of the paper came out with two main articles. The first was a report covering all the details of what Snatcher had been up to, and the second an article on the fact that buttocks were 'OUT!'

'Quel horreur!'

Next morning, as Arthur made his way to the laundry, he approached the towpath and discovered it was thronging with the ladies of the town. After a struggle he managed to

make his way past them till he reached the gangplank. Kipper and a number of the bigger pirates were holding back the crowd who were trying to get on the ship. Kipper saw Arthur, grabbed him and lifted him aboard. Here he found Tom and Marjorie looking very worried.

'What's happening?' shouted Arthur over the noise of the crowd.

'We are not sure, but it has something to do with my resizing machine. They have heard we have got one here,' squeaked Marjorie.

Kipper saw Arthur, grabbed him and lifted him aboard

'Quick! You've got to come and deal with them!' shouted Kipper. 'We can't hold them back for much longer.'

'What are you going to do?' asked Arthur.

'I don't know . . . ' panicked Marjorie.

'Let one of them up here and see what they are after?' suggested Tom. 'It might be the only way to stop a riot.'

They all nodded and then Tom called out to Kipper to let one of the ladies through. Kipper did as he was ordered and a very cross looking woman strode up the gangplank, and as she did the din died down.

'How can I help you?' Marjorie squeaked.

'I've read that you have a machine like the one that Snatcher had, that can shrink things?' It was Ms Hawkins.

'Er . . . Yes?' Marjorie replied.

'I want you to shrink my buttocks! And that is not a request but an order!' said Ms Hawkins.

Marjorie looked astonished. 'Umm . . . Are you sure?' she squeaked.

'I am not leaving here till you do,' she replied. 'You can

use my boxtroll to put the size into,' she went on, thrusting a tiny boxtroll towards Marjorie.

'I want you to shrink my buttocks!'

'All right, if you insist . . . ' Marjorie smiled. 'But I do charge!'

'I don't care. I want my buttocks reduced at any price,' Ms Hawkins insisted.

'How about ten groats a pound . . . and your boxtroll?' Marjorie said.

'Done!' Ms Hawkins snapped, and took out her purse. 'Who'd want a big boxtroll anyway, it's only the small ones that are fashionable!'

'Very well then!' Marjorie squeaked. Then she turned to Tom and Arthur. 'Can you rig up a screen for the ladies and take the money?' They nodded. 'We need something for them to go behind and it needs a hole in it big enough for the funnel on my resizer.'

Marjorie turned back to Ms Hawkins. 'I've got to go and get my machine, and while I am away I want you to go behind the screen and prepare yourself. When I get back I am going to put the funnel through the hole, and you must place a buttock against it. I'll extract the size, and then you'll have to place the other buttock against the funnel. When I have done that one, I'll upsize the boxtroll.'

Marjorie disappeared below deck, while Tom finished putting up the screen with the aid of the crows, and Arthur took the money. One of the pirates found a pair of scissors and cut a hole in the screen. Ms Hawkins huffed, placed the boxtroll on the deck, and then disappeared behind the screen.

Tom finished putting up the screen with the aid of the crows

Marjorie returned, struggling with her machine. 'Tom, can you get one of the pirates to operate the resizer? I don't think I am big enough.'

Tom found a volunteer and Marjorie ordered him to push the funnel through the hole in the screen.

'Are you ready? Please place your first buttock against the funnel!'

'Ready!' came the cry from behind the screen.

'Extract the size!' Marjorie ordered the pirate. The pirate pulled the trigger and there was a flash and puff of smoke from behind the screen. This was followed by a delighted titter.

'Please place your second buttock against the funnel!'

'Ready!'

'Extract the size!' There was another flash and puff of smoke and yet another titter of delight.

Ms Hawkins appeared from behind the screen to gasps of admiration from the women standing at the top of the gangplank. Where once her buttocks had stood, her figure was now as straight as a board.

Where once her buttocks had stood, her figure was now as straight as a board

With no word of thanks she marched past her fashion rivals, flaunting her non-existent buttocks, down the gangplank and disappeared.

Marjorie now ordered the pirate to point the other funnel at the tiny boxtroll on the deck.

'Do you understand what we are doing?' she asked the boxtroll. The boxtroll nodded and grinned.

'All right, release the size!' Marjorie ordered. There was another flash and instantly the boxtroll grew about three inches.

There was another flash and instantly the boxtroll grew about three inches

'Well done!' Marjorie said to the boxtroll, who was looking very pleased.

Over the course of the day many ladies were treated, including a large number who didn't have underlings as pets. This enabled Marjorie to get all the creatures back to their original size. There were cabbageheads and boxtrolls, and several women turned up with buckets containing fresh-water sea-cows. These proved a little more difficult to resize, as they had to be taken out of their bucket and kept wet

On deck there were swarms of full-size underlings

during the process, then gently lifted over the side and lowered into the canal.

By late afternoon Arthur had had to find somewhere to put all the money. He now had a large barrel almost full of banknotes and coins, while on deck there were swarms of full-size underlings.

There was still a queue of ladies on the towpath, but none of them had pet underlings.

'Where are you going to put the size?' asked Arthur.

'We need to find some more shrunken underlings,' said Marjorie.

'Shall I go and get Match from the shop, and the little cabbagehead that Titus is looking after?' Tom asked.

'Yes, and what about the fresh-water sea-cow that was here on the boat?' Marjorie asked.

'We did her hours ago,' Tom smiled.

'Well, what shall I do while I'm waiting? There are still loads of ladies on the towpath . . . '

'Isn't that obvious?' asked Tom.

'No,' replied Marjorie.

'Don't you want to get back to normal?' Tom asked.

'Of course. It had gone clean out of my head.'

Tom went off and returned half an hour later with

everybody from the shop, to see a full-size Marjorie standing on deck, accompanied by full-size versions of Pickles and Levi.

Marjorie grinned at Willbury as he arrived.

Marjorie grinned at Willbury as he arrived

'I am not sure I approve of this,' said Willbury.

'We didn't have much choice in the matter,' said a much less squeaky Marjorie. 'I think we would have been lynched if we had refused to co-operate. And look at all the underlings!'

Willbury looked around at all the happy big underlings standing around the deck.

He smiled. 'Well, let's finish this off. Fish, can you bring Match here? We are going to get his size back.'

Fish came forward and placed Match on the deck in front of the screen, and Marjorie ordered the pirate to let another lady through.

Over the next few minutes the queue of ladies on the towpath disappeared and Match and Titus's friend regained their size.

'That's the last one!' said Marjorie triumphantly. 'Everyone's back up to full size!'

'Right!' said Willbury. 'Marjorie, could you lend me your machine for a minute.' Marjorie looked curious, but handed the machine over. Willbury placed it on the deck.

'Herbert, could you do the honours with your walloper, please?'

'But . . . ' Marjorie cried and started to move forward to get her machine.

Willbury raised a hand. 'No! We have had enough of all this resizing. I am going to get Herbert to destroy the resizer and I want you to promise you are not going to try to build a new one.'

Marjorie looked rather sad. 'I suppose so . . . '

'All right then. Herbert, wallop the machine!'

Herbert walloping the machine

There was a mighty crash and the resizer lay bent beyond recovery on the deck.

'Thank you, Herbert!'

Marjorie stood staring at the ruins of her machine, while Willbury stared at the barrel full of money near Arthur.

'Don't complain! I think you have made rather a lot of money out of this. Perhaps you could put it to some more useful purpose than just changing the size of things.'

'And maybe something that causes less trouble,' added Grandfather, looking up at the smog that was starting to settle over the town. 'Have you ever thought about going into pollution prevention?'

'I did have an idea about how to distil oil and run a motor off it. It would be a lot cleaner than steam engines.' Marjorie grinned.

'Do you think I could help?' asked Arthur.

'Of course you could. I need an bright assistant.'

That night a party was held on the laundry. The crows played harmonium, vast quantities of cocoa were drunk, everybody danced, and complaints were made about the noise to the Squeakers, who did nothing about it. As the party died down, Arthur wandered onto the towpath with his friends Fish, Tom, and Kipper for a little peace away from the crows' music. As they walked along the bank they saw Willbury and Grandfather sitting on the bank with Titus.

'What are they doing?' asked Arthur.

That night a party was held on the laundry

'Looks like throwing weeds in the canal,' replied Kipper.

As they approached, Willbury put his fingers to his lips to keep them quiet, then pointed out into the canal.

There was the mother fresh-water sea-cow and her size-restored calves, feeding on the weed that Willbury and Grandfather had been throwing in.

They watched until the sea-cows had had their fill and had turned and swum off down the canal. Willbury and Arthur helped Grandfather to his feet and they all waved as the little group of sea-cows slowly disappeared into the distance.

'You know, for all its failings, I rather like Ratbridge,' said Willbury.

'It's not all bad, is it?' replied Grandfather as he gave Arthur a wink.

HERE BE MONSTERS!

www.here-be-monsters.com

Come in and explore the wonderful world of Ratbridge at our HERE BE MONSTERS! website. Inside Willbury's shop, you'll find all sorts of bits and bobs to keep you as happy as a boxtroll in a pile of nuts and bolts. Website includes:

- A crazy HERE BE MONSTERS! animated game featuring cabbageheads, boxtrolls, and cheeses galore!
- Screensavers to brighten up your computer
- A competition to spot Arthur and win a fantastic prize
- Movie clips from the HERE BE MONSTERS! film
- A downloadable toy theatre—have the HERE BE MONSTERS! characters live in your living room
- Maps of Ratbridge—investigate all those nooks and crannies and find out what happens when the book cover is closed

And much, much more!

www.here-be-monsters.com